BACON AND EGG MAN

BACON AND EGG MAN

by
KEN WHEATON

Premier Digital Publishing - Los Angeles

Bacon and Egg Man
ISBN: 978-1-62467-111-1

Published by Premier Digital Publishing
www.PremierDigitalPublishing.com
Follow us on Twitter @PDigitalPub
Follow us on Facebook: Premier Digital Publishing

ACKNOWLEDGMENTS

When the initial seeds of this book were planted back in the 1990s, it was little more than a twisted fantasy of a paranoid junk-food fiend. So I guess I should thank Michael Bloomberg and Center for Science in the Public Interest and other such crusaders for making it seem plausible.

As always, much thanks to Jason Primm and Jacquelin Cangro for being the dynamic duo of first readers. Thanks especially to Simon Dumenco for a killer round of edits. And gratitude to my agent, Cynthia Manson, who didn't necessarily sign up for this book, but has shown remarkable patience with my genre jumping.

1

Monday. Monday meant bacon and eggs.

Wes Montgomery threw back the covers, his skin prickling in the cold air of the house, and sighed. He'd moped around for weeks, starving himself and working out. Starving himself wasn't hard. When Hillary disappeared, his appetite went with her. Which wasn't the worst thing in the world. He'd done enough damage during their time together, to his supply, to his body, so much he'd had to bribe Dr. Halpern to fudge the cholesterol and carb levels on his monthly report. "Five pounds in a month," she'd said, "Getting harder to hide."

That five pounds was gone and then some. Working out two to three times a day helped. Helped shed the pounds. Helped exorcise the neurosis as he punished himself for his weaknesses: physical and emotional. Helped him sleep at night. Dr. Halpern had offered him a plethora of pills and topical patches, but he'd declined.

Now, finally, he felt a grumble in his stomach, a recollection of true hunger. Maybe he'd rounded a curve.

Bacon and eggs.

To be more precise, three strips of bacon, two eggs sunny-side up—just like in the old picture books—and one slice of wheat toast to sop up the yolk. On the few occasions he felt he could spare it, he slathered his one piece of toast in butter. Today was one of those days, a bread-and-butter day. A phantom smell of frying butter drifted around his bedroom, and his stomach growled again.

"Good man," he said, rubbing it.

As he hopped out of bed, the frigid morning air chased away the little lingering clouds of self-loathing. The hard wood floor was cold on his feet. He pulled on a University of Phoenix sweatshirt and peeked out the window. Two feet of snow was on the ground and still coming down. A five-foot drift of gray ice blocked his view of the road.

He stopped in the bathroom to empty his bladder. While there, he poked at the mirror, pulling up a four-week old image of himself in the glass. He squinted his eyes, stretched his neck, tugged on his cheeks. Definitely a difference. The older picture was that of a contented face, slightly bloated from eating and drinking too much. That face was now skinnier. Miserable, mostly, but skinnier. His face always gave him away.

After checking to make sure the bedroom window was shut, he padded downstairs and checked all the others. All were locked tight, and all offered the same view: snow, snow and more snow. The temperature hadn't been above 25 in two weeks.

"This is now three weeks in a row the temperature hasn't climbed above 25. Looks like 2050 is going to be another for the record books," Gawker's weatherman corrected him when he flipped on the kitchen-counter monitors.

"And it's just October," said the woman sitting behind the anchor desk with fake cheer. The look in her eyes gave her away, made it clear that the prospect of another seven months of this had her right on the edge.

"Yes," answered the weatherman, "Just a reminder of the not-so-subtle dangers of Global Freezing."

It was too much for the anchor. "Well, Jim, the rest of the globe seems pretty hot enough," she said, her laugh laced with venom. "Maybe we could trade them."

"Good girl," Wes said, knowing full well that before day's end she'd be issuing an apology for publicly doubting Global Freezing.

"Global Warming" had been a favorite target of his old man, who at one time was capable of thousand-word written rants on the subject, rants in which the word "green" became a curse, and some old politician named Gore was Satan incarnate. Also on the old man's hit list were King Mike, the Federation and, on a level more relevant to this Monday, the dangers of women and neurotic behavior—the former leading directly to the latter.

But the old man had always been full of shit. From what Wes could remember anyway. That was long ago.

Wes shook his head clear.

"Bacon and eggs," he said. He called up a Google Live Earth shot of his house. He needed to know if anything was out there. The screen came up blank except for a text notice: "Service Error: No Data Available."

"Shit!" He reloaded a few times, each with the same result. He tried his mobile. No luck. What to do? Proceeding without an aerial shot of his home threw off the entire breakfast ritual.

He flipped through vid screens. The other feeds were working. A survival show from the ash heaps of California, a live weather cam from the air-conditioned domes in the baked wastelands of West Texas. There's your Global Freezing, he thought. The Federation media was bordering on hysterics about Global Freezing—all but lobbying Congress to revert to gas-powered cars, to blow up some of the carbon trapping stations—but what about the rest of the world? It was practically on fire.

"Go away old man," he whispered as if to an actual presence, a specter that visited in times of trouble. He wasn't going to turn into the old man, into someone who yelled at the video screen. It was a good thing they no longer spoke. He'd have given his father an aneurysm by now.

He flipped along. The Suffolk News and Review, where he worked, was reporting a raid on an unlicensed dairy farm hidden somewhere just outside of Amagansett. Not only had the farmers been selling unlicensed, unpasteurized milk, there were unconfirmed rumors the cows were eventually used for meat. How'd they manage to acquire cows, much less hide them?

Good story—made him jealous. It didn't have a byline attached to it, so he wondered if Lou, his boss, had broken it. He wondered, too, how much it was killing Lou to break the story on screen, rather than in print.

FoxNews in the South was pointing out everything wrong with the Northeast, and a few hundred Gawker channels served him streaming news, gossip, reality shows and hidden-camera views of in-breds shopping in an Alabama Walmart. Everyone was worried about the Brazilians taking over the country and China's civil war spreading beyond Asia. On The Gawker's personal feed was a taped recording of the man—three hundred pounds and covered in the makeup and clothes of a deranged clown—railing about the inequities of "so-called Real America, where knuckle-draggers rule and the minds of the people shrivel in a stew of fat and poisonous media."

Too early for that. Then again, it was too early for highlights from the previous night's debates, pitting the current King Mike against the ten whack-jobs running against him.

He tried Google's Live Earth again. Down. Down across all of Peconic, Suffolk and most of Nassau counties.

He settled on a live video feed of Saint Bernadoodle puppies streaming from somewhere just north of Manhattan and tried to nudge his mind out of this particular ritual's very specific rut. He could practically taste the bacon. Maybe he was being too superstitious, overly cautious.

"Screw it." He ran down to the basement for his cast-iron fry pan, hung on the pegboards amidst a wall of hammers, wrenches, screw drivers and pliers. Back upstairs, he set it on the stove and opened the fridge. A pitcher of water, half gallon of soy milk, three bricks of tofu, a host of smelly Asian condiments meant to make the tofu taste like something other than tofu.

And a watermelon. A fake watermelon.

But fake as it was, it felt real—had a watermelon's heft and, when placed on the counter, a pleasant thump that would do any ripe watermelon proud. A gift from his artist friend Jules, it was among Wes' most-treasured belongings, right up there with his cast-iron cookware. For within that watermelon were the seeds of joy, of hope, of good fortune.

"Watermelon time," he said.

He lifted the top half from his fake watermelon, paused out of respect, like a priest opening the tabernacle doors, and gazed upon half a dozen eggs and a half-pound package of 100% pork bacon.

For the first time in weeks, Wes smiled.

He wasn't a religious man, but before lighting a fire under the skillet, he uttered a brief prayer. "Rub a dub dub, thank God for the grub."

Within minutes, the smell of bacon filled the kitchen. Always the bacon first. It saved the trouble of using oil or wasting butter. So what if the eggs were browned by the grease? They tasted so much better.

Moved by emotion, Wes did his bacon dance, which involved little more than bending over, sticking his ass out and shaking it around a bit. Done with the dance, he plated the bacon, dropped in the eggs and fetched the butter from its hiding place before realizing there was no way he'd be able to wait to eat it all at the same time. The bacon was sitting there, slutty little strips just asking for it.

"So be it," he said with a shrug, and proceeded to eat while keeping an eye on his eggs.

Halfway through the third strip of bacon, an explosion rocked the front of his house. Standing there, pork poking out of his mouth like a dog's tongue, a spatula in his right hand, Wes watched as his front door flew through the foyer, followed by a blast of cold air and the stomping of boots.

"No, no, no," he muttered, swallowing the rest of the bacon and chucking the sizzling eggs into the sink. "Nooooo."

Watermelon now in hand, he turned just as five fully-armed SWAT members fought each other through his kitchen doorway. Before they could squeeze through, Wes found his voice.

"Don't you fucking move!" he screamed.

They stopped shoving long enough for him to belt one in the goggles with a raw egg. Then they were scrambling again. By the time he'd chucked the remaining three eggs at them, they were through the door, pointing what he hoped were stun rifles and not real guns.

"Wes Montgomery, you are under arrest for possession of illegal substances. Put down the watermelon and put your hands in the air."

Wes looked at his watermelon, looked back at the man with egg dripping off his goggles. Wes raised his right hand, as if to signal surrender, then brought it back down to the watermelon.

"I'm going to put this on the counter," he said. "Just keep calm."

He turned, put the watermelon down and considered the half-pound of uncooked bacon within. Such a fucking shame.

"Mr. Montgomery, turn around and put your hands on top of your head," the SWAT leader shouted.

"There's a fine line between bravery and stupidity," the old man had once written. "Thing is, you usually don't know what side you've landed on until the dust settles." But that was a debate Wes had no time for. He moved his hands to the inside of the watermelon, trying his best to look submissive and defeated.

"Mr. Montgomery, hands up," the SWAT leader said. Then to his team: "Three-quarters charge."

Wes heard the high-pitched whine of the rifles. At least they weren't using bullets. Yet.

"Mr. Montgomery, I'm required by law to tell you that we are considering firing upon you."

"Fine," Wes said. "I hear you"

The thing was, Wes really wanted to put his hands on top of his head. But looking at the bacon, something came over him.

"We are considering firing upon you, Mr. Montgomery. Second warning. This shot is not designed to be lethal, but it will hurt. In some cases, the charge has proven lethal. The government is not responsible for any damages to your person or property. Do you understand this?"

Wes had heard acquaintances recite the speech, but this was his own first time on the receiving end. Had he been outside, he might have made a run for it, get a good 50-yard start while the cops finished up the legalese.

"Yeah, yeah, yeah," Wes said. Then, in one motion, he yanked the bacon out of the plastic sleeve, balled it up and crammed all of it into his mouth. Fuck them if they were going to get his pig.

"Mr. Montgomery, we will now fire at you," the SWAT leader said.

Wes started chewing.

"Fire!"

He'd managed three or four good chews before the first shock burned through his body. And Goddamn if it didn't smell like the bacon was frying in his mouth. "There are worse ways to die," was the last thought he had before falling unconscious.

2

Wes woke from a vivid dream that he was a lone piece of bacon sizzling in its own grease. Smelled nice enough, but being fried hurt like hell.

As his eyes fluttered open, the phantom aroma disappeared but the pain remained. It felt like someone had kicked his ass from the inside out. To top it all off, his hands were shackled to the bed.

He took in his surroundings.

A standard-issue placard depicting the flags of the Northeastern Federation arranged around a photo of old King Mike, the man who'd so left his mark on the Federation the people called his successors, the government itself, King Mike—the legacy of some editorial cartoonist carrying down through the years.

A 62-inch in-wall monitor with multiple Gawker networks and search feeds—including The Gawker himself staring down at Wes.

A scrawny uniformed cop snoring in a chair in the corner.

A keypad on the bed's railing that he could just reach. He flipped over to Deadspin, which was covering the Monday Night Football game between the Toronto Bills and the Jacksonville Jaguars. There were playing in Florida, which meant an orgy of supplemental coverage from outside the stadium. It was like watching video from a different planet, one populated by morbidly obese people with bad skin and worse hair.

The camera crew found and focused on a group of fit Torontonians, burned lobster red from a sun they were unaccustomed to. Wes could see they were about to cross the border from pleasantly inebriated to dangerously drunk. The problem was they were partying with

Jacksonville natives, six couples, each sporting triple-extra-large Jaguar regalia pulled over their 300-pound frames. The monitor showed a temperature reading of 97 degrees and 100% humidity even at this time of night. For a moment, Wes thanked God for the cooling effects of volcanic ash. He wondered how people could get so fat in that kind of heat, but the camera answered that question. Four smokers were going—a whole pig on one, chickens on another, burgers, steaks, chops, dogs on the third and fourth. The meat glistened. The people did too.

The Jag fans were guzzling booze out of 72-ounce cups. Professional gluttons, they laughed and backslapped the increasingly ill-looking Canadians as sweat rolled off their red faces. The Floridians would probably be dead of coronaries within the next five years. Wes imagined grabbing a screen shot and sending it to his old man with a note attached: "What was it you were saying about balance? Maybe the Federation has a point."

The bathroom door popped open and through it came a plain-clothes detective.

"Look at it come down. Not even December yet. Gets earlier every year." Outside, snow flurries seemed to be strengthening into blizzard conditions.

The detective was typical of the breed. Close-cropped hair offset by a broom-sized mustache. A fitted dress shirt stretched out over a torso seemingly chiseled from granite. Yet there was something lithe about the package, a dancer's body that tapered down to the waist then out again at muscular thighs wrapped in black slacks. Years of training combined with a government-regimented diet did that to a body. Wes sometimes wondered if cops got the body because of the job or the job because of the body.

Plain Clothes smiled at Wes, hooked his thumbs in his belt loops and turned to Uniform.

"Wake the fuck up!" he barked.

"Sorry sir!" the kid said, wiping his drool on the back of his hand.

Plain-clothes considered him. "You tired from training or from a shit diet, Gomez?"

"Training, sir."

"You're not into caffeine again, are you? That looked like a caffeine crash. That shit messes with your metabolism. Makes you crash. It's not worth it. Gonna be illegal soon enough anyway, so might as well cut it out now."

"No sir. It's the training, sir. I swear." As if to prove it, Gomez performed a couple of elaborate stretches that cops two generations prior would have thought unmanly—and found impossible.

"Good work, Gomez. Now get the hell out of here."

"Yes sir." On his way out, Gomez shot Wes a glance. It was meant to condemn, but the outrage couldn't quite cover up the curiosity.

Wes knew he'd just watched an easy mark walk out of the room.

The detective shook his head. "Good kid. Gonna go far if he keeps out of Starbucks." He popped a stick of sugarless into his mouth and smiled again.

"I can get you the real thing," Wes said, motioning to the pack of gum in the cop's hand.

Where had that come from? He'd made a career out of not pissing off cops, but suddenly he didn't seem to care much.

Plain Clothes stopped chewing. "Come again."

"Real thing. I can get you real gum with real sugar. Or high fructose if that's your thing. Any flavor you want—wild berry, bubble gum, cinnamon. But you strike me as a no-nonsense, wintergreen kind of guy. Minty fresh!"

Even as he fought to control his own mouth, Wes chuckled at the joke.

The detective replaced his shit-eating fake smile with a real one. Despite his obvious delight, he moved his hands up to massage his temples as if he'd suddenly developed a stress headache.

"So continue, Mr. Montgomery. Tell me about that gum."

Wes laughed again. "Oh, you want me to start over now that you've started recording?"

Plain Clothes quit smiling.

"Really?" Wes said. "You're gonna piss this case away by trying to record me on the sly?" Somewhere in the back of his head a little voice was shouting, "Shut up, Wes. Shut up, now!" But he couldn't stop. "And the arresting officers were so good. By the book. They won't be happy about this. No, not at all."

As if in response, two men in dark suits walked into the room. Built like Plain Clothes, they were older, but neither sported mustaches.

"Goddamnit, Mulrooney," said one, snatching Plain Clothes by the collar and dragging him out of the room.

"What?" Mulrooney said. "I had it under control!"

"See you later, Mulrooney," Wes shouted after him.

The other suit walked over to the bed and yanked a white patch off Wes' shoulder, taking with it a spot of hair.

"Ow! Shit! Why'd you do that?"

But the answer became clear within two minutes. As the new cop stood by in silence, the dull ache throughout Wes' body became more acute, and the little voice in his head, the one that normally told him to shut the hell up and otherwise kept him out of trouble, reasserted itself.

When Wes grimaced—out of shame as much as pain—the new guy spoke.

"Wes Montgomery, I'm going to turn my recorder on. Is that clear?"

"Yeah," Wes muttered, wondering for the first time about the severity of the situation.

The cop squeezed the bridge of his nose and blinked three times. "Wes Montgomery, my name is Detective Darley. I am now recording this conversation. Is that clear?"

"Yes," Wes said.

"You have a right to record this conversation as well. Is that clear, Mr. Montgomery?"

"Yes," Wes said. He didn't have an implant, and they knew it.

"Now, Mr. Montgomery, I've also removed your med patch. As you may have been under the influence of pain killers earlier, your discussion with Officer Mulrooney will be erased."

"Great. Thanks."

The other detective returned, stomping into the room. "Darley, you recording this?"

Darley nodded.

"Okay. Good. We're all clear here." He turned his attention to Wes.

"Mr. Montgomery, I'm Detective Brant. I just want to make something clear. You are under arrest. You're only here in this suite until you can walk again, and you piss out the rest of the painkillers. After that, we're taking you to Chief Blunt. You'd do best not to talk to anyone else—not us, not your guards, not the doctors unless it's to answer questions about your condition. Understood?"

"Yes."

"Any questions?"

"Why was I arrested? It's a little hazy."

"Possession of banned food substances."

"Just possession?"

The two detectives looked at one another. Brant sighed. "Yes. Just possession."

Wes relaxed a little. If they weren't nailing him with intent to distribute then they hadn't found his stash. He sighed and settled into his bed, rearranged the covers.

Brant motioned to Darley, who squeezed the bridge of his nose, turning the recorder off. Brant then leaned in close to Wes. "I wouldn't start celebrating just yet, Wesley. We caught you. Blunt and his men are on the case. It's only a matter of time."

Underneath the layers of cologne, sugar-free gum and mouthwash, Wes smelled something on Brant's breath, a hint of illegality. Smokeless tobacco, that was it. He thought for a second about trying to work a deal, but with the painkillers now losing effect, he'd lost the courage. Besides, tobacco wasn't his scene anyway.

3

Excerpt from a letter to Wes Montgomery, signed, "Love, the Old Man," dated August 25, 2025

The bastards started with tobacco. Easiest thing for them to go after. Taxed the shit out of it. Sorry for the language, but if you're old enough for the story of how this mess came about—and God knows you won't get it from your mom or those damn schools—anyway, you're sure as hell old enough for the language.

But one day I'm paying $2.50 for a pack of smokes, next day I'm paying seven bucks—for 20 cigarettes! Then they're telling me I can't smoke at the office. Then in restaurants. Then it's bars. Which puts me in the position of driving two hours from Brooklyn to the Shinnecock Reservation out in Southampton to buy tax-free cartons so I could come back and stand in the freezing cold and smoke like a common bum.

And of course, nobody else defended tobacco. Hey, let's be honest, the shit rots you from the inside. It kills you. And if I were up there with you now and I caught you smoking, I'd beat you clear into next week.

Philip Morris and R.J. Reynolds and crew hadn't done themselves any favors with their three-thousand-mile paper trail and fifty-year history of dirty deeds and marketing to kids. On the off chance they never taught you about the great satan, Joe Camel, look it up online—if that's still legal. Hell, maybe they scrubbed him completely from history.

So the taxes are piling up, and you can't smoke anywhere. That woulda been fine for most politicians. You've got a tax base built on addicts. How fucking beautiful is that?

But the activists kept pushing. Their early battles with cigarettes led to victories in other arenas, which led to more victories against *tobacco. They were, in the words of one previous president, embiggened.*

Then the government got greedy—well, parts of it anyway. Hard up for cash, King Mike—who was still just Mayor Mike—started arresting black-market traffickers carrying in cartons from South Carolina and Long Island. (That was the first time I got knocked, before I married your mother, thank God.)

Then came the billion-dollar ad campaign paid for by Indian casinos. The feds had cut off their tax-free cigarettes and were eyeing their casinos. So it was time for a message—and revenge. The Indians ran a multi-million dollar ad campaign pointing out what a bunch of money-grubbing, cancer-enabling shits the politicians were. Super Bowl ads. American Idol. World Series. You name it. Painted them as child-murderers. "First it was small pox. Now this." Christ, it was brilliant. The politicians felt more and more pressure. Soon enough it wasn't just restaurants and bars you couldn't smoke in. Next it was your house, your car, within fifty feet of buildings, within a hundred feet of buildings, within ten feet of kids. The question became, why the hell not make it illegal once and for all?

I don't have to tell you how they answered that one.

4

Chief Detective Blunt's office suffered from multiple personality disorder. The desk, shelving and chairs wanted to be from a Sherlock Holmes novel. But as governmental offices were forbidden from using real, grown-in-a-forest wood, everything was made of a recycled laminate that made plastic seem warm. And Wes had only to take one look at the upholstery to know he was going to spend the duration of this interview trying not to slide off the fake leather.

They'd at least managed to program the light coming from the green-glass lamps correctly. But the warm glow did little good against the glare coming from the wall opposite the windows. It was dominated by a massive touch monitor broken into several smaller panels, some of them showing tables and charts, weather information in various places, a map of the Northeast Federation and, on the biggest panel, a Google Live Earth shot of Wes' house. The neighbor's dog, Legume, was taking a shit in his front yard.

Below the screen sat a control panel and another bank of processors of some sort.

To the right of the entry way was a gleaming office gym—stationary bike, elliptical, a rack of dumbbells and, oddly enough, a climbing wall that broke through the plane of the ceiling and into the third floor.

A voice called down from the top. "Just cuff him to the couch, Boggs. I'll be right down."

"Yes sir."

Boggs, who hadn't said a word to Wes on the ride over from the hospital, nudged him toward the couch, sat him down and clipped the cuffs to a chain leading from the floor.

"Rock climber, huh?" Wes asked.

"You shut your bacon-greased mouth," Boggs said, jabbing a finger into Wes' chest.

"Oooo-kayyy."

Boggs face turned red. "Chief Blunt's father died of obesity," he spat. "Because of junk pushers like you."

Wes let slip the leading edge of a laugh but pulled it back and tried to wipe the smile from his face. He put his hands up in surrender—had just enough slack in the chains to get them to ear level. "That's too bad," Wes said.

"Wait till he gets done with you," Boggs said, a single tear gleaming in his left eye.

He turned and left, his muscles quivering like sugar-free Jell-O.

Blunt climbed down from the ceiling, a sight to behold. But it wasn't the white hair and matching mustache that caught Wes' eye. And neither was it the chiseled climbers' shoulders and biceps rippling out of the tank top tucked into the spandex shorts. No, it was the protruding belly, the round hump stretching the tank top's fabric forward—and the love handles and lower back fat pushing out at the sides. Wes caught only a glimpse of it before Blunt slipped behind a screen where he issued instructions to someone on the other end of a comlink.

"Yeah, cancel that Pilates class. And can we sub out yoga for a weight-training class? Yeah. I know, Celine. I haven't been to Core Connection. Well, can you write down that I went to Pilates at least? You're my assistant, right? So assist me. Yes. I know it's the law. You don't think that I know it's the law, Celine? Of course I know it's the law. Never mind. Fine. I'll go to Core Connection. Yes. Okay. I said I'd go. Bye."

Not for the first time during this ordeal, Wes found himself wishing he had his own recording implant.

Blunt emerged from behind the screen in a dark double-breasted suit. Wes was no style maven, but even he knew that double-breasted had gone out of fashion twenty years prior. Still, the boxy look lent Blunt a distinguished air and, more important, hid the signs that he was letting himself go a little—or, Wes thought, dipping into the evidence room.

"Well Mr. Montgomery," Blunt said, falling into his chair and throwing his feet on his desk. "You're being recorded, I've alerted you to this, and you've waived your right to an attorney. Care to explain why?"

Wes shrugged. "I didn't think it was necessary just yet." As far as he could figure, it wasn't. They only had him on possession. As long as the words "intent" and "distribute" weren't flying around, he didn't need a lawyer. He'd be out in two days. It was his first offense. He had another eight to spare.

"I'm sure by now you're thinking we haven't found your stash," Blunt said.

Wes didn't bite.

"We found just under ten pounds of bacon, two dozen eggs and a case of beer in a crawl space in your house. A similar size stash we found in an unused septic tank in your backyard—interesting choice of hiding place, and we probably wouldn't have found it on our own." He paused. "But yes, you're only being charged with possession. For now."

Wes kept quiet. Found it on their own?

"Nothing to say?"

"No sir."

Blunt took his feet off his desk, spun the chair around and launched himself toward the wall monitors.

"I'll give you this much, Mr. Montgomery. You weren't an easy catch. You have no implants to monitor. Your electronic traffic is slight. Your private travel unsuspicious. Your monthlies are impeccable, though I guess we might be chatting with Dr. Halpern about that. We monitor everything. We have the best technology. All within legal limits, of course. Reasonable cause and all that. But none of it did us much good. So we tried a fairly old-fashioned approach."

Blunt touched a control panel, pulling up before-and-after photos of a woman.

"Fuck me in the ass," Wes moaned.

"I see you recognize Hillary Halstead," Blunt smiled.

5

When he'd met her at a party she looked like the before picture—blond hair cut into a bob, perky tits and just on this side of skinny. Better yet, she looked clean, healthy.

The problem with Wes' side job was that he usually ended up with eaters who didn't take care of themselves. They bounced around from dealer to dealer, eating what they could, then puking themselves silly or getting colonics or going on purge diets to maintain the illusion of a balanced diet. It always showed in their complexion. Why they couldn't just strike a balance—eat a little of the good stuff, maintain an exercise program—was beyond him. As the old man would say, "A little self-fucking-control would make this world a better place."

Those girls were never more than flings, mutual-using agreements. He needed to get laid, they wanted to get fed. Certainly nothing to get neurotic over. And the minute one of them started to exhibit signs of neurosis or drama, he made himself scarce. He wondered sometimes if this obsession with avoiding neurosis was a neurosis itself.

When they met, Hillary told him she was an aspiring model pessimistic about her chances. Fifty years earlier, she might have qualified as a supermodel—well, had she been 18 back then. She was too old for that now. And in this day and age, in this part of the world, she was too skinny. With a ban on meat, most fats, processed foods and sugars in anything other than fruit, not to mention a cornucopia of anti-obesity meds, skinny was common. Not so common were women who could gain weight and carry that excess flesh in just the right places. The supermodels these days—those in the Federation at any rate—tended to have Mediterranean or Hispanic influences, women given a genetic head start on the posterior portion of the equation. Most were brunettes with coal-black eyes. They sported love handles, plump arms, and breasts that cried out for the support of a sturdy bra.

And they were all eaters. That was the not-so-hidden secret. Just as there was a time when celebrities and models kept weight off with cocaine and puking—and everyone knew it, but pretended they were natural beauties—these girls kept weight on by eating illegal food, swilling high-fat, high-protein shakes and, in some cases, boozing. Everyone knew it but pretended these girls were all natural.

Wes always wondered why some savvy Southern businesswoman didn't grow such girls on trees—print calendars and shoot porn for a Federation market. But the rest of the country was a different place, where food was still legal and skinny girls ruled and coffee-table books of Ruben paintings weren't sold as jerk-off fodder. In the rest of the country, women like Hillary were the jerk-off material. Wes, a product of his society, liked his women carrying a little weight.

But a pretty face—a fresh, clean healthy one—was still a pretty face.

So he'd insinuated himself into a conversation with Hillary. "Why don't you move? Try your luck in-country?"

"Not my scene," she'd said. "Even if I could afford the exit visa. Land of savages and all. Besides, with all that food floating around, I doubt I'd maintain this figure for long."

"If you put on too much weight, you could just move back here and be a supermodel," he joked.

"They'd arrest me at the border," she said. "They'd commit me to an asylum. Move back here after fattening up in the land of milk and honey? Savages or not, I don't know that I'd be able to give it up once I had access to it."

He'd seen her around the circuit, but this was his first time talking to her. What he liked immediately—aside from her eyes and smile or boobs and ass—was that she stayed in the conversation. She wasn't toying with her implant, checking incoming messages, sending outgoing ones, updating her status.

As if on cue, someone shouted "Hey, everyone, check out Gawker

Feed 25." The room fell silent as people adjusted their chip sets to pull up something—whatever it was—on the heads-up-displays generated inside their field of vision or on the skin-based screen systems on their forearms.

An implant would have made his own life convenient. But being one of the last guys on Long Island to not have a comchip in his head gave him a certain rebellious edge. Besides, he didn't trust the damn things, figured they were too easy to tap or hack or track. Google was already sharing all the data moving into or out of his phone directly to government databases, why give either of them direct access to his head.

More, the whole concept just bugged him. He lived in a world where it was now commonplace for a man to walk down the street babbling like a schizophrenic hosting happy hour for demons, angels, saints and sinister dogs. Parties tended to be the worst. Gone were natural pauses in conversations, those tide-like waves of sound that had one time marked the breathing of a party. Now, it was nonstop noise, a cacophony of multitasking as any one guest was chatting to the person immediately in front of him, someone across the room, another person across town, to complete strangers on the web.

The brief moment of silence created by the video ended as there was a mad dash for those at the party to make the wittiest comments on whatever it was they'd all just watched. If silence was an endangered species, listening was completely extinct. Talk, talk, talk—but no real conversation and certainly—most definitely—no listening.

Except Hillary seemed to listen.

"So you like food?" Wes asked, distracted more by her attention than by the crowd noise.

What seemed a stupid question was typically the first step in a poorly coded dealing ritual. He might not be looking for money, but it was a ritual all the same.

She was sipping from a can of beer. "Yup. I think I risk beer parties for the carbs more than the alcohol."

"That so?"

"And sometimes, if I'm lucky, I'll meet someone who dabbles in something other than booze."

"Is that right?"

"That is right. But it's been pretty dry lately. Guess the cops are cracking down."

It was true. Wes was working his regulars, but he'd given up freelancing. For two months he hadn't dared take on new business. The cops hadn't started bothering with parties yet—however much the concept of private property had been eroded, it still existed, enough of it at any rate to make party raids a hassle for the cops involved.

"That's too bad," he said, turning away from her and scanning the crowd. "So what's your poison?"

"Hmmmm," she said, in a way that gave him an instant erection.

There was something earnest about her. She spoke in straightforward sentences, and while the "hmmmm" sounded sexy, it occurred to him she was actually considering the answer.

"In descending order. Bacon. Steak. Pork. Dessert. Ice cream." She paused. "Then again, I'd say breakfast is what I dream about. I can't remember the last time I had a real egg."

"Ever had one fried in butter?"

"No. I have not."

He turned back to her, leaned in. "Turn your implant off."

Her green eyes searched his. "I'm not recording."

"Right. But just turn the system off. Entirely. I've got an important question for you. I wouldn't want any incoming traffic interrupting."

She pressed the small bump on her temple to shut off the transmitter, then reached up and touched the side of his head. "You don't have one, do you?"

"I like to focus on what's in front of me. Can't have all those voices in my head driving me crazy."

"I think you're the only person I know without implants."

He bit his tongue. If he got going, he'd start ranting like the old man. Besides, it was his experience that proclaiming yourself morally superior to the rest of the world—like those people who bragged about never watching video—never did anything to impress a woman. Not the sort who showered on a regular basis and shaved her legs. Better to shrug it off, give her a smirk and let her bask in his independent, free-thinking aura.

"Many women fall for that whole off-the-grid, silent macho pose you're striking now?" she asked, waving her hands at him.

He blushed. He didn't like to think of himself as a blusher.

"The processor, too," he said, trying to regain composure. "All of it."

She pulled the waistband of her jeans away from her hip, giving Wes a glimpse of panty fabric.

"You can do the honors," she said. "It's right there on the hip bone."

"Is that where you keep it?" he asked, putting his beer down on the counter. He rubbed his finger along the edge of her hip until he found the position of the implant processor and pressed it firmly.

A shiver ran through her body.

"I don't think that's supposed to happen," he said.

"It's all in my head. And before you get any ideas, it happens all the time."

"I wasn't getting any ideas."

"So, what's this important question?"

"How do you feel about breakfast at my place?"

"I thought you weren't getting any ideas."

"Sorry, let me rephrase that. How do you feel about breakfast at midnight?"

"Wheat grass and whole grains keep me up at night."

"How about eggs fried in butter?"

She said nothing. Looked into his eyes to see whether or not he was joking.

"Side of pork sausage," he added.

"Don't tease." She pulled him toward her. There was nothing semi about his erection at the moment. And there was no point in hiding it. If she noticed or cared, she didn't let on.

"And hash browns," he added.

"Must be a damn good connection you have," she said.

"That's one way of putting it."

6

Just talking about the food was foreplay enough for her. When they kissed briefly before leaving the party, he thought she was going to mistake his face for the egg breakfast he'd promised. On the drive back to his place, she tailgated, blew her horn and flashed her brights until he dialed her car and told her to cool it down.

"I don't want the cops following us," he said, trying not to sound like a scold.

"Fuck the police," she said, laughing.

"It's usually the other way around," he said.

"You don't know the half of it."

"What?"

"Nothing," she laughed again. "I'll be good."

And so she was for the rest of the drive. But the minute they stepped through his front door, she jumped him.

"I have a bed," he said.

"There'll be time for that later."

So they went at it in the foyer like a couple of animals. It had been a while, but he managed not to embarrass himself. It helped that as she rode him, she kept shouting out "bacon and eggs" and referring to his penis as "pork sausage." It wasn't quite the same as thinking of grandma and baseball statistics, but it helped.

When he came, he almost blacked out—and not only because she was banging his head against the hard-wood floor. He immediately thought of the explosion that resulted from biting into a perfectly prepared hamburger and knew he was in trouble. The only other time in his life he'd thought of a woman and a perfect hamburger simultaneously, he'd fallen in love. He tried to remember something, anything, about drama, neurosis and mistakes, but came up with nothing. Post-sex brain chemistry asserted itself, drowning out his concerns. So what if he fell in love? Look at her, he thought. She's hot and mixes food and sex metaphors.

He was slipping into a pleasant post-coital coma, Hillary draped over him like a blanket, when she sat up and shook him awake.

"Wake up. My ass cheeks are freezing, and you promised me breakfast." She launched herself off him and onto her feet. After doing a set of naked jumping jacks, she dropped to the floor and did twenty push ups.

"What the hell are you doing?" he groaned as he summoned the will to sit up.

"Pre-emptive calorie burning," she smiled.

"Christ." Had he been wrong about her? "You're not going to puke up my food ten minutes after you eat it, are you?"

"No," she said, rolling her eyes. "I'm not one of your groupies. Are you going to stand there staring, or are you going to get me some clothes?"

He found her a pair of sweats and a fleece pullover. It was cool in the house, fall reaching its fingers into early August this year.

"This keeps up, July's going to be the only month for the beach," he said.

"Beach is just good for skin cancer," she answered.

"Okay, King Mike," he said, but otherwise clamped down the urge to fight about it. He pulled on sweatpants and a shirt.

She tugged at his pants. "You're not going to cook for me in the nude?"

"Have you ever fried anything in your life?" he asked.

"No," she said, putting her hand in his pants. "Is it dangerous?" She was mocking him.

"If you consider hot grease splattering on your business parts dangerous, then yes, it's dangerous."

"You're putting your life on the line for me, is that right? A big hero?"

"Hardly."

She bit his lip then let go. "I'm hungry," she said, twisting her own into a pout.

"Why don't you release that?" He motioned downward with his eyes. "Playing with it isn't exactly an incentive to get a move on."

She pushed him toward the fridge. "Fine. Get going."

He pulled out his fake watermelon, plopped it on the counter and removed the top.

"Very sneaky," she said, coming over to inspect. "Six eggs? I don't want to wipe you out?"

"Don't worry about that. But my watermelon has run dry of sausage, it seems."

"That's okay," she said. "Eggs are plenty for me. Besides, I've had enough …"

"Okay," he laughed. "That'll be enough of the word play. I don't want to think about penis every time I eat sausage."

He was overcome with the need to impress her. It was risky letting anyone know he kept anything in the house. It was folly to let on that he kept more than this. Possession vs. distribution. Simple as that. But looking at her standing there in the kitchen light, hugging herself with anticipation as she stared down at his eggs—he wanted to flex, to puff out his chest, fan out his tail feathers.

"I'll be right back," he said and ran down into the basement. He snatched his skillet off the peg board, then went into the storage closet, pulled a panel off the back wall, spun the old combination lock and grabbed a couple of individually wrapped sausage patties and a half pound of links from the freezer.

He ran back upstairs, where he found her gently handling one of the eggs, rubbing its shell with her fingers, rubbing her face with the shell.

She turned to him, stared at his pork products as if they were precious gems. "Can I hold them?"

"We'll have to make do with patties tonight," he said by way of apology. "The links would take too long to cook, and I don't want to ruin them in the microwave."

"So you have more than a connection, I'm guessing."

"You could say that."

"And what you're also saying is I can have breakfast tonight. Then breakfast again tomorrow."

"Yeah. But you'd have to sleep over."

"Well played," she said. "Well played."

7

What followed was two months of sex interrupted by eating—or the other way around. And the more they ate, the hornier he became. Her curves grew curvier, more prominent. Her hair seemed to shine, her skin glow. She was softer in all the right places.

He wanted to take her out to parties and show her off, but he couldn't keep his hands off of her any more than she could keep her hands off of the food.

Unlike all the recent women in his life, she didn't seem that interested in the party scene. She wasn't addicted to the lifestyle. She never once asked where his main stash was hidden, never asked to go with him on rounds. Considering her seemingly constant hunger and plain old curiosity, he knew it must have been hard for her not to bug him about it. Hell, it almost made him want to tell her all his secrets. The food, though, when it was around, made her a maniac. It was as if the experience—seasoning, chopping, stirring, letting a roast cook for four hours while the house filled with smells—did something to her body chemistry.

And just when he was thinking she liked him only for the food, she'd spend two hours asking him questions about everything non-food related. That earnest tone would return to her voice. She wasn't as quick to laugh—he had to work harder at his jokes. But she listened intently, watched every move he made. She was as interested in his day job as a reporter as she was in the dealing. She'd turn her implant off and just lay in bed with him watching videos or trying to read his articles.

"That's some exciting school-board proceedings," she'd say. "And to think, the last ink-and-paper newspaper in the entire Northeast is devoted to Long Island politics."

"Hey, it's honest work and a fine tradition."

"A real reporter. Do the bloggers point and laugh at you guys?" What would have been sarcasm from anyone else came off as a serious question.

"Nah. They see us more as museum pieces than anything else, I guess. What about your friends? What do you tell them about me?"

"That you're a no-good bacon-dealer and live a life of crime. They're all horribly jealous."

"I bet," he said.

He hadn't met any of her friends. He didn't know if she had any—something he saw not as a warning sign, but as a positive omen, proof she was a kindred spirit. She was the epitome of a homebody. He'd set out a ration of food before leaving for work and when he'd return home there was dinner on the table and the kitchen was clean—the only evidence of her daily struggles, the piles of print cookbooks in the kitchen. None of his illicit foods were packaged with the RFID chips that would automatically generate recipes in the counter-top glass, and he'd specifically told her never to search for such recipes from the home network.

Other than that, he didn't quite know what she did with her days. Normally the jealous sort, he hadn't seen any red flags. His previous adventures with food girls followed a pattern: they met, and after a week or two of frenzied fucking during which she ate him out of house and home, she'd get bored and start visiting with friends, who invariably happened to be dealers of some other sort, then she'd leave for a guy who ran booze or tobacco.

He was rarely heartbroken over such proceedings. The truth was most of them were, as his mom would have put it, "landfill—not even worth recycling." They were vacant-eyed shells who seemed to be shoveling down food and whatever else in an attempt to fill a void. The worst of them inevitably grew fat and—still being gnawed at by something they couldn't identify—they'd switch to something harder than food. Sooner or later they all ended up in rehab or jail, and it was better they were with someone else when their lives fell apart. Drama wasn't only bad for his health, it was bad for business.

Hillary, he thought, was different. She liked the food. She was putting on weight, but kept herself toned. Shallow as that observation was, it was an indication she could strike a balance, that there was something going on with her other than ravenous consumption.

And she was—how to put this—quickly becoming his best friend. Because of his lines of work and his nature, he didn't make friends easily. He could count his friends on one hand and still have a few fingers to spare. The only difference between Wes and a shut-in was that he left the house. He didn't want or need any more friends, he told himself. But having someone there every day to talk to when he woke up in the morning, when he returned home from work, before he turned out the lights...

"This is nice," he said, one night.

"What's that?" she asked.

"Us?" he said

"Us?" she asked.

He'd been suddenly overcome with two competing urges. First, to say "I love you." Second, the overwhelming suspicion he'd spook her if he did so. It was too soon. Entirely too soon. For him. For her.

Before he could speak, she turned to him. "It's really nice to have a friend, isn't it?"

At that moment, he knew he was done for. He was hers to deliver or demolish.

Her lack of friends wasn't the only mystery. She seemed to have some purpose in life—some drive at least—but for the life of him he couldn't figure out what it was. Pushed, she'd answer with vague notions of settling down, having a family, maybe turning the failed modeling into a failed fashion career.

"You don't seem to be doing much modeling at the moment," he'd pointed out.

"Taking a break," she said, rubbing her belly. "Besides, I have money saved."

None of it really mattered. He was happy playing house. He came home after work, she was there. He made an unannounced stop for lunch, she was there. Always seemed happy to see him. And he was happy to watch her eat. He knew better than to burn through his own inventory like that, but he could afford it.

"I think you could give those supermodels a run for their money," he said one night while running his fingers through the pile of hair just below her waistline, overgrown shrubbery being fashionable at the moment.

"Yeah? You think so?" It was a tentative response. She didn't seem the insecure type, but it made sense that a model didn't take supermodel comments lightly.

"God yes," he said. "Look in the mirror. Firstly, you're a super fox. Secondly, there aren't that many blonde ones out there. You'd probably make a killing."

"I'm too old."

"Too old? Old is in. Thirty-five is the new 15!"

She climbed out of bed to consider her figure in the full-length mirror on the closet door. She lifted her ass cheeks, let them drop. "Maybe you're right," she said, seriously. "It's funny. I see the extra weight, but I don't feel that different."

"Well, what did you expect? That you'd hear your arteries clogging? That you'd catch an instant heart attack?"

"I don't know."

"We probably shouldn't be eating like this every day—and you'll get tired of it soon enough. Or I'll run out of food. But as long as you strike a balance, you'll be fine."

"But this shit's bad for you. It's supposed to kill you," she said.

"Yeah, yeah, yeah. Sooner or later they'll prove that breathing will kill you. It's a lot of hysteria over nothing."

"I guess." She didn't sound convinced.

"Anyway, just look at you. God. Damn."

"I *am* a fox," she said, smiling again. "Maybe I could run off to Manhattan."

He instantly regretted broaching the subject.

"Yeah," he said, the excitement gone from his voice. "You'd do great in Manhattan."

She turned to him and pounced back onto the bed. "Don't worry. You're not getting rid of me any time soon."

But three weeks ago, she'd disappeared. No note. No explanation. No nothing. He'd come home from work and found a sink full of dirty dishes.

He never did tell her he loved her.

One morning soon after—it was all a bit of a blur—he found himself standing in the kitchen, the house creaking as it settled in the cold, not quite sure what time it was, what he'd gone to the kitchen for, what he'd been thinking the minute before. There was no room for coherent thought. Her absence took up all the room in his head.

"Fuck me," he said. "Fuck her." He went out for a run. Twelve miles—too far and too fast. Punishing himself for getting sucked in, for getting suckered.

He'd moped around the house and work, starving himself. He ran. He worked out. He tried to burn her out of his system like excess calories—or, failing that, numb the pain by punishing his body. Even then, he lay awake at night in a sweat of self-pity and self-loathing.

And when his appetite finally returned, this.

More worrying than finding himself cuffed to a police-station chair was that upon seeing the photo, the pain came flooding back. That and a glimmer of hope. Perhaps she hadn't run off to Manhattan. Maybe she'd just been picked up by the cops. She'd ratted him out, but lord knew what kind of interrogation she'd been subjected to.

He stared at her photos on the monitor. God, she was something to behold.

"What did you pick her up for?" he asked.

Blunt turned to him.

"Pick her up?" He grinned. "We didn't pick her up. She's one of ours."

8

Excerpt from a letter to Wes Montgomery, signed, "Love, the Old Man" dated Sept. 25, 2025

The second time I got pinched by the cops, it was your mother's fault. She turned me in. "For my own good," she said. Imagine that shit. Look, I know you're just a kid, and God only knows what she's been saying about me, but you're old enough for some truth. No use going through life like those idiot kids who believe the Potemkin village their parents try to build around them. I sure as hell hope you've found out by now that Santa Claus is fake. And his compadre, Jesus, too. Sooner you let go of those two illusions, you can get about growing up without your head clouded by lunacy.

You know who else is fake? Your mom.

Sorry. That was a bit uncouth and ungentlemanly. But true fact, Wesley: Your parents are morons just like everybody else stumbling across this planet. Yes, I include myself in that category. And you probably do, too. You should. Just be sure to remember that despite her saintly virtues, your mom's got her own skeletons in her closet.

At any rate, at this point in time, I was running black-market baked goods and high-fructose soda up from South Carolina. I'd drive down in a U-Haul and load up on Twinkies, Ding Dongs, Oreos, Sno Balls, Fudge Rounds, Yodels. You fucking name it. And cases of Coca-Cola, Dr Pepper, Mr. Pibb, Pepsi, Fanta—in grape, orange and strawberry—man, the Puerto Ricans went nuts for that shit. Then, I'd drive the truck back up. If I'd ever flipped it or wrecked it, I'da been eaten by ants or carried off by bees before anyone arrived at the scene.

I'd park in an abandoned lot in Jersey, somewhere near the Holland

Tunnel. Old King Mike—he was just Governor Mike at that point—was already on a rampage about black-market goods, so no way I'd drive that truck into the city. They searched every other U-Haul—as if Twinkies were more dangerous than terrorists. The cops in Jersey in those days could still be counted on to do the right thing and look the other way—especially if you gave them a cut and a case of soda for the kids.

Some time after midnight, my customers would arrive, one by one, in their cars or vans. They'd grab their order and off they went, back to their bodegas or Korean groceries or Taquerias.

See, at that point the cupcakes and Cokes were still legal. But you know what they say: "First, they came for the cigarettes, and I did nothing. Then they came for the transfats, and I did nothing ..."

There were some massive budget holes King Mike had to fill. Say what you will about the man, but he knew how to balance the books. So they came for the soda. Anyway, you could still buy and sell soda in New York State, but you had to pay a 50% tax on the full-sugar varieties and a 75% tax on high-fructose. This on top of the standard sales tax.

Which presented an opportunity for a wily businessman such as your father.

I'd drive down South, buy my sodas from a Walmart or Sam's Club for eight bucks a case. I'd sell a case to the bodega bunch for $24. Sounds like a lot, but I could have gotten $48 for it.

I was lucky. None of my guys ever were caught. None of them ever snitched. Mine was a small, profitable operation. I never got greedy. No semi trucks for me. No entanglements with chain stores or regional grocers. No partners. It was supplemental income. Just enough to make up for all the fucking taxes the government took out of my regular paycheck. "Free" counseling. "Free" healthcare. "Free" employment services. "Free" food. There's no such thing as a free lunch. Keep that in mind. Somewhere, somehow, somebody is paying. For everything.

Trouble started when I switched from two runs to four. Until that point, your mom had no idea. None. I was, of all things, a copywriter for a marketing consulting firm. I wrote pages and pages of bullshit web copy for bullshit companies, one of which was in Boston. As far as she knew, I was in Boston twice a month dealing with clients.

But when I started doing four runs a month, she started getting suspicious, asking what she thought were subtle questions designed to get me to confess. I knew it wouldn't be long before she accused me of cheating—that's what women always assume.

So, like an idiot, I told her the truth.

I should have known better. She was a bona fide, big-government liberal. Anyway, I unburdened my soul about my cola and cupcake enterprise and she, as they say, flipped her shit. Tears. Screaming. Accusations. I was poisoning children—POISONING!—with fructose. I was robbing them of the tax money that could save their little lives and give them an education.

I pointed out that that poison was what allowed me to purchase the three-bedroom apartment in Cobble Hill. Because otherwise the Feds, the State and the precious fucking children were siphoning off over half my fucking paycheck. She told me to shut up. To stop. I didn't like her tone. I told her to piss off. We didn't speak for a week or two.

Just when she seemed to be getting over it, it was time for another run. I had commitments to keep. She wasn't the boss of me.

And I was pulled over by a task force of Jersey State Troopers and the New York City Vice Squad. The Jersey boys couldn't look the other way when a tip had been called in.

"I did it for your own good," she told me when she visited me in jail.

I'm not proud to say this, but I punched the plastic divider. And if that hadn't been there, I might have punched her too. I screamed like a mad man. "You have no idea what you've just done. None. You stupid fucking cow." I pounded on the glass. Called her every name under the sun until the guard dragged me out of the room.

You'll go through a lot in life, up and downs, troubles at school, problems at work. Girls will break your heart and drive you crazy.

But I hope you never ever know what it's like to be betrayed like that by the person you love most.

Christ. I'm going to end this letter now. All these years later and just thinking about it makes me heart sick all over again. I just want to puke.

9

Blunt tapped at one of the screens on his desk. The door to his office opened and in walked Hillary, wearing a tight navy pantsuit over a white shirt stretched across her breasts. She looked like a woman who was trying too hard to fit in her old clothes—which is exactly what she was. Instead of seeming slightly pathetic, it came off as a little bit trashy and a whole lot sexy.

Wes flinched when she walked in. He didn't know whether to cry, fight, or run. Almost involuntarily he tried to stand up, forgetting he was shackled to the couch. The chains bit into his wrist, snapped him back down so that he fell forward to his knees on the floor.

"Fuck me!" he screamed, unable to stop himself. He stared down at the floor, rubbing his wrists, shrugging his shoulders as if checking for damage. What he was really doing was making sure he had no tears in his eyes, no quiver in his lip when he sat back up and faced her. Tears? Fucking tears? What had she done to him? This bust. This betrayal. This reduction to a weak little man on his knees trying not to cry.

In an attempt to focus, he thought about the broken eggs, the wasted butter. But the urge to cry was as much about abject rage and betrayal as it was about a broken heart and humiliation—or the emotions were so entangled as to be indistinguishable from each other. "Goddamnit, focus, Wes," he whispered to himself.

So he thought about work—his day job—about the task of reporting and writing dull stories about local events that never would be read outside of a hundred-mile radius yet seemed of paramount importance to those who did read them. School boards, town boards, zoning boards. Building codes, dietary restrictions. These were where the first assaults on freedom occurred on a daily basis. He thought, too, about walking back to the printing plant with Lou, his boss, both the press and Lou being the last of dying breeds, touchstones in an off-kilter world. The press was the last functioning privately owned press in the Northeast. Newsprint—for private companies at any rate—was a thing of the past, too environmentally unfriendly, too expensive. Yet it clanked along, churning out Suffolk News & Review and, during the summer, beach supplements for the North and South Forks. And Lou, a chain-smoking (when he could get them), foul-mouthed gray-hair who somehow slipped through every bit of sensitivity training and self-esteem class in the last 50 years. On printing days, Wes and Lou would walk into the plant and watch in silence as Lou sneaked a smoke, Wes gnawed on a bit of jerky, and they both listened to the old girl hum along. It was their shared "om," centering them. Thinking about it now calmed him enough to face Blunt and Hillary. He pushed himself off his knees and back onto the couch, flicked his hair out of his eyes as best he could, and looked straight ahead at the wall behind Blunt's desk.

"I'm sure you remember Detective Halstead," Blunt said. Wes could practically hear the smirk on his face.

"Of course."

"Hello, Wes," she said flatly, neither disdain nor fondness showing in her voice.

He looked at her, fighting hard to steady his voice. "Hi," was all he could manage.

"Looks like the weight's starting to come off, Halstead," Blunt said to her.

"I'm trying, sir."

Blunt motioned for her to sit, and she dropped onto the couch next to Wes. He scooted away, afraid to touch her. But he could feel the heat, the force emanating from that well-shaped thigh. A few weeks ago that had been his thigh, his to touch, stroke, bite or ignore. Now he could do none of that.

"Just calm down, Wes," she said, giving his leg a friendly pat.

He flinched, as if her touch had physically wounded him. He turned to look at her. And what he saw was her eyes, the curl of her lips, the faint fuzz on her cheeks.

"I want my lawyer," he started to say, but between the word "want" and "lawyer," both Blunt and Hillary had reached up to turn off their chips.

"Mr. Montgomery, let's not get ahead of ourselves," said Blunt. He put his big hand up in a calming motion.

"You heard me," Wes said. He could feel the first threads of panic unspooling. No way he'd be able to keep his head straight with her in the room. "I want my lawyer. I don't care if you're recording or not."

"Mr. Montgomery, if you'd listen, I have a proposition you might be interested in." Blunt's smirk was fading, but he still looked like a man in control of the situation.

"Lawyer. Now. I'll start screaming," Wes said. "I'll hurt myself and claim torture."

The word "torture" struck a nerve with Blunt.

"Now look, you. You calm down right this minute. I'll start throwing so many charges at you—"

"I. Want," Wes started, getting louder with each word.

Hillary put one hand on his knee and another over his mouth, turning his head toward her while she did so.

"Wes," she said, gently. "Wes. Calm down. Listen."

He tried to shake her off, but she held firm. His breath shot out through his nostrils in short bursts. Once. Twice. Three times. An enraged bull. But her eyes worked on him. They seemed to be saying something she wasn't allowed to say in front of Blunt. That, of course, was according to his inner moron. "She can't be trusted," the rational part of his brain pointed out. "Awww, she sure is pretty," said the moron.

She kept talking. "Just calm down. Listen to what Chief Blunt has to say. Doesn't hurt to listen. You might like his options better than what your lawyer has to offer. Just listen."

Her hands smelled like cheap soap, but it was the loveliest smell in the world. He was pretty sure she was saying something that he should be listening to her.

"And if you don't like what he has to say, then we'll turn our recorders back on, and you can request your lawyer, okay?"

Wes stared at her.

"Wes? Okay?"

He nodded slowly, watched her hand as she pulled it away and placed it back on her thigh.

"Mr. Montgomery," Blunt said.

Wes shook his head clear. "Yeah. Fine. Okay."

Blunt leaned back in his chair, threw his feet on his desk and let Hillary do the talking.

"So option one is, obviously, you call your lawyer. You walk out of here. We all know I didn't get enough on you to stick you with much more than possession. And a good lawyer might take issue with." She paused, looking away as she sought the right word. "Our tactics."

"You don't say," Wes said. "Which tactics specifically do you think might not be kosher?"

"Let her finish, Mr. Montgomery."

She picked up where she left off. "You also know that even if you walk, we'll be following you much more closely, openly even. Now we have probable cause."

"How convenient," he said.

"So you can go back to business and get busted, or you can try to wait us out and watch all your inventory go to waste—rot in some hole somewhere when the generator dies out."

Wes smiled. He finally had something on her. "As much as bacon gone bad breaks my heart, that's not an issue."

Blunt took his feet off the desk and leaned forward.

"Now what's that supposed to mean?" he said.

"Means my generator isn't going to run down any time in the next 60 years. Maybe I won't be able to get to it—but neither will you."

"Wes, did you just admit to having a nuclear generator?"

"I didn't admit anything."

"Nuclear?" said Blunt. "But nuclear's illegal."

Hillary's face tightened up as she tried not to roll her eyes.

"Know what else is illegal?" Wes asked. "Donuts."

He noticed Blunt flinch and knew he'd scored a hit. He continued. "Amazing how slapping an illegal tag on something doesn't just make it disappear. They sell home nuclear generators in Japanese Walmarts. You don't think I can get my hands on a couple? You don't think maybe a lot of those homes out on Dune road aren't getting their power from something other than solar panels or hydro?"

"Now listen here," Blunt said, unleashing his pointing finger again.

"Chief," Hillary said.

He put his hands back down on his desk and shut up.

"Wes, you're not doing yourself any favors. So you wait us out? How long? And even if you had a backup plan in place, who's to say you'll ever get your hands on the cash? So then what?"

The cash wasn't a problem, either. The bulk of it was in accounts in the South, waiting for him, growing. Out of the reach of these clowns. Of course, he couldn't get at it from up here. And despite the particulars, she was right. They had him. The money he had available in accounts up here was mostly what he'd made at his real job. And he'd burn through that in no time if this ended up in court.

He could make a break for the South. Migrating had always been part of the plan. But never this soon. The goal—fuzzy as it was—had always been 45, not 35. Yeah, he had a healthy stockpile of cash, but was it enough to retire in comfort, much less luxury? He'd always pictured a wife, a dog, maybe a kid somewhere near a beach. Instead, he had a sudden clear image of living alone, three hours inland, on some scrubby hill in Bumfuck, Mississippi, supplementing his retirement income by working as a greeter at Walmart. No longer trying to hide the fact he was slinging bacon and eggs, no longer trying to convince the law he was an upstanding healthy citizen, he'd gone to fat. There was an angry patch of acne on his face and what little hair he had left hung limply from under his Walmart cap, that century-old smiley face mocking him. His neighbors were all morbidly obese and watched Fox News without an ounce of ironic intent. Sure, they had freedom of choice, but they'd all die too young from the poor choices they made. Young and broke after spending their life savings on medical bills for conditions they could have prevented in the first place. And Wes would become one of them.

Or he could track down the old man.

He shuddered.

Of course it wouldn't be anything that drastic. Wes probably could retire in comfort, in the right locale. He'd just conjured up an image of the U.S. as unfair as the stereotypes of Federation citizens as effete drones. Aside from dietary and travel restrictions in the Federation and reproductive and religious restrictions there, most people went about their daily lives with little drama, too busy to spend too much time obsessing over the philosophical underpinnings of their respective governments.

Maybe escaping had always been a fantasy anyway, equal parts boredom and subliminal programming by the old man. But now it didn't seem he had much of a choice. It was get out or get ruined.

He had a sneaking suspicion that the current crop of excuses for not leaving were being piled up by that pathetic part of him that wanted to stay for one reason: Hillary. "There was something there," it whined. "No way she's that good of an actress."

But there was a very good chance he'd get caught trying to get out. Then what?

That was the most valid opposition he could think of. He had the closest thing he knew to a foolproof escape plan. But that plan hadn't involved this level of surveillance. The problem would be setting it in motion without getting busted. And God only knew what they'd do to him then.

"So what's the other option?"

It was Blunt's turn to talk. "We can all help each other. See if you can stay with me. There's a task force working on a case right now. We're trying to crack the Manhattan ring."

"The Manhattan ring?" Wes laughed. "That's the biggest operation there is. It practically operates in the open. Doesn't seem like it would be that hard to break. Follow the celebrities. Follow the bloggers. That's the whole allure of the city. The laws don't apply to rebels—as long as the rebels are rich and famous enough."

"That's exactly the fucking point," Blunt blurted, slapping the desk and standing up, suddenly looking like a man in the grip of a religious experience. "These people just flaunt the law. What kind of message does that send? The wrong kind, that's the kind. The capital of the Federation, a seething pit of sugar and saturated fat. And if I could just break that ring, well then! The rest of you cockroaches would be out of luck, wouldn't you?"

Wes kept his mouth shut, afraid Blunt had come completely unhinged.

"Chief," Hillary said in a soothing voice.

Blunt looked at her, as if he'd just come out of a trance. He looked back at Wes. Cleared his throat, took a deep breath, swiveled his head around and rolled his shoulders. "Listen," he said, trying to start over again. "None of this is official. It's all off the record." He paused. "It's a deep-cover operation."

Wes wasn't quite sure he'd heard right. "Come again?"

"King Mike doesn't know about our task force," Hillary said.

"Oh dear lord," Wes said. "So who is it angling for the promotion, for the Federation-level appointment?"

Blunt started to breathe heavily again. Hillary looked down at the floor. "Listen here, you little shit," he said.

"Chief," Hillary said.

"You do *not* know what you're playing with," Blunt said.

"Chief," she said again.

He fell silent, glaring now at both of them.

"Listen, Wes," she said. "It's not like that at all. Trust me."

"Trust you?" Wes asked. "Did you just ask me to trust you?"

"Forget it," Hillary said.

Wes turned to Blunt. "I don't see how you have anything remotely resembling jurisdiction here."

"Let us worry about jurisdiction," Blunt said.

"It's complicated," Hillary added.

Wes looked at both of them.

"So if I'm understanding this, you're asking a small-time regional dealer to infiltrate Manhattan's inner circle and somehow bring down a dealer who's been operating under King Mike's nose for at least two decades. All so that King Mike 3.0 can stay in power long enough to transfer it to 4.0, which will guarantee the nanny state marches bravely into the future. Them meddling in what I eat, how I prepare my food, restricting my travel and everyday energy consumption. I'm not quite sure I see how I benefit in all of this."

Christ. He was channeling classic, unadulterated old man. Or preaching like Blunt.

"You stay out of jail for one," said Hillary. "And as long as you're working with us, you're allowed to carry on business as usual."

"And when—if—the case ever ends?"

"Full amnesty," Blunt answered.

"And free passage to the South. Or wherever else you were thinking of heading," Hillary offered.

"Free? As in free to take my chances and sneak out? Or free as in you'll pay the exit Visa fees and allow me to do it legally."

"Whichever you prefer."

"Again. Pressing question. I'm supposed to trust you?"

Blunt let out a fake laugh. "It's not like you have much of a choice."

Wes knew Blunt was right. Still, he sat in silence, chin in hands as if running through his options, weighing the pros and cons.

"There's one other benefit to our plan," Blunt said.

"What's that?"

"You'll be partnered with Detective Halstead." His lips curled into a smile that would have made Satan proud. "I doubt it will be quite the same, but I understand you enjoyed your previous time together."

Wes, his head feeling as if it were going to explode, turned to Hillary. She stared at the wall behind Blunt's desk, a Mona Lisa smile on her face, anger in her eyes and a blush creeping up from her chest to her neck.

"Fuck me," Wes said, dropping his head back into his hands.

"We'll see, won't we?" Blunt said. "But for now, let's talk over this plan."

It was straightforward as far as Hillary and Blunt were concerned. Passing as a couple, Hillary and Wes would journey into Manhattan and fall in with the blogging and celebrity circles, then sniff out the trail and follow it to the source, avoiding New York City cops and the Federation police who worked in the jurisdiction.

"Are you kidding me?" Wes asked.

"What?"

"How the hell are we supposed to insinuate ourselves into *that* circle? Like they'll just open their arms to two rubes from the East End?"

Hillary blushed again as Blunt explained that for her part, she was going to pose as a model new to the scene.

Wes couldn't help himself. "So what, she's going to fuck her way through Manhattan?"

"There's no need for that language, Mr. Montgomery," Blunt said. "She'll be posing as your girlfriend."

"What am I supposed to be?"

"I'm sure you'll figure something out."

"You make it sound so easy," Wes said. "And a timeline?"

"As long as it takes," Blunt said.

"Fuck," Wes said. He had a sudden horrifying vision of being partnered with Hillary forever—he a common criminal, a dog on a very short leash, while she went on with her life, her real life. In this vision, they sat in a car on a stakeout of some sort. The doors were locked, he was cuffed to the arm rest. And over a cup of coffee, she prattled on and on about her marital problems to a rich, fat guy named Jeff.

Blunt looked up at Wes, smiling a little now, as if he'd had a glimpse of Wes' vision and was finding some small delight in it. He nodded at Hillary. "You can unshackle him. Get him out of here."

As they walked out the door, Blunt called out. "There's one last thing."

"Now what?"

"You're getting an implant."

"Oh hell no, I'm not," Wes said. "Absolutely not." The word "implant" set off a panic, and he made a break for the door. It was locked, but he started kicking at it.

"Halstead," Blunt said, and with a cat-like quickness she was on him.

She slammed him against the wall and pinned his arm behind his back. "Just calm down, Wes. It's going to be okay. We'll be home in no time."

"Home?!" he said, "What the hell are you talking about?"

She didn't answer, instead slapping a tranquilizer patch on the back of his neck. "Shhhh," she said. "Shhhh."

10

After Halstead wheeled her new partner out of the office, the door sooshing behind them, Blunt flattened his palms against the desk's top, closed his eyes and exhaled, trying to calm himself. Somewhere between the back of his closed eyelids and his optic nerve, a little red heart appeared. Blinking.

"Heart rate elevated. Blood pressure elevated," a soft voice chimed.

"Off," Blunt said through gritted teeth.

The heart disappeared. He pushed up from his desk, ran his hands through his hair and walked slowly toward the heavy bag hanging from the ceiling. He took another deep breath. Considered the bag. What would punching it solve? Nothing.

Still, he struck out, a full-forced punch, perfect form. But not perfect aim. His bare knuckles glanced off the bag, leaving a layer of skin behind.

He hissed like a kettle—"Ffffffffffffff"—before letting loose with a loud "Fuck."

And without even thinking about it, he'd grabbed an aluminum baseball bat and was swinging it at the bag.

Thwap! "Fuck!" Thwap! "Fuck!" Thwap! "Fuck!"

Blunt was at full boil now and knew well enough that he wouldn't be able to stop until he'd exhausted himself. And when his vitals were uploaded to the department system at week's end, both the medical staff and the psych staff were going to want an explanation for such a huge spike occurring outside of a scheduled workout. That would lead to meetings and, worse, worried glances. "Fuck! Fuck! Fuck!"

The door swished open and Hillary was standing before him.

"Chief?" she said.

He knew why she was there. She'd come to talk her way out of the assignment, to turn those big eyes of hers on him, use her powers to get herself out of an awful situation. She'd always gotten her way with him before. "Before" was the key word. Those days were over. She had to have known that. Or did she have so little respect for him that she expected him to roll over even after all this?

Well, there she was. And so was he, red-faced, panting, a maniac with a baseball bat held over his head.

"What?" he demanded.

"I thought maybe." Her voice trailed off.

"You thought you'd come in here," he pointed the bat at her. "And be all 'Mew-mew-mew. I don't want to do this.' And you thought I'd say, 'Why, sure, Halstead. Anything you want. Anything at all. Don't want to work the biggest case of the decade? By all means. Hell. Why don't you take another vacation? This last one worked out so well for you.' That's what you thought."

"Well," she started.

He'd called it exactly, and now she didn't know what to say.

"Not this time," he said. "Not this time. Not ever again."

It felt good denying her, to be in charge once again. It was a small consolation.

"Listen to me," he continued. "You're fucked. Plain and simple. Six ways from Sunday, you're fucked. I own you, you hear me? You and that bit of filth you picked up on vacation. One false move on this case, you're going to rot under the jail cell that I throw him in. You want to remain a free, productive member of society, you're going to do exactly what I say. So get your ass out of my face and go attend to your new partner. Get a chip in him and get on the fucking job."

He was standing toe to toe with her now, looking down into her face, frozen now in shock. It was only the second time he'd seen her wear the expression. The first was four weeks ago when he called her into his office and played his hand.

"Any questions?" he asked.

She looked down at her feet. "No," she said, barely audible.

"We understand each other?"

She paused. "I guess I don't understand the hostility," she said, looking into his eyes again.

"You understand perfectly well," he said. "Don't try to play stupid now."

"I guess I thought you were better than that."

She just always had to get the last word in, twist the knife one more turn.

"I should take the high road? Is that it? I tried that. Guess what. The high road is a dead-end street."

She started to speak, but he cut her off. "Get the fuck out of my face. Not another word. Get out now."

11

Now she'd done it. Those years in the academy, ten years on the force, she'd managed to avoid entanglement, affairs internal and otherwise. It was a lonely life, to be sure, but a simple one. KISS. Keep It Simple Stupid. She'd found a vintage print of the phrase, had it framed and placed prominently in her living room.

And then this? Whatever it was, it wasn't simple, what with Wes falling for her, Blunt turning it into some sort of Federal-level sting operation and, well, what about her?

She didn't know. For perhaps the first time in her life, she didn't know what she was feeling. All she'd wanted was some simple companionship, a friend—something, anything—outside of the force. After working a few undercover stings at local food parties, she'd started going on her own. An hour here or there. Nothing too much. Nothing that would get her in trouble. She'd just claim to be doing a little freelance if it ever came up.

And she'd run into Wes Montgomery. Something had drawn Hillary to him, an animal magnetism so strong—and so obviously reciprocated—that it scared her. It wasn't something she'd ever allowed herself to experience and she'd tried to keep the thought of it at bay. But even during the first week or so after meeting him— especially in the first week or so—her detective's mind wouldn't quite let it go. It was a case. It needed solving.

She filed away the obvious. He was handsome—enough. So what? She'd had plenty of handsome men throw themselves at her. Clowns and charmers as well. She considered herself immune to it all. And yet.

So during their time together, she started snooping around his place for clues to find out what made him tick. She was disappointed that it took her only one sweep of his house. There, in his underwear drawer, barely hidden away, was a box stuffed full of handwritten and typed letters, all of them signed, "Love, The Old Man." The rantings of a reprobate, they seemed. The kind of man who'd never been to half a sensitivity session, who'd never sat for a minute with analyst or therapist, who've never taken five milligrams of Stabil-U or a patch of Even-Keel. It was like a museum exhibit, a look at unreformed man.

She couldn't stop reading them. When she arrived at the last one, she found herself wanting more and so started over again.

Then it hit her: Wes wasn't raised right. Not in the modern Federation sense. She knew his old man hadn't been around, that Wes hadn't been molded by him. Not directly. Wes had never told her about the letters, only that the old man had left during the secession movement. This abandonment drew them together. Her own mother had bailed out. It gave them something to talk about in those late-night hours as they lay in bed, legs entwined, staring at the ceiling. She couldn't very well talk about her real job. So they talked childhood, both in a detached, bemused manner. It wasn't something he railed against. It just was. She liked this about him. She didn't see herself as a victim. He didn't claim to be one, either.

But even a few weeks into the relationship, after having read the letters, she could recognize the strands of the father woven through the son, like polycarbon fibers through a skyscraper. Hell, if the old man had been around, Wes likely would have rejected every ounce of this foolishness. Instead, at some point in his life, he'd been receptive, had let it in. And whatever had caused the letters to stop, however Wes might resist the notion that he was his father's son, it was too late now. He had a strong undercurrent of unreconstructed 20th Century man running through him.

She liked that about him, too.

What had she ever known but men so in touch with their feelings or neutralized by chemicals as to be eunuchs? Sure, the Federation had its fair share of knuckle-draggers. Plenty of smart women fell for them, too. No doubt about it. Or, in an act of rebellion, embraced it. She knew from rebellion. She knew from daddy issues.

Her own father had been the pinnacle of Federation manhood, a man tuned like a fine instrument to the emotional and intellectual needs of women. On paper at any rate. He was a therapist. At one point a brilliant one. And a consummate nerd. Women had been a test that he set out to ace. And, in the form of her mother, Madison, he had. Temporarily.

How did Hillary know all of this? It was her first case, the evidence strewn about in the wreckage of her parents' marriage.

It had been a matter of passion, of sexual tension. There was none. Barry and Madison's relationship had no highs and lows—that without the benefit of psychotropic drugs. It was her father's nature to eschew drama, to put the woman first, to sublimate his own needs. He'd do anything he was asked. Anything. But he never initiated. One of the few things Hillary remembered of her mother was the resigned refrain, "I don't know, Barry. Why don't you tell me what you want?" His answer, without fail: "I want what you want."

Madison, without causing a scene, without fighting for more, without trying to change him, walked out the door, never to be heard from again.

Barry cried some, upped his medications, insisted it was her mother's right as a fully-formed Federation woman to abandon them both. Then he set about shaping his daughter into the sort of woman who would never do such a thing.

He rid the house of video and forbade implants in an attempt to keep her out of the clutches of anything resembling Fourth-Wave Feminism, the jumble of politics, consumerism, sexual predation and excess he attributed to his wife's exit. But he did succeed in planting the seed in Hillary's head, and she would forever harbor her own hatred of the movement for stealing her mother away—even when she grew old enough to know better.

He spoke to her about feelings and intellect, told her that while she was one of the prettiest girls in her classes, those looks were sure to fade away. He began to preach a bastardized western Buddhism, urging her to let go of the material, the physical, the real. He wanted for her a desexualized world in which the soul, that poorly defined thing, trumped all. Worse, he began to want this for other people as well. It seeped into his practice and scared off patients—the important ones, the ones who paid with cash.

In other words, he created a veritable convent.

As she grew older, every fiber in her body wanted to rebel, to fight him, to run. How easy it would have been to rush into the arms of some boy. That was what daughters did, right? But so many of those boys were simply miniature versions of her father.

And the dumb ones with the sexy animal stares? It took only one run-in to learn that particular lesson. Anthony D'Amato. Great smile, horrible grades. Parked deep in the Pine Barrens, he'd made his move, all teeth and spit. When she tried to stop him, he chose to see it as a game. He'd likely have raped her, too, if he'd had the strength for it. But he'd spent the week sitting in a sauna while wearing a sweat bag, trying to lose weight for an upcoming fitness competition. Still, it was a close struggle, and a formative one.

But she didn't tell her dad she signed up for the mixed-martial arts classes. Neither did she rebel. After all, he was her father. He'd suffered enough for one lifetime. She didn't fight him. Didn't sneak out. Didn't slut around. She kept the house clean, kept him fed, worked a part-time job and read his increasingly wild and less frequently published papers. She bided her time. Went through high school on the periphery of that particular society.

But break his heart, she would. The spring of her senior year, she applied to the University of Phoenix's criminal justice program. The thinking man's daughter was done with the intangibles of the soul. She was going to be a cop. Not only was she going to embrace the black-and-white world of law, she was going to enforce it.

Then one night, all these years later, at a party she had no business attending, she'd busted Wes staring at her ass. She was talking to a dopey blond guy about the latest Gawker reality show—"Tattooed Testicles"—when she noticed. She caught Wes' eye. He didn't turn away, didn't blush or apologize. He shrugged, grinned and walked right over to her.

Funnily enough, Blunt—who was always in her implant when she was working undercover—had never picked Wes out of the crowd at any of these parties. She pushed the thought out of her head, to focus on Wes as much as he was focusing on her. If it came down to a fight, he'd be a tough one. But unless he'd taken specialized martial-arts training, she was pretty sure she'd beat him. What she wasn't sure of was his age. His face was young, as were his hazel eyes. But a splash of salt and pepper in his black hair threw her off. Premature gray or not? Was he 28 or 38?

"How old are you?" she asked.

It caught him off guard. Only for a second, but it was obvious. This happened. The Federation's subjects were conditioned to expect an opening salvo of irony or sarcasm. As the media outlets to the south put it, it was the Federation's chief export.

"Thirty-seven," he answered.

Two years older than she was. But it didn't matter. Whatever she was doing at the party, it wasn't looking for a boyfriend. Still, she found herself, what? What was she doing? Flirting? Acting?

Then he went and mentioned the eggs.

12

Wes massaged his temple where the new implant sat, felt on his hip bone for the processor switch but found nothing. Of course. Between the tranquilizer patch and the local anesthesia, his stint in the police infirmary was hazy. It could have been five minutes ago or two hours. An image of the red-headed technician leaning over him, warning him "this will pinch" or "you'll feel a slight tug" as she worked on his head. "Just like piercing an ear or getting a tattoo," she'd added. He wasn't so sure that phrase was comforting considering what she'd actually been doing was minor brain surgery. She'd consulted a pad, poked at it with her fingers and said, "Okay, then, no switch for you, they say." And with that she'd left.

Not only had they stuck him with an implant, they had complete control over it. For now, though, he neither saw nor heard anything out of the ordinary.

He was waiting in the lobby of the police headquarters as Hillary received last-minute instructions from Blunt. She came out, unshackled him from the chair.

"If you're wondering," she said, "all implant activity is down for the time being. Operating system and server upgrades. So you get an extra bit of reprieve."

Together they walked out into the parking lot. Wes blinked against the bright winter sunlight magnified by the three-foot high drifts gathered around the edges of the lot.

"Son of a bitch," he said. It was the first time since his arrest he'd been outside.

He took a deep breath, let it go and realized he had no idea what to do next. He hadn't mentally processed his arrest, much less figured out how the hell he was going to move forward with this ridiculous plan to bring down Manhattan's biggest dealer while pretending to be the boyfriend of the woman who'd betrayed him.

That woman sped through the parking lot toward her car in stern silence. Wes had to skip to catch up to her.

She turned on him. "Where are you going?"

"I don't know. With you?"

"Says who?"

"Blunt, I guess. Don't we have a case to crack or something."

She glared at him.

"What?" he said.

"Fuck my way through Manhattan?"

"Look."

She pushed him. Hard. "Fuck my way through Manhattan?!" She punched him in the arm. A swift, straight jab. It wasn't meant playfully, was not a love-tap.

"Ow. Shit. That hurt."

Two uniformed officers walking by paused long enough to laugh. "She's going to fuck that dude up," one said.

"That hurt?" she asked. "How about this?" This time she hit him with a cross, twisting her hips, putting her weight into the punch. He tried to get out of her range. "How do you think that felt in there? Fuck my way through Manhattan?" She punched him again. He wasn't going to be able to move his arm if this kept up.

"Are you insane?" he demanded, running now to the other side of the car. She followed, but he kept circling, keeping it between them. "I'm sorry," he said. "Jesus."

"I bet," she said.

"Well, I am." He could feel the guilt oozing over him. It was an awful thing to have said. His mother hadn't raised him to talk that way about women.

"Get in," she said, unlocking the car.

"You going to hit me again?"

"Just get in."

They climbed in and she was already backing out of the space when he realized what had just happened.

"Wait a minute!" he screamed. "Stop the car."

"What?" she said.

"Stop the fucking car!"

"No."

Wes reached for the wheel, grabbed it. The car wobbled back and forth, and they fought for control.

"Quit being crazy," she said, slapping at his hands.

"Stop this fucking car right now."

When she did, he hopped out, started walking, not even sure where he was going. He heard her door open and close, her feet slapping the pavement as she followed.

"What is wrong with you?" she asked.

"What's wrong with me?" He turned. "With me? Oh, I don't know. My girlfriend—or what I thought was my girlfriend—not only turns out to be a liar, she's an undercover cop. She has me arrested, ropes me into some harebrained undercover operation likely to get me killed, has a fucking com-set implanted in my head. And I'm the one apologizing? Because I hurt your feelings? What the fuck is that about? My door was kicked in. I was tazed. I almost choked to death on bacon. And I'm apologizing? Me? I'm the bad guy?"

He was puffing out little clouds of steam in the cold air.

"You done?" she asked.

"I'm the one who should be punching you," he added. "In the face!"

"I'd like to see you try."

Another two uniforms walked by. They slowed, reached for their Tasers. She waved them off.

"This is bullshit," he hissed. "Crap in a bucket."

She considered him a moment longer then shrugged her shoulders. "I'm sorry."

"That's it?"

"I said I'm sorry."

"Well, okay then. I wouldn't want you to get too emotional about it. Wouldn't want you to break down in public."

"I was just doing my job," she said, looking into the distance.

"So were the North Koreans," Wes said.

She rolled her eyes. "Get in the car."

He stood staring at her, his eyes watering in the cold, his skin starting to hurt. They'd brought him in without a coat.

"Get in," she said again.

"Fine." He opened the door and threw himself down into the seat. Like a pouting child, he crossed his arms over his chest. "Where we going?"

"Home," she said.

"Har dee har har," he answered.

They drove the rest of the way without further words. When they pulled into his driveway, he spoke.

"At least someone fixed the fucking door."

"Yes," she said. "Someone did. Someone also chased all the raccoons out and cleaned the place up."

"That totally makes us even. Nothing like a little housecleaning to make a guy forget about home invasion, assault and arrest."

"You do seem to forget you were in violation of multiple laws."

He said nothing in return.

Already the sun was going down and the temperature seemed to be dropping a degree a minute. Wes wrapped his arms around himself and ran to the porch. He fumbled the keys out of his pocket and tried to open the door.

"Had to replace the whole thing," she called out after him. "Made you a copy, but it's in the house."

She handed him a box and fished her keys out of her pocket, mumbling something about digital key pads and retinal scanners. Door open, she took the box and walked into the kitchen.

"Make yourself at home!" he shouted after her.

The house was warm and, at first glance, in good condition. As if nothing had happened.

"I had the walls repainted," she said.

He ignored her and ran down to the basement. There he found something more akin to the mess he'd been expecting: boxes strewn about, the door to his stash hanging on the hinge, his tools pulled down from the wall and scattered about the floor.

His skillet. It was gone.

Of course. Last he'd had it was in the kitchen, so logically it wouldn't be down here. Still, he felt a panic begin to grip him as the weight of the situation finally began to force itself on him. He ran back up the stairs and looked out into the backyard. A gaping crater where the old cesspool used to be, his backup home stash. His mouth was dry. His head spun a little. He made his way into the kitchen.

"What?" she asked.

"I." He stopped. It hadn't felt real until now, until he saw the physical evidence of the disruption, this reordering of his life. In the police station, it had been something happening around him— something incidental to his emotional drama with Hillary. Now, back in his home, he realized, he was in the center of something that scared the bejeebus out of him. There was no escaping.

Was this how his old man had felt after his mom ratted him out? He'd never quite understood the story on an emotional level. That betrayal was a plot point in someone else's story, an abstract concept that never really resonated. After all, he'd grown up with his mom, she was the sole provider. She fed him, clothed him, put him to bed at night, taught him right from wrong—real-world right from wrong, not the wholesale horseshit the old man peddled in his letters.

That's what she'd called it: "wholesale horseshit."

She never stopped them from communicating, never took the letters. She only asked that Wes give her the general gist of the letters so that she could offer a counterpoint. When he'd confronted her with the charge of betrayal, of sending the old man to prison, she didn't flinch from his accusatory glare. "He was breaking the law, Wesley."

"But he was your husband."

"Which is why I expected more from him."

"Do you believe all that stuff about the Federation and food?" The fact was, she'd taken to sneaking him chicken once a month. And for his birthday the previous year, she'd cooked him a steak. She didn't tell him where it came from and told him not to ask if he wanted it ever again.

"People change, Wes," she said. They must, he figured. Because she never seemed anything like the old man made her out to be. Years later, he came to the conclusion that without the old man around, she didn't have to prove him wrong all the time.

"Would you tell on me if I broke the law?" he'd asked, wondering about the limits of her loyalty.

"Only one way to find out," she'd said, laughing and mussing his hair.

He laughed for her, but he hadn't really found it funny. Or comforting.

"Wes," Hillary said, bringing him back into the moment.

"My skillet," he said, bracing himself, one arm against the door jamb, the other hand on his chest. It was all he could think to say.

"Shit," she said. She grabbed a kitchen chair. "Here. Sit down. Let me get you some water."

"Water," he repeated. Water. Times like this didn't call for water. Something else. But he couldn't remember what. Or where he put it. Probably wasn't there anyway. He took the glass handed to him and just held it.

She rifled through the box she'd brought in from the car. "I didn't have time to tidy up the basement. The skillet was taken in as evidence."

He looked up at her. He thought he might cry.

"But look," she said, excited all of a sudden. "I rescued it for you." She pulled it out of the box with a flourish, as if it were Excalibur. She pressed it into his hands, pressed his hands against his chest.

"It's okay," she whispered, suddenly gentle and caring. "I know this is crap in a bucket." The phrase was one of their couple phrases. "I'm sorry. We'll sort it out."

He held the skillet, rubbed his fingers over the handle, across its knobby bottom. A little rust came off on his fingers. Black iron had to be cared for. They hadn't cleaned it or dried it properly. No problem. That could be fixed. He held it up to his nose, breathed in all the years of oil cooked into the iron, inside and out, remembered the meals and tried to calm down. He closed his eyes. After a while, something else took hold of him. Something just as primal as panic.

He opened his eyes. She was squatting in front of him, worried.

"I'm starving," he said, quietly.

"Me too," she said, relief creeping into her voice. "Me too."

Of course, the only thing in the house was tofu, spinach, veggie burger. It was enough to make him want to cry again.

"I'm sorry," she said.

He shook it off and dug around until he found a jar of almond butter.

"Bread?" he asked.

She produced a loaf. He made them each a sandwich. He shoved his into his face, eating while standing. He felt like he hadn't eaten in days.

13

Excerpt from a letter to Wes Montgomery, signed, "Love, the Old Man" dated October 25, 2025

Why did I go back to your mother? Because even on a good day, your old man's a fucking idiot. People in love are stupid. People trying to save love may as well be loaded on a short bus and driven to the medal podium at the Special Olympics for a gold in "retarded."

Also there's a lot to be said for vindication, for the ability to say "I told you so."

They shut down our bank accounts.

"I told you so," I said.

Despite the assurances they'd given her when she called in the tip, they kept me locked up six months.

"I told you so."

They took our house.

"I told you so."

My credit, obviously, was ruined. So was hers.

"I told you so."

Pyrrhic victory to be sure. (Look that up.)

"You're the one who broke the law," she said, confused by it all.

"You're the one who trusted the government," I said. "You're the one who snitched."

"But you broke the law."

"You betrayed me."

And round and round it went.

But we had no one else. Two crazy kids in a crazy world and all that.

Besides, we were still—how shall I say this without planting unpleasant images in your head that may require therapy at a later date—we were still attracted to one another. And, for a hundred and one reasons that make no damn sense at all, being angry at one another sometimes makes grown-ups extremely, extremely attracted to one another.

Aside from that, we still had our good moments, tinged by sadness as they were. When we weren't busy accusing the other of getting us into this mess, we still made each other laugh. We still had moments of tenderness.

But those moments were rare.

The thing is, we were broke. And while I'm on a mission to dispel myths society may be implanting in your tender little skull, let me set you straight on one thing: money can buy you happiness. Or at least the peace of mind to carry on like a civilized human being. Lack of money can buy you only misery.

I picked up freelance work with my old agency and managed to pull some strings to get her on as a copywriter with another shop. It was enough for us to rent a two bedroom on the ass end of Prospect Heights. Ironically enough, she was put on a beer account. Fart jokes for frat boys and all that. It was one of the last bits of business the agency had. Truth be told, she got hired so easily because no one wanted to go near the place figuring it wouldn't be long for the world. They'd made their name helping companies sell soda, candy, chips— and, once upon a time, cigarettes. Now, all of that was on the way out. The feds weren't only taxing the merchandise, they'd started taxing the ads as well. Most of those marketers, cast as demons by King Mike and his media cohort, basically told New York City to go fuck itself and moved their accounts to shops in Atlanta and Texas.

It's not exactly a mystery where this one's headed, is it? The mystery is how the alcohol companies held out so long. Sure, sure, sure. Lobbying groups and all that. But the cigarette boys once had the most powerful lobbying groups known to mankind. And look what good it did them. If money was oxygen for politicians, maybe alcohol was their blood.

Cigarettes were now illegal across the land. Fast food was illegal in New York, Connecticut and Vermont. Sodas and snacks containing high-fructose corn syrup were on the verge of being illegal. And just when the sugar-cane farmers were starting to gloat, the obesity taxes on items containing real sugar started to spread out from New York, like a ravenous cancer. New Jersey, Connecticut, Vermont, Massachusetts. Pissing off the farm states may have been the first serious, irredeemable crack in the country.

California, of course, wouldn't be left behind in a social-engineering race. It taxed all beer and booze at a rate of 1500%. That is not a typo. And that's no way to treat your populace when the entire state seemed to be burning down around them, clouds of ash blotting out the sun.

King Mike, who'd somehow gotten himself elected governor of New York, wasn't going to let California outdo him. He enacted his own set of booze taxes and, to prove his integrity—that he was doing it for the health of the electorate—threw the New York vineyards under the wheels of the tax bus.

Now, I hadn't gone back to dealing. I wasn't happy about it. And it wasn't because of your mother. I'd have done it just to spite her. As much progress as we'd both made in forgiving one another, I'd still be overcome with moments of blinding rage. I could see the blue flashers of the cruisers. Could smell the inside of the prison. Could hear her say, "I did it for your own good." Sometimes I wished she'd done something more forgivable—like fuck my best friend or cut off my testicles.

Fact of the matter was, even after my house arrest was over, I was still being followed by the police everywhere I went. I'd been banned in all the local bodegas because if I so much as walked into one, there was a vice squad in there the next week checking the inventory and going over the books with a magnifying glass.

Which meant paying retail at chain stores.

So one afternoon, I walk into the apartment with a six-pack of beer that I'd just paid thirty bucks for. Middle of the day and I walk in and find your mother on the couch, sitting there looking at her hands as if she'd never seen the damn things before.

"What are you doing home?" I ask.

"We lost the beer account," she says. "They let everyone go. Shut the whole place down."

I just couldn't help myself. "I told you so," I said, before walking into the kitchen and opening up a beer. I thought for sure she'd follow me to the kitchen in a blind rage, screaming about forgiveness, communication, compassion—all that sort of silliness. But halfway through the beer and she's still in the living room. Back in I walk and find her frozen in the same position on the couch. I'll never forget the way she looked. Sitting there crying, she looked up, wiped her nose with the heel of her palm.

That's when she told me she was pregnant.

"Maybe I should buy a bottle of champagne," I told her, trying not to let on I was suddenly pants-pissing scared and lottery-winning excited all at the same time.

I handed her the bottle. "Here. It's the champagne of beers. Supposedly."

We couldn't have afforded real champagne anyway.

14

The sandwich hadn't been nearly enough to fill Wes' needs.

Done, he took a deep breath. "Okay," he said. "Get your keys. We're going for a ride."

He stood up and headed for the door, taking his skillet with him, unwilling to let it out of his sight. She followed him. He stood by the driver's side door.

"I'll drive," he said.

"Where we going?" She tried to shake off the cold that had attached itself to her on the brief walk from the front door. She stomped her feet.

"Get supplies," he said. He shivered. "Why don't you run back in and grab a couple sweaters, couple of hats and two coats. We'll need 'em."

She ran in and out, returning with her arms loaded. "Surprised you didn't make a break for it," she said.

It hadn't even occurred to him. Clearly, his head wasn't functioning. He needed no more evidence than the fact he was driving out to resupply this early in the evening. With a passenger. With a cop. In the car, he hesitated before pushing the ignition button. What, really, was there to lose? They had him, right? By the short and curlies, as they used to say. Maybe he should have called a lawyer, but they'd thrown him off with Hillary. It was too late now. He'd agreed to do this. Either way he was damn hungry.

"Wes, turn on the car. It's freezing."

He turned to Hillary. His stomach turned a little flip. He should have been choking her to death with his bare hands. Yet, he sat there thinking she looked kind of cute in that stupid hat, shivering in the cold. He was about to drive her out to Montauk. Perhaps it was some top secret pheromone they'd developed. They were using it on him to keep him in her thrall.

More likely he was just an idiot.

He pushed start and began to drive.

After cutting through the dinner-time traffic in Hampton Bays and Southampton, he had open cruising. A full moon rose in the sky, making it seem as if the potato fields on either side of Sunrise Highway were made of frosted silver glass.

"It's so quiet," she whispered.

Normally, for this stretch at least, he was gunning along on gas power, the old Suffolk County News & Review truck engine humming through the night air. Delivery vehicles with three or more axels had been given special dispensation. You could run them with a gas-hybrid engine—as long as you had the proper commercial license and paid the indulgences due the state by way of taxes and fees. Because of their size and the aging technology, they typically ran on gas 90% of the time, which was why more than a few bored, rich guys bought them just to have them. Try as they might, the feds couldn't get rid of the almost instinctual need—which sprung up in the short hundred fifty years of gas-powered vehicles—to hear the growl of an internal-combustion engine.

The paper had four of them. A gentleman's agreement with one of the drivers meant Wes had access to the Montauk truck as needed. Driver got a night off and two pounds of bacon. Wes got the delivery truck as something approaching a convincing cover. He dropped off the papers at three in the morning, put the truck in electric, then slipped off to his bunker. Wes also got another customer out of the bargain. It wasn't long before the driver was placing his own orders and selling the goods to friends and family at twice the already ridiculous prices Wes charged.

But no gas engine roaring through the icy air tonight. They drove in silent electricity, cutting through the preserved charm of East Hampton. Soon enough, the trees gave way to dunes as they neared Montauk.

"It's kind of spooky," Hillary said.

"Yeah."

"Mind if I turn on the radio?"

"Yeah."

"Oh," she said, shocked a little, but making no protest. "Okay."

She was treating him with kid gloves. It slightly confused him. What did she care? She was a cop with a criminal in custody. Had she wanted to be an actress when she grew up? Was she playing the role of a lifetime? Was she so damn dedicated to her job, to the state, that she'd lived with him for two months, made him fall in love with her and was now still pretending she was concerned?

15

"So, tell me something," he said. "You're a cop, right? I know you guys have mandatory weekly therapy sessions. I come up at all?"

"The therapy," she said. She figured she might not like the turn this conversation was about to take.

There was plenty to be disappointed about in the police force. It should have been the most masculine field outside of the military. But, no. It hadn't taken her long to discover that it, too, had been transformed into a sorority of over-sensitive pretty boys.

But worse was the therapy.

"Yes, the therapy," Wes said.

"Maybe I should have joined the fire department," she answered.

"What's that mean?"

"I wasn't lying when I said I hated therapy."

This had been another thing they bonded over—a shared hatred for sitting in a room, spilling your guts, mewling over your problems. Because her own father had been a therapist, she'd been able to skip all the mandatory evaluations that had come up throughout high school and beyond. Barry had wanted her to see someone else, but she'd played to his ego, batted her eyelashes, and that was all it took to get Daddy to sign off on his little girl's mental health. Wes had been insanely jealous that she'd made it through her formative years without forced confessions.

Of course, she had left out the part that she was a cop and was now forced into it once a week.

"That wasn't my question," he said. "Did I come up at all?"

"No. Of course not."

"Of course not?"

"I don't talk about real things in therapy."

Her first months on the force, it was her weekly sessions with Dr. Vasquez that had taken the most getting used to. She felt almost as if she were cheating on her father. But therapists, it turned out, were remarkably similar. Dr. Vasquez might as well have been Barry—an earlier version of him, before he'd started getting loopy—in a dress. All Hillary had to do was toss out some little worry or neurosis and Dr. Vasquez would massage it from mole hill to mountain and back down to mole hill again.

"After the hour's up, we both feel like we've accomplished something," Hillary said.

She detected a hint of a smile on Wes' face. She turned and looked out the window. "And she's obsessed with how the men on the force treat me. Always with the 'You fitting in okay? They treating you okay?'"

"Are they?"

"They're men," she said.

"Meaning?"

She tried to explain how Boggs wasted half an hour of her life on Monday mornings asking about her weekend. And another half hour on Friday afternoon, trying to maneuver a conversation about the coming weekend to such a point that Hillary might suggest getting together. It was against the rules for him to ask her out.

"Not that'd I'd say yes," she said, if only to ease the envy she could see etched across Wes' face. "Not that he'd have the balls to do it anyway."

She told him how Mulrooney was always moping about how his marriage was falling apart, how he wasn't ashamed to admit that, yeah, sometimes he cried in the bathroom at work over the sorry state of things.

"All a ploy, I'm sure, to see how I feel about the possibility of an affair."

Worse was Darcey and his stories about his crazy Fourth-Wave wife, a maniac in the sack. The shit she wouldn't do, Darcey was always saying. Adventurous didn't even begin to describe it.

"Which is his subtle way to lure me into a threesome," Hillary finished.

"So what do you tell the therapist?"

"I tell her what a great bunch of guys they are. That they have my back, keep an eye out for me."

"Why?"

"Because they do. Because I knew what I was getting myself into."

She'd learned pretty quickly in college and the academy that a woman had to be careful around men. It wasn't that they'd harm her in anyway. Not these guys. No. But laugh too much at their jokes, try to be buddies with them, let them into your confidence, and next thing you know, they're asking you on a date or crying outside your dorm room at three in the morning saying, "I thought we had something special," no matter how many times you'd stressed you were just friends.

And she'd wanted friends. She wasn't so antisocial as to not want basic companionship. But ultimately it became too much of a risk, too much damn work to walk the friendship line and always, at some point, have to push back. So she kept her head down. Did her job. Kept her after-work socializing to a minimum. Barely chuckled at even the funny jokes. She was no-nonsense Halstead.

"They still try, but they've got no reason for hope. And I'm sure in the locker room they call me a cold bitch. But better that than a tease."

Wes allowed himself a glance at her. "I guess it must be tough."

"It is what it is," she said.

She didn't tell him about Blunt. How he came along, how she figured he'd be safe. Old enough to be her dad. Still devoted to his dead wife. A mentor who played by the book. A friend? Maybe? Then one day in the evidence room, he's sticking his tongue down her throat. Worse, it had been so long since she'd had any kind of contact, she'd come within an inch of acquiescing, just for the moment. But she knew better, knew once again she'd have to be the one to do the right thing.

Blunt. It drove her crazy. It wasn't her fault. Of that much, she was certain. As certain as she was that he blamed her for it. And while he may have gone home that night broken-hearted and distraught, she'd gone home and, for once in her life, allowed herself to cry.

"So our thing?" Wes asked.

"Our thing?"

"Yeah, you know, that whole two or three months there? That thing?"

"It was," she started to say.

"If you say 'It was what it was' I will run this car into a ditch right now."

"It was nice," she said.

He took his eyes off the road to look at her. She looked back at him. He shook his head. "Unbelievable."

16

Hillary sighed, leaned her head against the window and looked out at the moon again.

The road lifted and they climbed out of the dunes onto the elevated bit of land at the very end of Long Island. Grass and trees appeared on either side of the road again. They entered the town of Montauk, drove through it.

"Where the hell are we going?" she said, more to herself than Wes. "The only thing left is the lighthouse. You're stash isn't in the lighthouse, is it? That would be pretty cool. Against the law, but cool."

"Not quite," he said.

So they really had no idea where his stash was? And he was leading them right to it. He pulled onto the shoulder of the highway just beyond a horse ranch. He had only to turn right down the next dirt road, drive to its end and his best kept secret would be a secret no longer.

"We here? Where is it?" she was losing patience, overcome with excitement.

"Just," he started, clutching the steering the wheel, his knuckles turning white. He took a deep breath, exhaled and released his grip. He turned to her, tried to smile and forced himself to pat her thigh—her firm, shapely thighs, between which he'd nestled his head on many a night. "Just give me a moment."

She didn't look down at his hand, didn't ask him to remove it. But he did anyway.

"Okay," he sighed. "Let's do this."

He turned right on the dirt road and killed the lights. Even without the full moon, he knew the road well enough to drive it in the darkest conditions. The empty branches of trees closed like skeletal fingers forming a tunnel over them.

"Where's the snow?" she asked, noticing the drifts piled up on either side, wondering why someone had bothered to plow a dirt road.

"It gets taken care of."

"How?"

"Don't want to talk about it." This time he wasn't guarding a secret, other than the rage that ensued every time he thought of the details of that particular deal. The plow guy was a state worker, a union guy, so he didn't come cheap. Every year, as if Wes were some sort of governmental unit bound by contractual negotiations, he demanded more, going on about having a family to feed and the risks he was taking, insinuating it would be a shame if he had to give it all up, turn it over to someone who might not be so good at keeping secrets. What really pissed Wes off was that the guy lived with his mother—no wife, no kids. There were costs involved with doing business, but it just chapped his ass. Wes changed his mind. "Actually, his name's Vincent Colliccio. Works for the highway department. He came recommended, so I imagine he's got his hands in other things as well. If you take him in, tell him to say hi to his mother for me."

Hillary looked at him.

"What?" he asked.

"And you lecture me about betrayal?"

"Don't start with me," he said, reaching the end of the dirt road, where it turned into a grass track. "Besides, he works for the government. Not like he's a real person." He kept driving, slower now, hoping the car wouldn't bottom out. They drove by a rusted-out gate bearing bright yellow and black signs.

"Was that a radiation sign?"

"Yup."

"And what was the other one?"

"Biohazard, I think."

"Is this safe?"

"I haven't grown a second head yet."

He flicked the lights back on. There was no one back here to see the lights, the path became tricky, and it took only one night of cleaning the splattered remains of deer carcass from the grill of a vehicle to determine that you never wanted to do that again.

They passed the remains of a guard booth.

"What the fuck?" Hillary whispered.

"Look up there," he said.

"Jesus."

He pulled to a stop in front of a three-story tower of cinder blocks rising out of the remains of what was once the other ten or so stories that rose into the sky. A radar dish—once half as long as a football field—rusted in pieces on the ground. To the left of the tower were a metal-frame structure and two more concrete buildings.

"If you look back there, just through the trees, you can see the old neighborhood."

She looked around, taking it all in. "This is seriously, seriously creepy."

Wes explained that what they were looking at was once known as Camp Hero, an Army Air Corps radar installation built during World War Two to protect America from invading Nazis. The housing area was made to look like a New England fishing village on the off chance German bombers found their way across the Atlantic.

"Sounds very melodramatic," she said, laughing.

"Nothing melodramatic about it. Fact is, at one point during the war, a handful of Germans were dropped off by submarine on Long Island. But they were caught."

"What happened to them?"

"What do you think? President ordered a military tribunal, and they were put to death."

"Roosevelt?"

"The one and only," he answered. "Anyway," he continued, brushing away the tangent and continuing with the history of Camp Hero.

According to official reports, the base was used by one branch or another until 1980 and then shut down, a victim of outdated technology and bureaucratic squabbling between the Army and the Air Force. According to unofficial "reports"—sublimely ridiculous conspiracy theorizing in a series of books called "The Montauk Project"—the base was used as a top-secret installation where time-travel and extra-dimensional experimentation was conducted. The mad scientists who roamed the grounds of Camp Hero were responsible for the Philadelphia Experiment, in which an entire battleship was cloaked and instantaneously teleported hundreds of miles—with disastrous bone-melting results for many of the crew. Like any good conspiracy, everyone was in on it—the Army, the local politicians, the Feds, the Free Masons, the guy who played Luke Skywalker in the original version of Star Wars. Even Martian Jesus.

"Martian Jesus?" Hillary asked.

"Yes."

"So what happened to them?"

"Martian Jesus went back to Mars. The others didn't go anywhere. They're still here, toiling away in underground laboratories in a parallel dimension. So if you feel anything brush against you, it's probably not your imagination."

"That's funny," she said.

"And yet, you're not laughing."

She shrugged.

"It's okay. The place does that to you. They're ruins, but not quite old enough to be classic. You almost expect to see someone walking out of those houses back there."

After they shut down the base, the hands of time started the process of slowly picking the place apart. Time was helped along by weekend whackjobs scouring the base—the radar tower in particular—for the outdated electronics necessary to build their own nonfunctioning time portals or whatever. Drunk high school and college kids climbed the tower in the middle of the night wondering if they could get a view of Manhattan, dared one another to ferret out the guard booths and underground bunkers.

At some point in the 1990s, the Feds handed the property over to the state to do with as it pleased. Plans were immediately set in place to turn it into a golf course, but the state ran out of money, and Montauk was hit by a drought. There wasn't enough water for the Fire

Department to put out a trailer fire, much less enough to water greens eight hours a day.

So the plans were abandoned, Camp Hero left alone, its radar array towering above the trees the only reminder—until that too succumbed to weather and time and collapsed. With that out of sight, the base was forgotten.

"The end," Wes said.

"How did you find all that out?"

"Books. Newspapers. Library. Some of it, I may have just made up."

"But how did you even think to look it up to begin with?"

"My old man. He used to come back here when he was a kid."

"He ever take you?"

"Left before he had a chance, I guess," Wes said.

He killed the car's auxiliary functions and shuddered as the heat went off.

"How much farther do we have to go?" she asked, the unbroken snow now more a concern than the history of the base.

"Half a mile."

She looked down at her shoes. They may have been sensible for the office, but they wouldn't cut it for long out here.

"You could have told me to bring boots or something."

"Don't worry about it. Let's go."

They stepped out into the night air.

"Fuck me," he said.

"Shit," she added.

What had been an inconvenience back in Hampton Bays now felt like a knife slicing away bits of skin. The Montauk Point wind blasted in from the ocean and whipped around them, whistling through the remains of the base. Chains and loose siding banged in the night.

Wes started off for a low-slung concrete building with a garage door. It was a hundred or so yards in the distance, slow going as they struggled through the snow, breaking through the crusted surface and sinking with each step.

"Wes' big secret stash," she said.

"Hardly," he answered.

He yanked on the building's garage door, and it slid up and away on well-greased tracks, clattering in the cold night air. Sitting in the bay of the garage was an electric snowmobile with a trailer attached to it. Next to that sat an electric all-terrain vehicle.

"Impressive," Hillary said. "But doesn't that snowmobile leave tracks?"

"There's a brush on the trailer that covers them. Wouldn't fool anyone on the ground but it does good enough for drone flyovers."

They climbed aboard, Wes started it up, and they drove up onto the snow and out into the night, the hum of the electric drive and the rattling of the treads and trailer the only noise in the night. Wes pointed the machine toward two hills, humpbacks of snow rising out of the white fields surrounding them. They slid by the first, cut between them and rounded the far side of the second before pulling to a stop at what looked like the entrance to a mausoleum sealed shut with concrete. In the face of the slab was a jagged opening.

"What is this?" Hillary asked.

"This," he said, motioning grandly, "is my underground lair."

"Are you shitting me?"

"Most decidedly not."

"We're going in there?"

"Most decidedly so."

17

He hopped off the snowmobile and started for the opening. "If it's any consolation, they're not technically underground. They just built concrete structures and piled dirt on top of them."

"Oh, well that changes everything," she said, following him in.

Her last syllable bounced off the walls in the entry room and down the length of the bunker before dying. Except for the moonlight spilling in through the opening, the place was pitch black and smelled of dust, mice and bird shit. The only thing that gave away its size was the echo.

In that vast darkness could have been an army of slobbering perverts, and he and Hillary wouldn't have been any the wiser.

Hillary dropped her voice to a whisper. "I know you have a flashlight. How about you use it?"

"For a cop, you seem pretty fraidy cat."

She reached out a hand, felt for his back, then delivered a sharp punch to his kidney.

"Ow!" he yelled.

"Turn on the light."

"Fine. You didn't have to hit me!"

He fished the flashlight out of his pocket. He flicked it on, revealing a cavernous room with two wide hallways leading off either side. Wes headed for the one on their right. The hallways would have been large in a standard office building, but compared to the vastness of the entry vault, they looked like rat tunnels.

Hillary clutched Wes' belt, stopping him short. "How far does this go?"

"About a hundred yards," he said, walking again.

He waved the light to the left and right, showing her the rooms on either side—old offices cluttered with military furniture. Desk drawers had been pulled out and filing cabinets tipped over. Papers were strewn everywhere. "Southampton College Class of 95 Tidewater Expeditionary Force" had been spray painted in blue on a wall. In red paint on another wall: "Is checkers still illegal in the future?"

Wes was glad to have company. As often as he'd made the trip over the years, he never had completely conquered his fear of the place. That he only slightly wanted to crap his pants at the moment was a vast improvement. The dread, though, was still there, unshakeable. Partly it was a fear of dark places and being buried alive. And, too, it was the ghostly scene set by the offices abandoned as if some avenging angel had come through and just whisked everyone away, knocking over the furniture in the process. Ruins were meant to consist of tumbled down stones, lettered with dead languages—not mid-20th century office furniture stuffed with purchase orders and invoices. And if forced to, he'd admit that all of those aliens and extra-dimensional beasties— and Martian Jesus, too—ran wild in his imagination when he was down here.

Run or walk—and he usually ran—he moved through the hall, hands shaking, forgetting to breathe. Tonight was no different.

He was just about to tell her this, when he heard a voice in the darkness.

"Wesley, Wesley, Wesley."

Wes stopped dead in his tracks, clenched his cheeks as tight as he could, quit breathing, said nothing.

"Wes? Is that you?" A man's voice.

He swung around toward Hillary, the light slashing through the dark.

"What's wrong?" she asked.

"Did you hear that?" he whispered.

"Of course I did," the voice answered. "I said it."

"Yeah," Hillary said. "Listen, Wes—"

The voice spoke again. "Wes. It's me." Drunk, playful—and in the darkness, sinister—it came from all directions at once. Wes pictured something Gollum-like, bug-eyed and wiry, crawling toward them on big, slimy toe-pads, a former mid-level military bureaucrat who refused to leave his desk when the base was decommissioned. Then the image changed. Now it was a morbidly obese, slightly retarded pervert, standing there with a huge erection poking through his blood-stained clown suit.

Wes swung the light around again.

"Who the fuck said that?" he screamed, his stomach doing flips. "Where are you?"

"Wow," the voice said and started laughing.

"Wes?" It was Hillary this time.

He turned back to her. She put her hand up against the light.

"You didn't hear that?" he demanded, but didn't wait for an answer. Then, shouting again, "I'm here with a cop. She's armed!"

The voice, wherever it was, laughed louder. "A cop? What the fuck are you doing with a cop, Wes?"

"Come out, Goddamnit!"

"Oh my, my, my." The laughter was verging on hysterical.

"Wes," Hillary said. "Listen to me." She reached out and touched him on the arm.

"Fuck this," he said, grabbed her hand and bolted, almost yanking her off her feet.

"Wes," she shouted. "Damn it, Wes. Stop."

But he wasn't listening. He was running full speed toward the end of the hall. He should have made for the exit, but something more primal in him had demanded light—lots of it and immediately. So he made for his storage facility. As fast as he ran, the voice kept up. "Are you running?" it asked in what sounded like amazement. It was laughing so hard, so loud in his head, Wes hoped maybe it would choke on its own mirth.

He ran faster, then banged with a loud crash into the metal cage at the end of the hall, bounced back and fell on the floor.

The laughter stopped. "What the fuck was that?" it asked.

"Wes, you okay?" Hillary asked.

He slapped her hand away, dug the key out of his pocket, opened the lock, threw her in and followed, locking the cage door behind them. He flicked the light switch, flooding the room with bright white light, intensified by its reflection off the rows of stainless-steel refrigerators and freezers.

"Shit," Hillary said. "My eyes."

Wes screamed into the darkness outside the cage. "Okay, you fucker. Now what? Show yourself!"

"What the hell has gotten into you?" the voice asked.

"Where are you?" Wes shouted.

"I'm in my house," the voice said. "Where the hell would I be?"

"Wes, calm down," Hillary said. "I'll slap you if I have to."

He ignored her.

"Who the hell are you?"

"It's Jules, you dumbass," the voice said.

Wes' brain froze for a minute, his fingers let go of the wire mesh of the cage. "What?"

"Jules," Hillary said.

Wes turned toward her. "Who the fuck is Jules?"

"Oh, who the fuck is Jules?" the voice asked. "That's lovely. That's gratitude for you."

Wes looked around, saw nothing but his facility gleaming in the light and darkness beyond it. "Jules?" Suddenly he remembered a Jules. Yes. Jules. A friend. And a customer. East Hampton artist.

"Yes, Wesley. Jules." The voice again, this time with concerned laughter. It did sort of sound like Jules.

Wes looked around, then back at Hillary. "What the fuck is Jules doing down here?" He looked back into the darkness. "Jules, what the fuck are you doing? How'd you find this place? Where are you?"

"I told you, I'm at home."

"Home?" Wes repeated the word as if it meant nothing to him.

Hillary caught his attention, pointed toward her temple. "You have an implant, now, genius. The system's come back online."

He opened his mouth to say something, but no words came out. An implant. Son of a bitch. Son of a bitch and motherfucker.

Finally, he found his voice.

"Can you hear everything?" he asked Hillary.

Jules answered. "Well, duh."

Hillary nodded.

"Well, why didn't you say anything earlier?"

"What are you talking about?" Jules asked. "I did say something. And then you had a hissy."

Hillary whispered. "I don't know. It's second nature to me, I guess." She paused. "And you scared me. I didn't know what was going on."

"Sorry," he said.

"It's okay," Jules said.

Wes shook his head. "I." He stopped. "I just got this implant today."

"Well, yes, Wes. That's what allowed me to speak to you across time and space, you Luddite. Saw your name pop up into the sync list, and I was so surprised I had to check it out."

"I guess I'm not used to it."

"Not used to it? You sounded like an Amazonian savage who'd just seen a video screen for the first time."

"Sorry," Wes said again. The shock was subsiding just enough for him to be properly embarrassed. "You're my very first caller."

"I'm honored," Jules said, laughing again. "They didn't test the thing out in the store?"

Hillary caught his attention, nodded frantically.

"Yeah. But that was in the store, the light of day. I'm down here in the dark. Middle of nowhere. Monsters abound."

"Down where?" Jules asked.

Hillary shook her head. That's right. If he had been foolish enough to get a stupid implant, he wouldn't be blabbing his whereabouts over the network.

"I'd rather not say."

Jules paused before speaking. "Ohhhh. You're meditating again."

"Huh?"

"You're in your special place."

"Oh, yeah." Wes tried to force a laugh. That was pretty clever, after all. But he was still shaking.

"Bring me back a souvenir from the other side," Jules said.

"A souvenir?"

"Remember what you brought back last time?"

What was Jules going on about? Wes looked at Hillary and shrugged, mouthed the words, "I don't know." She rolled her eyes, pointed to the fridges surrounding them, then mimed eating, bringing an imaginary fork to her mouth. He offered a weak smile and smacked his forehead. Duh. But fuck them both. One of the main reasons he'd avoided implants in the first place—aside from an attempt to drive his mother insane—was so he didn't have to speak in fucking code.

"Oh, yeah," he finally said. "One of those."

"Better make it three," Jules said.

Three? What the hell?

"I'll have to check my suppl—" He stopped himself. "I'll have to see if the souvenir store has that many in stock."

Jules laughed. "Lord."

"Sorry," Wes said, slowly finding his own voice again. "I'm just not used to this fucking thing."

"Whatever did possess you to join the 21st century?" Jules asked. "Should I be worried? This isn't like you."

Hillary made her eyes big in warning. Apparently, "The cops drugged me and surgically implanted a bug into my brain" wasn't an acceptable response.

"This chick I'm seeing," Wes said. "She's been on my ass about it for the last three months and wasn't taking no for an answer."

"Wow. So Wesley Montgomery gets an implant for a lady. Must be love or some shit."

"Some shit's a good way to put it," Wes said.

She rolled her eyes again.

"Some shit? Listen to the tough guy," Jules said. "Five minutes ago, you were screaming like a little girl in the dark."

"Ha!" Hillary laughed, unable to help herself. She fell back on her ass.

"Keep it up," Wes snapped. "I'll leave your ass down here."

"Well, well, well," said Jules. "She's down there? You brought her to your special place?"

"Yeah," Wes said.

"So, not only is this serious, she witnessed that entire hissy fit?"

"Yes. And I'd like to thank you for that. She'll probably leave me the minute we get back to Hampton Bays, and I'll be alone and stuck with this fucking implant."

"Sorry," Jules said.

"You should be."

"Look. Let me make it up to you. I'm going into Manhattan for a couple of weeks. Leaving in two days. You two can come for the weekend—stay at my place. All you have to do is pay your way in. We'll party. I'll show you two how the other half lives. Chicks are always impressed with that shit."

"I don't know," Wes started. "Manhattan?"

Hillary punched him in the thigh. "Fuckin hell?"

"What happened?" Jules asked.

"She just hit me."

"She should. What were you going to do, spend another weekend snowed in at home in Hamster Bays watching video?"

"I don't know," Wes repeated.

Hillary raised her hand again to strike.

"If you aren't the biggest chickenshit," Jules said. "C'mon. We'll do the circuit. The bloggers will love you."

At the mention of bloggers, Hillary made her eyes wide and motioned as if to say, "See?"

"Yeah, well," Wes said.

"A real-life print journalist from out in the sticks? You'll be the talk of the town."

"Fine. Okay," Wes said.

"Really?"

"Yeah, I guess I owe her."

"Most excellent. Bring your bags—and my souvenirs. Hell, why don't you two come over tomorrow night, sleep over, we'll leave Friday morning."

Hillary nodded frantically.

"Let me make sure I can get off of work," Wes said. "Shouldn't be a problem."

"Great. Smell ya later," Jules said.

A faint pop signaled he'd signed off.

Wes and Hillary stared at one another.

"What the fuck?" he said.

"I know," she said, excitedly slapping him on the thigh. "What a lucky break."

"Break? What are you talking about?"

"Someone offers to take us into Manhattan and party with bloggers. That's a hell of a cover. What were you talking about?"

"This," he said. "This whole thing. This deal. This lying to my friends, spying on clients. This." He tapped the side of his head. "This fucking implant. And you can hear everything. Can you see everything, too?"

"Of course," she said.

"Of course," he spat back at her. "So I've got absolutely zero privacy."

"What did you expect?"

He kicked a box. "All that and I'm stuck with you." He'd meant it to sound mean and angry, but by the time the words left his lips, they sounded pathetic, hurt. He was suddenly tired again. His muscles were stiff and his bones practically hurt.

"What's that supposed to mean?"

He looked up at her, dug deep for a smirk. "Is there a special cop class you people take in Missing the Obvious?"

"You know what, Wes? I don't care what they say in sensitivity training, but this wounded, emotional side isn't attractive at all."

"And? What the hell does that have to do with anything?"

She shook her head and muttered, "I'm the one missing the obvious."

"Come again."

"Nothing. Forget it."

They sat quietly for a while, the refrigerators and light bulbs humming along. The sound of papers rattling came down the long hallway.

Hillary looked up. Too exhausted to operate the irrational corners of his imagination, Wes' mind cranked out the most likely explanation.

"Rat," he said. "Maybe a raccoon."

"Oh," she said. She pushed herself off the floor. "I thought you were hungry."

He'd forgotten. But at the mention of the word, his stomach reasserted itself. She offered a hand to pull him up and he took it.

"Let's get moving," he said, grabbing a couple of plastic bins. She followed him around as he opened refrigerator and freezer doors. Eggs, cow's milk, butter, bacon, pork chops and sausage of various types, including boudin—a rice and meat-stuffed delicacy from South Louisiana. Paired with pig-skin cracklins and a cold Coca-Cola, it was perhaps the best breakfast a man could ever hope for. Wes was the only one who carried boudin or cracklins on the East End. And they were Jules' special addiction. That he'd ordered three times the usual amount probably meant he was throwing a party in Manhattan.

Hillary wandered off to poke around some more.

"If you want to dig, combination is 318," he said, over his shoulder.

He reached into a freezer and pulled out a two-pack of rib-eyes. He ran his palm across the cellophane packaging. Yes, this would do nicely. He placed them in a defrosting unit imported from Japan.

"Are there potatoes in the house?" he asked.

"Yeah," she said.

He could already hear them bubbling in oil. Oil. He grabbed a big bottle of vegetable oil. That, too, had been declared evil. Guilt by association with deep-fried foods or because it simply lacked the cachet of olive oil, he wasn't quite sure.

"Is this the reactor?" Hillary asked, standing in front of a six-foot-tall box covered with a bright blue tarp.

"Hardly," Wes said. He pointed to a knee-high contraption that looked like a cross between a fire hydrant and a porcupine. "That's the reactor."

"What's this?"

He yanked the tarp away, revealing a red glowing panel with white letters.

"Coke," she read. "So what is it? A piece of art?"

"Christ," he said. "It's a Coke machine."

"It makes soda?"

"It makes soda? What? No. Look." He grabbed eight quarters from a jar on a shelf and fed them into the coin slot.

"Now what?" she asked.

"Press one of the buttons."

"Which one?"

"If it's your first time. Press Coke."

She pressed the button then jumped back with a yelp as the machine clunked out a cold red can of Coca-Cola.

"Cool," she said.

He opened the can and handed it to her. "You've never taken a sip of this? Never swiped one out of evidence?"

"No," she said. "Not this."

"Drink up."

She took a small, tentative sip. Then another one, bigger this time. And another. Her eyes grew wide, as if she'd seen the Baby Martian Jesus hovering in the air. "Wow," she said. "Wow."

"You're repeating yourself."

"This is something else."

"That there is over 100 calories of useless high-fructose corn syrup. Believe it or not, it tastes even better with real sugar."

"Wow."

"Wait," he said. He fed another eight quarters to the machine and hit another button. "Try this."

She read the can. "Fanta. Is it orange juice?"

"Just drink."

She took a sip. Then she downed half the can and let out a ripping burp. "Why haven't you shared this with me before? Why don't you keep it in the house?"

"You just finished two cans in five minutes. And it doesn't get any harder to drink. You start moving that kind of sugar, it's almost as bad as fried chicken in terms of weight gain. At least fried chicken makes you full at some point."

"So you're saying King Mike is right about at least one thing."

"I'm saying that I, personally, can get carried away with certain items if they're in the house. So, in order to exercise some self-control, I keep it out here as a special treat. If it was truly physically addictive, I'd be dead at the foot of that machine, my corpse rotting in a puddle of sweet goo."

She cast another glance at the machine. "Can I take one for the road?"

"Sure. Also, go in that locker over there and grab two bottles of red wine and a 12-pack of beer. Your choice."

"Jules won't need more than that?"

"I don't sell alcohol. That's my personal stash."

As she did that, he grabbed a clip board and an inventory sheet. "Now," he said. "The understanding is you people leave my operation alone while we work this case?"

"Yep."

"And I can trust you on this much at least?"

"As far as I know. Why? What are you doing?"

"Placing an order. I take. They replace."

"I see." She paused, as if thinking. "You seem to be ordering an awful lot."

He sighed. The implant. She could see what he was writing.

"Don't know how much I'll need to last us through. Just consider it insurance." He stopped writing and looked at her. "Can you always see what I'm doing?"

"Technically, yes. If I wanted. But it gets to be a bit much. I can do multiple audio feeds without going nuts, but video-wise, I have issues with motion sickness and just being able to concentrate on where I'm walking."

"Hmph," he said. "And it's always beaming directly to headquarters."

"That all depends. So how does this operation work, anyway?"

"Who wants to know?"

"Oh, I guess we all do. But I'm also curious."

"I'm not naming names."

"I'm not asking you to name names. Not yet. Unless your guy is the one who supplies Manhattan."

"You don't even know that much?"

"Do you?"

"Touché," he said, laughing. "But seriously, my guy doesn't."

"How do you know?"

He didn't, actually. "We have an exclusive arrangement. Besides, Manhattan is Manhattan. Everywhere else is everywhere else. I'm sure the challenges of keeping that place supplied would rule out running another operation."

"But how do you know for sure?"

"If you'd hear my guy talking about the Manhattan guy. They hate each other. In fact he went into business with me on the condition that I never do business in Manhattan, with Manhattan or talk to anyone there about this stuff. Best I figure, they have an uneasy truce. And questions aren't exactly encouraged."

"Fine," she said. "So you gonna tell me how the hell all this food gets out here? I'm wracking my brain here and I can't quite figure it out. Even if you could sneak a truck through the border, the chances of you carrying on all these years without one of them getting busted at a crossing or pulled over on the L.I.E. It doesn't add up."

He stalled. "Well, you see, Martian Jesus jumps from the sixth dimension into an undisclosed location in the South. With 12 of his 24 arms, he picks up a load from my supplier and hops back here."

She laughed, called him an asshole.

Showing her the stash was one thing. But going any farther? Hell, he might have taken her to a smaller stash, the one in Sag Harbor, if he hadn't been so hungry and fairly sure that that one was mostly empty.

"I have an organic farm in that other bunker," he said. "It's staffed by 200 refugee Iranians. They're not crazy about raising pigs, but they don't steal the product."

"You're going to hell," she said.

He really wanted to show her. Pathetic as it was, he still had this overwhelming urge to impress her. But this was his best-kept secret, the coolest thing in the world, something he'd fought hard to keep quiet about over the years because it was just killing him not to tell someone, anyone. That he never did was a spot of pride. Not that anyone would have believed him anyway.

"You wouldn't believe me anyway," he said.

"Wes."

"I don't want to blow my secret," he admitted. "I don't want Blunt and his goons down here pawing all over everything."

"I am one of his goons," she said. "And I think you're going to have to accept the situation at some point. You've been busted. Life as you know it is not going ahead as previously scheduled. Besides, if you don't show me, Blunt and his goons, when they do get in here, will tear the place apart looking for clues."

She had a way with words, Hillary did.

"Fine."

He walked to the wall, pressed a button and the Coke machine slid to the side. His predecessor had attached runners to the wall, put wheels on the machine and basically turned it into a garage door.

"Whoa," she said.

"Hold your applause till the end of the show," he said.

The soda machine had been hiding a three-by-four foot metal plate in the floor and a couple of switches on the wall immediately behind it. He stepped on the plate and flipped the top switch.

"What's that for?" she asked.

"Lights."

"Lights where?"

He held out a hand. "Climb aboard."

Without taking his hand, she stepped onto the plate. He flipped the second switch and the metal plate shuddered, then started to sink slowly into the floor. The walls slid by slowly, then disappeared as the panel brought them into a concrete room with a metal grate floor. In the middle of the room, there was a large opening in the floor where a pool of inky water sloshed.

"Crap in a bucket," she said, stepping off the platform and walking to the water's edge. She squatted and put her hand in the water.

"Don't get too close," he said. "You fall in, you'll die of hypothermia in no time."

She backed quickly away from the pool, tapping the side of her head as she did so.

"What's wrong?" he asked.

"The chips aren't transmitting down here."

"And?"

"Let's get out of here."

What the hell was she talking about? Oh. That.

"Yeah, maybe I should chuck you in, let you die. Barricade myself in and wait for escape."

He smiled. She didn't.

"Oh, come on," he said. "I'd be well within my rights to drown you for what you did to me. But if I was going to start a career in murdering people, I don't think my first would be someone I slept with."

She opened her mouth to speak, then closed it. If he didn't know any better, she'd looked hurt for a moment, almost like she was going to tell him something. The moment passed.

"Can we get out of here?" she asked, stepping onto the metal plate.

He flipped the switch and up they went. This time, she didn't hold on. She didn't speak again until they'd packed up, stowed the snowmobile and gotten the food in the car.

Once in the car with the heater running, she turned to him. "So you've got a submarine lair?"

"So you're transmitting again," he said. Oddly enough, now that it was out in the open, he didn't much care.

She shrugged. "You've got your stash in an underground bunker in Montauk, and your supplier delivers via submarine to a level below that?"

"A submarine lair? Underwater delivery? That's just insane," he said, trying not to smile. "I'm a fucking journalist. I sell bacon and eggs on the side. What do you think this is, some kind of movie or something? A submarine. Ha! Even if there was some sort of crazy underground submarine dock, where would my supplier get his hands on a vintage World War II era diesel submarine? Preposterous. I guess next you'll be believing in Martian Jesus."

She was trying to glare at him. But the more he went on, the harder it was for her to keep her face rigid.

"I told you. I have all my food grown by Guatemalans on a farm in the next bunker. Hydroponic sugar cane. Albino pigs. But all my Guatemalans are sleeping right now. They don't like to be woken up."

"I thought you said they were Iranians." She struggled not to laugh. It wasn't something she did often, but when she did it was a small victory, something he felt he'd earned.

"Iranians. Guatemalans. Hard to tell them apart."

"Fine," she said, turning away from him and looking out the window. "You got all that? Good. End transmission."

He sighed. "So are you done for tonight?"

"Transmitting, yes. Recording, not necessarily. If my signal completely disappears for longer than a minute, Blunt's notified. He completely lost it after that little trip down to the dock."

"Awww, that's too bad."

"He's been screaming in my ear for the last half an hour. You could have killed me down there."

"But I didn't. That should be noted in my file."

She hit him in the arm. "Drive. I'm hungry."

"You can't eat this food. It's illegal and highly dangerous."

"Drive," she said.

18

Blunt sat fuming in his car, the right half of his field of vision crowded with alerts and warnings. The red heart blinked, accompanied by readouts of heart rate and blood pressure. A sleep warning flashed now, as well. Because his heart rate hadn't gone down much, if any, since the afternoon, the system overrode his ability to turn it off. Save for the few hours in the afternoon when the network was taken down for updating, he'd had no peace. And, as predicted, these alerts prompted a host of messages suggesting or requesting meetings and appointments.

He placed a call to the overnight tech guy.

"Jimmy, can you clear all these fucking alerts out of my AR?"

"I don't know, Chief. I'd need authorization."

"I'm the fucking chief. I'm on a case, and I can't see out of my right eye."

Blunt knew he was putting Jimmy in a bad spot. There were protocols in place for the department's augmented-reality system—especially if psych and med alerts were being signaled.

"C'mon, Jimmy. Do the old man a favor."

"I guess I could override the alerts on your end. But I'm going to have to let internal affairs know about those psych trips."

"Fine, whatever," Blunt said. "And I promise you, I'll run in for an appointment as soon as I can get off this stakeout."

Just like that, the alerts disappeared.

"How's that?" Jimmy asked.

"Better, thanks. Is everything else still working?"

"Should be. I just disabled that part of the heads-up display on your end. It'll still be compiling data and uploading. So don't go crazy in the evidence room."

"You're a funny guy, Jimmy. You should try standup. Thanks for helping anyway."

"You all right, Chief? Everything okay?"

Blunt sighed. "Yeah, Jimmy. Everything's fine."

Of course everything was far from fine. The God's honest truth was he could go for a couple hours on the therapist's couch.

He'd had a mandatory hour a week since puberty. Like most boys that age, he was convinced he'd hate it—sitting with a stranger and talking. It sounded so girly. But he'd taken to it immediately. Part of it was that his first therapist was a man, a much-needed father figure after he'd watched his own father die of an obesity-related heart attack on the living room floor, fifty years of bad habits shaking like a Jell-o earthquake as dad's eyes rolled back into his head and bloody foam bubbled out of his mouth. All these years later, he could call up that scene as vividly as the day it happened, almost as if he were watching a video through the implant.

The scrawny therapist with the wire-frame glasses was no replacement for his father, but it was a male role model—and one who helped him get a handle on the rage building in him from that early age. It wasn't long before skipping a therapy session was as unthinkable as his mother skipping Sunday Mass.

"Which do you think is better?" he'd asked her once.

"Oh, therapy's better than Mass, I guess. In Mass you never know for sure if God's paying attention—and you have to share your time with a hundred other people. But confession's better than therapy, because you're expected to atone for your stupid behavior rather than sit there and blame it all on your parents."

So it was an hour a week his entire adult life. Until his wife died. He then upped it to two hours a week at the suggestion of the department therapist. He saw the sense in it immediately. It had taken years for him to get over his anger at his dad for killing himself slowly with food. But that rage had a clear target. The rage that swelled in him after Janice's death, though? That was something else entirely.

To lose his wife of 20 years to a heart attack? Janice—a vegetarian who worked out an hour a day, who never put a single foul thing in her body, who lived in and believed in the most nutritionally advanced society in the world. And she came up short in some stupid genetic lottery. There she was on the floor, dying at the exact same age of the exact same thing as his father.

It made no sense.

Perhaps that's why, five years after her death, Blunt found himself in the evidence room with his newest detective, Hillary Halstead. He was infatuated with her youth, her beauty, her intelligence. He'd taken her under wing, and she was eager to learn. She asked questions, laughed at his jokes, hung around in his office after her shift was over, gave him reason to hope. Late into middle age, he was suffering the side effects that ambitious, pretty young women have on a man. It was the first secret he kept from his therapists, bottling up his feelings until he was overcome with a sudden need to do something reckless to impress her.

They were in the evidence room, cataloguing a box of donuts—apple cinnamon, fresh from a morning raid.

"The smell," she said. "It's almost intoxicating."

She'd been standing right next to him. Even now he remembered the feel of her shoulder against his, the scent of the shampoo in her hair.

"Have you ever?" she asked.

"Never. In 30 years, never a nibble. Never a sip."

"Impressive," she said.

And for what?

He opened the box, the smell now overpowering him.

"What are you doing?" she asked.

He didn't answer. He picked up a donut, surprised at the way it felt—the springy nature of it, heavy yet airy at the same time. The grit of the sugar and the powdery feel of the cinnamon.

He bit into it, immediately filled with a powerful mixture of self-loathing and ecstasy as the powder tickled his nose, and the soft, cakey morsels dissolved in his mouth. It reminded him of his first tries at masturbation—pure physical, cellular delight mixed with an equally pure existential and spiritual dread. He'd be caught. He'd be punished. Humiliated, killed and, to top it off, roasted in the fires of hell for all eternity.

"How is it?" she whispered.

He raised the other half to her mouth. She closed her eyes and took it. She moaned. Finally, she opened her eyes, a changed woman. He'd never seen her betray emotion of any sort.

And when he leaned in and kissed her, she gave ground for two heart-lifting seconds before her hand was on his chest, pushing him away gently.

"Chief, we shouldn't."

He studied her eyes, hoping to find doubt, conflict, that secret glint that meant she only wanted him to try a little harder. He saw only panic. And pity.

He found his voice. "No. I guess you're right."

He'd thrown away a lifetime of principled abstention, to impress an underling, to make the sort of move that could have him out on the streets in a heartbeat had she decided to file a complaint.

"I don't know what came over me," he said. "I'm sorry."

That sorrow only grew. At times he almost wished she'd file a complaint. Every day in her presence was a new, exquisite form of torture as he fell more and more in love with this forbidden fruit. He was a foolish old man with a heart-sick teenager locked inside him. Worse, after all those years of detailing every little problem, examining every little neurotic tic with one therapist or another, he couldn't say anything about this new problem in his life. To admit it to a department shrink would be to ignite an inquiry and have her removed from his chain of command—something he knew he needed, but something he knew he couldn't stand.

So it festered and grew. He worked out harder and harder to try to deal with the rage all on his own. But what she had done with Wesley Montgomery, that she had fallen so far, spurning him at the same time. Even now—while she and Montgomery were up to their eyeballs in trouble—she seemed to be flirting with the dealer. He seethed. A white-hot flame burned inside him and he had no idea how to handle it, no clue how to channel it.

Except towards Wesley Montgomery.

Didn't Montgomery represent all that was wrong with the world? Hadn't Blunt's old man died from the kind of shit that Montgomery and his ilk peddled on the streets? It was all mixed up in his head. That Goddamned donut. Hadn't his mom told him he had to watch himself, that the disease was genetic, that he came from a long line of sweet-tooths? And thank God the government had finally stepped in to save people from themselves. Hadn't Blunt promised her to not only follow the law to the letter, but to embrace it, to become an enforcer— to protect others from what had happened to his old man? But these dealers kept poisoning the well. He'd eaten that donut and, yes, it was his own fault, but the temptation wouldn't have been there in the first place if sleaze like Montgomery and the ring in Manhattan weren't importing it.

He'd get them both. Somehow. And if that didn't sate his need for revenge, dampen the rage burning inside of him—well, he'd worry about that when he came to it. First things first.

19

Wes and Hillary drove back to Hampton Bays, mostly in silence. She'd turned the audio on once, but when he said, "Really, must we?" she'd said "Fine," and turned it off without further protest. Fifteen seconds later, she was singing under her breath, listening to the music library channeling through her chip. He shot her a look. "It's my car," she said. "Besides, doesn't all this silence in the middle of nowhere freak you out?"

The cold outside, and the barren landscape gave the appearance of a dead planet. An over-active imagination could lead one to believe that there was no air out there, that if the windows broke, your head would implode in the vacuum, soundlessly.

He punched the audio button and said, "Revver." Out of the speakers came the synthesized rumble of a gas engine. He mashed the accelerator. The car sped up five miles per hour, and the speakers gave a throaty roar.

"Better?" he asked.

"It's still too quiet," she said and started singing again.

"Whatever. I need to think."

It was a half lie. He did need to think, untangle his emotions, process the mess in his head, figure out exactly what it was he was going to do. But planning wasn't his strong point. And Hillary sitting there, singing softly, she may as well have been naked and screaming at the top of her lungs for all the concentrating he could do.

The sound of the fake engine, the road swishing by underneath, the occasional pair of headlights drifting by silently like a ghost. It all went a little way toward soothing him. He was moving. It was something.

What did freak him out, though, was the quiet of the house when they returned, being alone with her and not quite knowing the next step. He turned the video on in the kitchen, but the first thing to pop up was a weather guy talking about global freezing.

"Jesus," he said, turning it off. "It's like they don't even acknowledge the rest of the globe." The old man was growing stronger in him. His beef had been with climate change going in another direction—and who knew which one of them was right, if either of them were—but there was no escaping the fact they were both men prone to yelling at the media about the weather coverage. Was it an inevitable process of aging, the son becoming the father? Or had the arrest knocked something loose in his head?

"What are you talking about?" she said. "The science is settled."

He pounded the countertop with the flats of his hands and turned to her. "Shut up" was on the tip of his tongue but he swallowed it. He took a deep breath.

"What?" she said.

"Just." He stopped himself. "Never mind." He started for the basement. "I'll be right back."

He returned five minutes later with a bottle of Jack Daniels.

"Where was that?" she asked.

"In the basement drain hole," he said, washing the bottle in the sink. She shook her head. "How much is that worth?"

"Here? If I sold it, I guess I could get whatever I asked. In Tennessee, it's probably worth about a hundred bucks."

He put ice in a glass, covered it with whiskey and handed it to her.

"I don't know," she said.

He hadn't gotten around to introducing her to whiskey.

"Oh, just fucking drink it. It's not going to kill you."

While he poured one for himself, she put the glass to her lips, tilted her head back and drained it before he could stop her. She let out a burst of air, blinked the tears out of her eyes. But otherwise she didn't let on she'd just scorched the back of her throat.

"You watch too much video," he said, shaking his head and taking a sip from his own glass. He let the warmth spread through him slowly, soothing him, before taking another sip. He'd be drunk when all was said and done, but he was going to be civilized about it at least. "Sit down. Have a beer. It'll make the pain go away."

"Okay," she whispered, putting the glass down gently as if it were a bomb that might go off.

He set to work, salting and peppering the steaks and letting them get to room temperature while he sliced the potatoes paper thin. He mashed up garlic. Found some spinach. On one burner, he sautéed that in olive oil and garlic.

"No butter?" she asked. "No bacon fat?"

"Skillet," he said, holding out his hand. She landed the handle in his palm, and he placed it in the broiler for five minutes before transferring it to the stove over a high flame. He rubbed a little oil on the steaks, then dropped them in the skillet. They hissed violently.

"Damn," she said.

He flipped the meat, seared the other side. He lit a fire under the pan of vegetable oil. Pulled the skillet from the stove and slid it into the broiler.

"You sure you don't want to wrap that in bacon?"

"Good steaks don't need it," he said, pouring them each another whiskey before dropping the potatoes. "Sip this time," he said.

Garlic, potatoes and seared beef—the smells layered in the kitchen air. When his stomach grumbled, he fed it some Jack. This was much like their first time—without all the sex on the floor or the hope for a long-lasting relationship. Still, he found himself worrying less about Hillary with each sip of whiskey.

"Open up a bottle of that red," he said. "Pour it in a carafe so it can breathe." In their two months together, she'd gotten good enough with the cork screw that he no longer had to run the wine through a strainer to sift out all the cork after she was done opening it.

While she did that, he yanked the steaks, tossed a quarter stick of butter in the super-heated pan and flipped the meat a couple of times before letting it sit. He pulled the fried chips and let them drain on paper towels, then rewarmed the spinach.

They were halfway through the meal, he eating like it was his last, she moaning periodically, before either spoke.

"I missed this," she said, without looking up.

He stopped, looked at her, poured them both another glass of wine and went back to the meal.

The food gone, the wine gone, they pushed back from the table and went back to the whiskey. She groaned with satisfaction. Offered him what looked like a genuine smile and did this thing where she stretched in the chair, from head to toe, arching her back just a little, looking for all the world like when she released, she'd melt onto the floor.

Now that he was full, his body satisfied, Wes was tired again. Tired and slightly sad. He'd been abandoned, betrayed, arrested, jailed, his life turned upside down. Throw in an ugly dead dog and he'd have the makings of a classic blues song. And the muse, the source of that deluge of sorrow sat directly across from him drinking his booze.

For the most part, he was glad she was there.

Pathetic. Pathetic and drunk.

"I'm tired," he said. It was the only thing he trusted himself to say without starting another fight or, worse, putting his self-pity on full display.

"Okay," she said. "I'll do the dishes."

"Thanks." He grabbed his glass and what was left of the bottle. "You'll find," he started.

"What?" she asked.

"Never mind," he said, trying to fake a laugh. "Almost forgot you already knew where everything is."

She smiled. "I'll find my way around."

He didn't turn on the lights in his room. The moonlight spilling in was more than adequate to strip down to his boxers. He found the edge of the bed and sat.

Her voice popped into his head. "I'm gonna have another beer." He winced, said "Okay."

Staring out the window, he put his hand on the pane. The cold shot through his arm and into his chest, where it became an ache solid and real.

"Shit," he said, putting the heel of his palm into his eye. Get it together, he told himself, momentarily horrified that the implant might let her read his thoughts. But nothing more came from downstairs than the sound of banging pots and running water. Outside, a scrawny deer picked its way gently through the snow.

Downstairs, the water was turned off. The music too. The house fell silent for a second before her footsteps started up the stairs, into the bathroom. He sat. He listened. She brushed her teeth, washed her face, opened the bathroom door. Her steps stopped outside his bedroom door.

"I probably shouldn't come in," she whispered, the voice in his head, coming through the chip.

"Probably not," he said, realizing just how drunk he was, that she was probably in worse shape. He didn't care.

"But I am," she said.

"Okay," he said.

The door opened. He looked over his shoulder and saw her standing naked and cold in the moonlight. He didn't move otherwise. Or speak.

She climbed into bed, put her warm hands on his neck and began kneading. He hadn't realized quite how much tension he'd been carrying.

"This is stupid," he said, but only because it was part of the ritual before two adults climbed into bed with clear foreknowledge of the regret-layered hangover waiting for them after the hormones had been worked out of their systems.

"You want me to stop?" she asked, moving a hand to his chest.

"Of course not," he said.

"Then shut up."

20

Wes was woken the next morning by the sound of the house-com ringing insistently. He sat up, hungover and sore. Christ, what had they done to one another? There were scratch marks all over his chest. He found the remote and pointed it at the wall to check the caller ID on the monitor.

A photo of Lou popped up, scowling. Lou had probably scowled on his own wedding day.

Wes bumped the call to voicemail and waited for the message.

"Four fucking days, Wesley. Better have a damn good explanation." And that was it.

Wes looked down at his chest, rubbed his fingers over the scratch marks. "Jesus," he said.

Hillary wasn't in the bed. He sat and listened but didn't hear noise in the house. A flash of panic gripped him: She'd abandoned him all over again. But it vanished as soon as he remembered she was monitoring him, that she wasn't going anywhere.

"Where are you this time?" he said out loud, talking to himself.

Her voice came through into his head, breathing heavily. "I'm out for a run," she said.

"Are you insane?" It was 20 degrees outside. And he knew if he was feeling this fuzzy she had to be in much worse condition.

"Hold on," she said. He listened as she threw up.

"Breakfast of champions," he said as she cleared her throat one final time and spat out the results. "You okay?"

"Yeah," she panted. "But look, I can't use this chip and run at the same time. Not in this condition. It's too much. I'll see you in half an hour."

"You're going to keep running?"

"Don't have much of a choice now. I'm four miles out."

"I can pick you up."

"No, I'll feel better after this and a shower."

The running he didn't understand, but the thought of her naked was something he could get behind. Literally. Repeatedly. "I can scrub you down," he said, playfully.

"I don't know about all that," she said and started throwing up again. "Just," she started. "Look, I gotta go."

I don't know about all that? What the hell was that supposed to mean? Was last night a pity fuck? Drunk meaningless sex? He dropped back into bed, stared up at the ceiling and began lecturing himself. She's a cop, dumbass. Get that through your thick skull. Even if she still remotely liked you, you can't trust her. She sold you out. And now she's watching your every move.

Except she wasn't. Not at this minute. He might be downloading to God knew where, but so far the set-up seemed to feed through her first. Still, what could he do in a half hour? He thought briefly about hauling ass but nixed the idea, telling himself it wasn't because he didn't want to leave her but because they'd catch him before he got far.

A knife to the skull could pry out the implant. Maybe. But surely she'd notice the screams and have back-up descend on his house. Besides, he didn't need a gaping wound in the side of his head.

What to do? What to do?

He looked around the room, noticed Lou's ugly mug on the monitor. "Lou," he said.

"What?" It was her voice again.

"Shit. Nothing."

"Turn it off," she said.

"You're the one with the control button," he answered.

"Fine," she said.

His head went silent. Excellent.

Still, he was afraid to call Lou. Maybe the implant was voice activated. Maybe he'd just turn it on accidentally. He scanned the room again, his eyes falling on the antique Mac set up in the corner.

That would have to do.

He hobbled over to it, pressed the on button and waited the eternal two minutes it took to boot up. All the programs were there. Either the police hadn't bothered with it when they ransacked his house, didn't find anything of interest or just couldn't figure out how to turn it on. Whatever the case, he didn't keep anything on it, and it was too old to network with anything, was compatible with nothing except the sorry printer. It reminded Wes less of the slick, well-designed piece of technology it once was and more of the hulking Zenith tube-TV his mom used to have in the basement. He'd told Hillary it was just for playing vintage games. A half truth. As a kid, he'd used it to reply to his old man's letters—two Luddites banging out toner-on-paper letters and entrusting them to the care of what was left of the postal system.

In the early days, it took Wes hours to draft a letter, finding the keys, poking them out, one at a time, until his mom took pity on him and taught him the antiquated skill of typing, using a Qwerty keyboard in an age of touch screens and voice commands. Boring lesson after boring lesson, interspersed with a game she always referred to as "Missile Command." In it, letters fell from the sky, threatening his city with nuclear annihilation. The only thing to stop them was to type the corresponding keys in the correct order.

Was that the legacy of the woman who raised him, cared for him, made him eat his tofu and vegetables, believed in the government and who was devoured in her prime by cancer? Her only son could type 75 words a minute without looking?

Of course not. There were the years of loving and caring. The very house he lived in. His basic decency. He always felt slightly ashamed of himself when he caught his mind chewing over the old man's words, the old man's letters, the old man's this, the old man's that—like he was betraying his mother somehow. But wasn't that always the way? You obsessed over those who weren't there for you, wondering why? He had a thousand mental images—and actual images—of his mom, but his mind sometimes only wanted to fill in the gap left by the old man.

One memory of her came back to him this morning. It was his senior year of high school, and they'd been arguing for weeks. She'd been urging him to get an implant, but he kept resisting—partly to be obstinate, partly because he didn't want to be a humpster. That's what they were called, the preening early adopters rushing out to be the first generation of the com sets before they were completely miniaturized. The unsightly bulge on the sides of their heads was played up in the media as sexy, a sign of progressive daring. To Wes, humpsters just looked like self-satisfied assholes. But the real reason he resisted? Put simply, he was afraid of the procedure—something he wasn't about to tell his mom.

Low-level bickering led to a shouting match, which resulted in her screaming, "You're just like your father!"

He responded, "Well, I guess I wouldn't know, would I? Thanks to you!"

She started crying. He ran off to his room to sulk.

Two hours later she knocked on the door. "Wes," she called.

Ashamed of his own behavior, he cracked the door. She was standing there in a print blouse and a skirt, looking like a woman half her age. As pretty as she was, her eyes were swollen and red from crying. Before he could apologize, she did.

"I'm sorry," she said. "I've been acting crazy. I'm just afraid I'm going to lose you."

He pretended not to know what she was talking about. After all, he himself had been ignoring the elephant in the room.

"Look, I know your dad is going to want you to move down there. I know he's hinted at it. He may have done more than hint at it. And I don't blame you if you want to leave."

He opened the door and let her into the bedroom. She sat on his bed. He sat next to her.

"Look, mom."

"Wes, let me finish. I know how it is. The Federation is—well, it's nice enough. And I can see how the other side would seem attractive. Hell, sometimes I feel like I made the wrong choice myself. You've been stuck on Long Island your whole life. I'm sure you want to get out and see the world."

He did. Of course he did. He was a kid with dreams. But travel to the other side was prohibitively expensive. And when he was finally old enough to travel internationally, a seemingly nonstop chain of volcanic eruptions in Iceland had choked the skies over the Atlantic and Europe with ash.

"And the only reason I'd want you to stay is purely selfish. There's more opportunity down there than there is here." She was crying again. "Christ, look at me. I'm a mess."

"Mom," he said, but he'd started crying, too. And he didn't know what to say. He didn't know his own heart, didn't know what decision to make, didn't know how to put her at ease.

"It's okay," she said. "It's a lot of pressure for a kid. Just do what you need to do. And always eat your vegetables. And remember who taught you how to wipe your butt and how to cook and how to read and write and type."

"Mom," he said.

She cut him off. "Shut up and give me a hug."

She'd backed off after that, tried to keep her own worry and melancholy to a minimum. Did a pretty good job of it as a matter of fact. But when she found the acceptance letter to University of Phoenix's journalism program in the mailbox and realized he'd decided to stay, she ran around the house in such a state of frenzied euphoria that she'd twisted her ankle and ended up on crutches for three weeks.

Of course, neither of them could have imagined it eventually leading to a gig at a print rag on the East End of Long Island working for Lou.

Shit.

Lou.

He needed to type a note to Lou. That's what he'd do.

He called up Word, stared at the screen, started to type but stopped after the "u" in "Lou." Better safe than sorry. On the chance Hillary decided to drop in on his head—or he accidentally switched the damn thing back on—he turned and looked out the window. Slowly, he started typing. He was sure there'd be mistakes, but it would have to do. Without looking, he hit the command and p keys at the same time, waited five seconds, then hit the enter key. He held his breath until he heard the paper working through the old laser printer. That done, he found the backspace key, held it down until the computer blooped angrily, as if to say, "Okay, asshole, there's nothing left to erase." Only then did he turn back to the screen. He switched everything off, grabbed the paper off the printer and, without looking, folded it and jammed it into his wallet.

Mission accomplished, he went downstairs, set the coffee brewing while he drank a pitcher of water. He took a shower and waited for Hillary.

21

Wes was playing around with the implant's dictionary, thesaurus and Gawkerpedia features when Hillary returned from her run. It was pretty cool, he had to admit. But how people could run these constantly while trying to do other things, he couldn't quite fathom. So far, it required concentration. And that was on a government unit. He knew that many of the sets available to the public—especially the ones that came with cheap or free data plans—were cluttered with hyper-targeted advertising.

Hillary stumbled through the door, sweating profusely through the layers she'd worn to protect herself from the cold. Her eyes bloodshot and her face an angry flushed red over a pale green, she looked like she'd been stricken by one of those old-timey diseases. The chip supplied a handy list: dysentery, ague, the grip, cholera, bubonic plague, malaria.

"Wow," he said, offering her a chair and moving to kiss her on the cheek. She declined the chair, yanked her head back as if he were a poisonous snake—an asp, an adder, a pit viper.

So much for falling into pre-arrest routine.

She poured herself a glass of water, gulped it down. Made a face.

He pulled open the utensil drawer, lifted the tray and found a little nest of foil packets. "You sure they searched this place?"

"Yes."

He didn't like her tone.

"Stir this into your water. You'll feel better."

"G?" She asked.

"G. Gatorade. Electrolytes. Sugar. University of Florida. Banned by Federation. Is it in you?"

"What?"

"Nothing. Playing with the implant. You can't see that?"

She took the glass. "I'm not accessing everything myself. Video. Incoming, outgoing calls. They'll log your surf patterns back at headquarters, sift through it later maybe if there's reason to. Once you get the hang of it, there'll be too much information for me to process by myself. But no, at the moment I'm not."

Hillary put her hand up, signaling him to wait. She stopped talking, gripped the edge of the counter and stuck her head in the sink, but didn't throw up—vomit, puke, wretch, hurl, yak, toss cookies.

"Toss cookies?" he said out loud.

"What?" she groaned.

"Toss cookies. I guess it was once a synonym for vomiting. That's weird."

"Fascinating."

He ran a video clip of a dog and her puppies. Bitch. Female dog. Domineering, unsavory woman.

Hillary straightened up. "I'm going to go shower. Quit watching puppy videos and start thinking of our next step."

She'd been peeking.

"Got it all figured out, chief," he said, trying to sound aloof—stand-offish, non-committal. He was starting to feel autistic.

"Can't wait to hear it."

"I'll make breakfast."

"How can you eat? Why aren't you hungover?"

Would he risk sounding pathetic to lay down a guilt trip? Of course he would. Even if he had to lie to do so.

"Let's just say I had a little practice with the bottle over the last couple of weeks."

She started back up the stairs, impervious to guilt. "Mature," she said.

"And you don't have an overnight bag stuffed full of mood stabilizers?" he countered.

His old man had a special hatred for them, felt they dulled real life, made it easier for the government to pass prohibition after prohibition. "Who needs booze, cigarettes, a nice glass of wine, a piece of chocolate when you're emotionally flat-lined?" he ranted in one letter. "Of course, considering the shit-show you've got up there, if you yanked all the pills today, you'd all kill each other within 24 hours. Don't know if it would be outright murder or a mass suicide pact, but mark my words, you'd all be dead."

Wes' comment had stopped her halfway on the stairs, where she was now glaring down at him from above. "Anything else to say?"

"Just go shower," he said. "I'll make breakfast. You want to feel better, you'll eat it. You want to keep punishing yourself for last night, you won't." Maybe that would provoke a response.

"Fine," she said and continued up the stairs.

She came down with a wet head, a tight t-shirt and extremely snug cotton pajama bottoms. Wes pulled up some images of corpses mangled in war, starving babies in Africa, natural disasters—just enough to tamp down his erection.

"You watch some interesting video," she said.

Shit.

The Cheshire smile she offered him as he served her a plate of bacon and eggs made him think she'd dressed like that specifically to disarm him. It was all he could do not to stab himself to stop his hand from reaching out and cupping the curve of her boob, pinching the nipple mocking him through the thin fabric of her shirt. But what was acceptable every-morning behavior just a few weeks ago—and for a brief time the night before—would likely get him a swift punch to the groin.

She ate slowly at first, obviously afraid food would be little more than ammunition for her wine-fueled puke launcher. After a few tentative bites, the salt and grease began to work their magic, and she ate with more confidence. By the time she was done, she seemed less hostile.

Perhaps if he found a way to keep a constant stream of calories flowing through her, he'd get her back.

"So what's your plan?"

"We'll go into Manhattan with Jules, infiltrate the bloggers, find their source."

"Why didn't I think of that?"

"What?"

"Your plan? This fell into your lap last night. That barely qualifies as a plan. That reminds me of the time the world's best scientists asked me how to get to the moon. That one was easy. I just told them they needed a rocket. I won the Nobel for that one."

"You got anything better?

That shut her up.

"But there's one thing I have to do first," he added.

"What's that?"

"Quit my day job."

"You're going to quit? What are you going to do when you get back?"

"Assuming I don't get killed in Manhattan? That you don't throw me back in jail?"

"You're not going to get killed. You're not going back to jail."

"Whatever. Either way, I'm not coming back. What do I have left here?"

She looked down at her plate. "I guess you're right."

What was that about? Was she sad at the thought of him leaving? Had she intended to turn him into an honest man? Or was she playing him like a chump? His head said the latter. His inner idiot insisted the 0.00009% chance of the former was a gamble he just couldn't pass up.

"Either way, I've disappeared off the face of the planet as far as work is concerned. To Lou, that might spell 'story,' and we definitely don't want him snooping around. He starts digging, our cover won't last for long. Besides, I owe the old guy an explanation."

"I guess," she said. "When do we want to do this?"

"We? I don't think you'll be tagging along to the office."

"You're a flight risk."

"A flight risk? We're on Long Island? How far am I going to get short of stealing a helicopter?"

"Or a submarine?"

"You can't just make a submarine appear at command. They're not underwater rockets. Besides, I couldn't stand to leave you." He knifed the last bit with sarcasm, leading to another stare down.

"It's cute when you try to act tough," she said.

"It's not cute when you pretend to care."

She didn't take the bait.

"You can stay here and spy on me through the damn implant. Lou's about the only person left who gives a shit about me anyway. This is going to break the old bastard's heart."

Hillary clasped her hands to her chest and smirked. Suddenly a snippet of Mozart's Requiem was blasting through his implant. "The pain," she whispered. "The heartbreak," she gasped.

"Bitch," he said, this time aloud.

22

He stomped through the driveway, climbed into the car. His implant started speaking.

"I see you're driving somewhere. If you give me your destination, I can help."

"Shut up," he said.

"I'm sorry. I don't recognize that destination."

"Fuck."

"I'm sorry. I don't recognize that destination."

"You know where you can go? You can go to hell!" he shouted into the car.

"Please turn left in point five miles."

"What? No!" What was happening? "That's not even the right way, you stupid cow!"

"Please turn left in point five miles."

"Fuck you! Fuck you! Fuck you!" He banged on the steering wheel.

"Pardon me while I recalculate your route."

"I don't want you to recalculate. I want you to shut the fuck up!"

"That hurts my feelings," it said. "Did you think about that for one minute? I'm just trying to help?"

"What the hell?"

Just as the joke dawned on him, Hillary started laughing. "That was awesome."

"Real mature," he said.

"Maybe not. But I laughed. Not with you, but at you."

Despite himself, he smiled a little. "You go to hell," he said. "You go to hell and die."

He put the car in drive and pointed it toward Riverhead where the office was. He turned on Revver, the gas-engine simulator, and cranked some music. Vintage rock. A band called Drive-by Truckers that his old man had always gone on about as if they were the biggest thing since Jesus. Wes preferred more current fare—Alpha Whores, Crinkle Cut Fries, Poo Fling You—but he liked Drive-by well enough, knew all the songs, had learned all the lyrics.

He blasted the band now as revenge. Hillary hated them. When they'd first started dating, he'd tried to impress her with his breadth of musical knowledge—as if he were a 19-year-old luring a girl back to his dorm room for a makeout session. She was having none of it.

"What is that?" she'd asked in a tone that suggested something hairy and many-legged had just crawled into her ears.

He explained that they came from the dawn of the 21st century, a key player in a long line of Southern rock.

"That's nice and all, but if you have any interest in getting laid tonight you'll turn it off," she'd said.

"No appreciation for the classics," he said, but turned it off immediately.

"The classics are fine," she said. "But I prefer the old Idol winners. Kelly Clarkson, David Cook, Coldplay, Clay Aiken, Johnny Cash."

"I'm pretty sure Clay Aiken never won American Idol," he told her.

"Yes he did."

"Look it up," he said, back in those golden days before he'd had his own implant.

She paused long enough to access her chip. "There it is. Gawkerpedia says he did. Oh, and Led Zeppelin. Almost forgot about them. Season six."

But she hated Drive-by Truckers. If she were in a decent mood, she'd clamp her hands over her ears and squeal, "Nooooo."

"Can you turn that shit off?" Her voice came through his implant.

"My car. My rules," he said and turned it up.

"Jackass," she said, then went silent.

Good. He didn't think she'd stay gone long, and figured she could watch the video without the sound. But he'd wanted to chase her off, wanted her out of his head. Hell, he wanted everything out of his head—including the prospects of his showdown with Lou.

At the thought of his boss' name, Wes' stomach clenched tight, and it felt like he might soil his skivvies.

Lou had always struck him as a dragon in a lair, waiting to devour anyone who crossed him. Sure, they had their break time together, Lou puffing on his cigarette, Wes gnawing on beef jerky as they watched the presses roll. But over the years, they'd shared about 20 words of conversation that didn't deal with politics, sports or the history of media. And yet, Wes considered Lou family and was pretty sure the feeling was mutual. Such was the bond between men.

What Wes knew about Lou was that the old man loved the Mets with a passion that bordered on embarrassing, had worked for The New York Times back when it existed as a print publication, and hated pretty much everything about King Mike, the real one back when he was alive and the government that had assumed his name after he died. Lou seemed like a man more suited for the South. But he might as well have been a tree in the pine barrens for all his ability to leave Long Island. Hell, he only just barely tolerated living in the City during his time there.

"If I can't be on my boat, engine running, within ten minutes," he'd say, "I start getting nervous."

Wes pulled into the parking lot of the massive building that served as the Suffolk News & Review's office, hundreds of empty spaces a reminder of a time when a newspaper could employ more than 15 people. Much of the rest of it had been walled off and rented to the government for storage of potatoes and other winter vegetables. He sat in the lot, delaying the confrontation, doing deep breathing exercises while the music played on. It was Thursday. Everyone would be cranking to get the stories done for the back pages and departments so they could clear Friday for the "real" stories, such as they were. It would print tomorrow, ship on Monday. If something big happened over the weekend—oh well. That's what video was for.

The wallet in his back pocket made his ass itch. He hoped the note would be enough to get him through.

When he walked through the doors, the other reporter, the copy editor and the designers and programmers popped their heads up from their cubicles, like meerkats on the savanna. As one, they all turned from Wes to Lou's office, then put their heads down as if they'd seen nothing. In any other office, two or three of them would have scrammed, not interested in witnessing the carnage. But these were journalists—or what passed for them these days, as Lou was fond of saying—and they'd no sooner miss a train wreck or a baby drowning.

Lou's lair sat on the other end of the newsroom, separated from the cubicle farm by a wall of glass with wire mesh running through it—as if it had been specifically designed to protect the reporters on that day when Lou finally flipped and flew into a furniture-throwing rampage.

Today might be that day.

Across the room, Lou sat in his office, barrel chest heaving, a bulk washed up from another time. He glared down at his desk, editing something on screen by tapping with gorilla-sized index fingers. Sensing a change in his newsroom, Lou looked up, locking eyes with Wes.

"Uh ohhhhhhhh." It was Hillary.

"So you're there?" he mumbled.

"Wouldn't miss this for the world."

"Great."

"God, he looks like a big old pile of stereotype."

"Archetype might be a better word for it," Wes said.

Wes could see Lou's face going red under his head of white hair. The glasses only magnified the anger rays beaming from his eyes. Lou lifted one of his gorilla fingers, pointed it at Wes, then crooked it. Once.

"Crap in a bucket."

"Good luck," Hillary said, suddenly sincere in her support.

Wes took one step, then another. In one terrifying blink, he was inside, moving to shut the door behind him.

"Leave it open," Lou said. "I wouldn't want to deprive them of this."

"Hey, Lou," Wes said.

Lou sat back and laced his hands behind his head, the chair groaning under his weight.

"Sorry I've been out."

"Sorry ain't gonna cut it, kid. Not a whole sack of sorries." He started out calm enough, establishing a base from which to build. "Four days with no explanation. No call. No text. No email." His voice inched up. "No stories from your beat. Here it is, Thursday, and I've got nothing from you. Nothing. At least Tim out there has decided to pull his head out of his ass long enough to turn in a couple of stories that don't immediately make me want to wipe my ass with them. And even if you did come in here with something, it'd take us six damn hours to edit into something a reader would recognize as English."

They both knew that wasn't true. Wes' stories made it to the page much in the condition they came in.

Lou turned the volume up another notch. It was a healthy yell, now. "But at least tell me you came in here with a story, Wesley. You *do* have a story, right? Perhaps even two. About how you were abducted by aliens? Or were trapped by a pervert in your basement getting ass-raped and whipped for days on end?"

Wes heard Hillary laugh on the other side. His back was to the newsroom, but knew without looking they too were all struggling not to laugh.

"So what is it, Wes? What did you come in here to tell me?"

Wes swallowed. Hard.

"I came," he started. "I came to tell you." He stopped again. "I'm quitting, Lou."

Lou unlaced his hands and sprung forward in his chair.

"What?" he whispered.

This was going to hurt. "I'm moving to Manhattan. Got a job on a blog."

"A blog?" Lou screamed, the volume up now to 11. He stood up and pounded on the desk. "Blog?" It sounded less like a word and more like a noise a rabid Tyrannosaurus would make. "A motherfucking blog? Are you fucking kidding me?"

Old-school as he was, Lou kept actual paper and books on his desk. These came in handy now as he swept them onto the floor.

"You little ungrateful cocksucker, you! After everything I've fucking taught you? The covers I gave you. The stories I put you on. You're the top fucking reporter at the last print papers in the Northeast."

Lou turned around and grabbed one of the statues Wes had won— for a profile of the school-board president who had a habit of blaming the students and parents for poor grades and also carried a Taser in a holster into board meetings. Lou threw it at the wall of glass, which to Wes' surprise, didn't break. The statue simply bounced off the window to the floor, its little wings broken now.

"And you're gonna squander it all in that viper's nest of fat-ass fags and transsexual cocksuckers in Manhattan?" He paused, walked to the door and stuck his head out. "Casey, Tony, I didn't mean that."

"It's okay," they both mumbled.

Lou turned back to Wes and got in his face. "As for you, you little cocksucking prick." Spittle flew from his mouth. A monstrous index finger was a centimeter from Wes' nose. "Why don't you just take a knife and run it through my chest, you cocksucking little cocksucker?"

"I guess I know what his go-to word is," Hillary said through the implant.

"No notice at all? Has nothing I taught you gotten through that thick fucking skull of yours?"

He raised a hand as if to smack Wes upside the head but thought better of it. He went back to his desk, leaned on it for support, panting, the veins in his neck throbbing.

"You," he said, catching his breath, readying for the next round. "You. You little."

As fluidly as possible, Wes looked up at the ceiling, reached for his wallet, took out the folded note and threw in on Lou's desk without looking.

"I'm sorry, Lou," he said, turning toward the newsroom. "I don't know what else to say." Behind his back, he made a circular motion with his hands, hoping Lou would understand it as "Hurry up and open that." Wes assumed the "Hurry up and open this" he'd scrawled on both sides of the note when Hillary was in the shower would help get the message across. That and the "Shhh. I'm bugged."

He heard the sound of paper crinkling.

"Sorry?" Lou said, now trying to keep up appearances. "I should shove that sorry up your ass. If I could fit it up there with all the cock that's in it already."

"Damn," Hillary said, laughing again. So much for her own sensitivity training. Whatever the case, she hadn't seen Wes drop the note on Lou's desk.

Lou fell silent as he read, his breathing still heavy and audible.

Lou,

Sorry I'm typing wihtou looking been busted by cops dor dealing. Gone to Manhattan undercover help with other bust. Can't talk imp[lanted with chip. Being monutored don't know if I'll be back. Hope to explain someday. Thanks for everything. You were like a dad. And its ok about all the yelling you probly just did. I understand. —Love Wes. P.S. I'm not a cocksucker.

"Son of a bitch," Lou muttered. He lumbered over to the door, shut it and turned a dial on the light-switch panel.

"Hot?" Wes asked, sheepishly.

Lou looked at him as if Wes were, to borrow one of Lou's other favorite phrases, a mental defective. He spoke slowly. "Yes, Wesley. I am hot and therefore I'm turning on the ceiling fan."

"There's no ceiling fan," Wes started to say. But as Lou turned the dial, static started hissing in Wes' head and grew louder the more Lou turned it.

"What the hell is going on?" Hillary asked before the static overtook her, drowned her out.

"That should do it," Lou said. "Step away from the window and you won't have a head full of static. They can't hear or see now."

"How?"

"Let's just say those wires in the glass weren't put there to stop bullets."

"Is that legal?"

"Was a time you could justify just about anything as freedom of the press. Now? Guess it would depend on which lawyer or politician went after me. It doesn't keep me up at night."

He picked up the letter and shook it at Wes. "Now what the fuck is this all about?"

"It's not a whole lot more complicated than that."

Lou shook his head. "I knew you were up to something on the side, but why go after someone like you? How big can your operation be?"

Wes shrugged. "I don't deal booze or cigarettes. But food? Riverhead and everything east of it on both the North and South Forks."

"No shit." Lou lowered himself into his chair. "How long?"

"Since after college. Right after mom died. So fifteen years, almost."

"And all I get out of it is a couple of steaks for Christmas every year?" Lou laughed. He looked out the window at the rest of the staff. "What about those useless sacks? You ever deal with them?"

"Hell no. Want to keep a secret, don't do business with reporters. Especially bad ones who have trouble finding their own stories."

Lou laughed again. "Good to see some of my prattling stuck in your head."

Wes sighed. "I'm sure I remember all of your prattling, Lou. Every word of it."

Fixing Wes with a stare, Lou said, "Don't start that shit. Not in my office."

They sat in silence for a while. Ever the reporter, Lou started in again with questions.

"How'd they get you?"

"Undercover," Wes said, hoping that would satisfy Lou, knowing it wouldn't.

"Fifteen years you don't get busted and suddenly an undercover busts you? Bullshit. Besides, they're so hemmed in by their own rules and stupidity, so how'd you fuck up?"

Wes looked down at his hands, overcome with shame.

Lou chuckled. "You stupid little cocksucker. They sent a woman after you."

Wes shrugged, found his voice and managed a "Yeah."

Lou slapped his desk and laughed. "Oh, Christ! It was that Hillary woman, wasn't it? And you fell in love with her?"

Wes looked at Lou, his eyes full of apology and self-loathing, begging almost to be put out of his misery.

"And judging by that hangdog look on your face, she's your handler now."

When Wes said yes, Lou had a laughing jag that seemed like it would go on forever—or until he had a stroke. Body shaking, his shoulders jackhammered up and down.

"I'm sorry," Lou finally said. "It *is* funny. And it's always you smart guys, isn't it? The ones who have all their shit together otherwise. You always get laid low by a pretty woman. Never fails. Competent in everything but love."

Wes started to protest, to try to muster some form of defense.

Lou put a hand up. "Save it," he said. "Besides, you've met my wife. I don't have a whole hell of a lot of room to talk."

Wes managed a fake laugh.

Lou reached into his desk, took out a notebook and a pen. "Now spill. Doubt I'll be able to do anything with this, but I want details."

Being on the wrong end of an interview was more than a little disconcerting. Even at the hands of a mentor and friend, Wes' palms went clammy. He was overcome with an urge—no, a need—to protect his information, clam up, withhold. Still, Wes spilled, detailing his business, how it operated, guestimates of the overall sums involved, how he was busted and the fuzzy details of their next move.

"So the locals are going into Teddy's backyard." Lou had known Theodore Bernstein before he'd assumed the mantle—and mocking nickname—from the second King Mike. "I don't know what kind of sense that makes—if it makes any. And this is Blunt you're dealing with?"

"Yeah," Wes answered.

Lou looked like he was puzzling things out, like he wanted to say more, but didn't want to talk, as he often said, out of his ass. "There was always something screwy about that one," was all he offered.

Wes continued. "To be honest, I have no idea what to do next. Even if this works and I help them nab this guy, then what?"

"Then you get the hell out of the Northeast, Wesley. That's not hard to figure out."

"I guess," he said. "They promised to let me keep operating if I helped them with the case."

"Was this before or after the woman you fell in love with revealed she was a cop sent specifically to trap you?"

"Yeah, yeah, yeah. I know."

"It doesn't sound like you know."

"I just don't know if I'm ready to move South yet."

"How ready do you have to be? You could get killed. Or you could blow the case. And who do you think will be the scapegoat? You need to pull your head out of that woman's vagina and come up for air, clear your mind. Hell, if you had any sense, you'd call for that submarine to pick your ass up in the middle of the night. Get out of here before any of this goes down."

"I thought about it," Wes lied.

"But?"

"I don't know?"

"Christ," Lou answered. "Where's your money? The real money?"

"In bank accounts in the South. My supplier has the dealer pick up cases of cash when he delivers. They take their cut, the rest is deposited."

Lou's eyebrows arched. "That's a hell of a supplier."

"One place where my trust hasn't been misplaced, I guess."

"And yet instead of hitching a ride, you're sitting in my office. Why the hell haven't you left, Wes?"

"They're watching me. First of all, they have me chipped. Secondly, where the hell would I make a call from without getting busted?"

"How about here?"

"You've got everything jammed in this office."

Lou reached into a desk drawer and pulled out an antique telephone, one with a cord attached.

"They don't even know this thing exists. Got any other excuses?"

No. He didn't. Not that he'd admit out loud.

"Fine."

Wes took the phone, dialed a number and left a message. "The party ends at midnight tonight. I might be too drunk to drive, so I'll need a ride. Midnight tonight. Probably be just me." Wes looked at his watch. It was 10 a.m. That gave him 14 hours to get to Montauk.

Lou shook his head. "Probably just you? Don't be stupid, Wes. It'll never work. Keep telling yourself this, 'She's a cop. She had me arrested. There's no hope for her.'"

"Yeah, okay," Wes said, a truculent teen all over again.

"Say it."

"She's a cop. She had me arrested. There's no hope for her."

"You don't even mean that," Lou said. He stuck out his bottom lip, blew out a puff of air that lifted the white hair that looped onto his forehead. "Now, get the hell out of here before squad cars start descending on the lot."

They stood up at the same time. Lou walked around the desk to show him out.

At the door to Lou's office, Wes turned to him.

"Thanks again. For everything."

"Don't mention it."

"And I was serious about what I said in the note."

"What's that?"

"You were like a dad to me."

Lou's face betrayed nothing. "You got some pretty low standards for parenting, Wesley."

Wes smiled. "Beggars can't be choosers.

Lou let slip a chuckle. Then, suddenly, he reached out an arm and wrapped it around Wes, pulled him in.

For a moment, Wes thought Lou was going to strangle him to death. He didn't know what was going on, had never been hugged by a man—not since he was two or three at any rate. His face was smashed up against Lou's chest, which was strangely soft, comforting almost. He faced the newsroom and wished he could take a photo of the horrified looks on the faces of his coworkers.

"You call if anything goes wrong," Lou said, pressing an old cellphone into Wes' hands. "I don't know what I'll be able to do, but I'll think of something."

23

That there wasn't an armada of squad cars waiting for him when he stepped from the office into the bright light of day surprised Wes. Were they watching him as closely as he thought? Could he have made a break for it, gotten a head start? The problem, he'd figured, was that the chip would give away his location no matter what he tried to do. The submarine was his best hope, but even if he had a rocket ship or a magic unicorn with wings, they'd catch him before he got to it. Maybe Dr. Halpern could remove it. But the visit itself would put his name into the Federal system, setting off an alarm for an unscheduled appointment. Maybe he should have had her come to Lou's office. Maybe he could try a veterinarian.

He didn't have much time to think it over. Hillary's car came buzzing into the parking lot like a giant angry bee.

"Don't get out of the car," he started to say.

But it was too late.

She was out, arms gesticulating wildly. Another day, another scene in a parking lot. She looked much like those old Donald Duck clips he watched on video. If she had feathers, they would have flown.

"What the hell was that? How did that happen? How did you?" Here she poked him in the chest. "Drop off my radar for that long? You don't know what you're toying with here, Wes. No idea! None!"

He couldn't help but see the humor in the scene. Especially as his coworkers had their faces pressed against the glass like school kids watching a playground fight. He waved at them. Lou shook his head, raised a mug and motioned as if to get on with the proceedings.

"Aww, you missed me," Wes said.

She balled her fist and pounded the hood of her car. Then his.

"You think this is funny? You're lucky I didn't call up half the force to come after you. You don't want to be on the wrong side of me. I give the word to Blunt and you'll rot under the jail. Do you hear me? Under it. In the jail, then under it."

"But you didn't call up anyone," he said.

That caught her short.

"What?"

"No squad cars. No all-points bulletin or Amber alert or whatever. And me off the grid for a whole half hour. So what gives?"

She was seething, her mind working. She wasn't going to answer the question. Not with anything resembling the truth.

"What did you tell Lou?" she asked.

So it was going to be like that.

"Don't worry about it," he said.

"I hope you didn't do anything stupid."

"You mean like dating someone who turned out to be a snitch?"

"Whatever. Just—whatever. We have enough on Lou to keep him quiet." She looked at the staffers gathered in the window. "And don't you worry about our protocol, Wes."

"That's twice now I go off the grid—one of those times taking you with—and no posse coming to the rescue."

"Look," she said, "you don't know the parameters of this case."

"The parameters."

"Calling in the troops is a last resort." Suddenly she was serious again. "We're deeper undercover than Blunt let on."

"Oh really?"

"No one else in our department knows."

That made no sense. What made even less sense was that she'd tell him. That also meant he could have run.

"So you could have run," she said, as if reading his mind. "At the same time, if some sort of accident were to befall you, trauma to the head, followed by death due to exposure, a stray bullet, a mugging by an overeager Taser carrier. Well, no one else would know that it happened right under our noses."

"Yeah, well what if I told Lou?"

"What if an old man had a nasty fall?"

"Jesus Christ."

"Don't know if he'll be of much help either."

Wes was at a loss. On the one hand, that was the scariest thing she'd said to him. On the other, she could be lying. Most likely was. Right? Could his judgment be that far off? Could he have fallen in love with a woman capable of leaving him for dead in the pine barrens? Nah. No way was she a black widow. Right?

He could practically hear Lou screaming at him, smacking him in the side of the head. "She turned you into the police. She is the police. She just told you straight up that they'd have you killed."

"Well, thanks for clearing that up," Wes finally said. He'd be on the first sub out tonight.

Hillary let her shoulders drop and the anger went out of her eyes. "Seriously, Wes. I'm just trying to help you, trying to protect you on this." She reached up and ran her fingers through his hair.

He tried to pull his head back, but she grabbed his ear and held on. Whatever else she was, he now had all the evidence he needed to declare her a schizophrenic.

"What the hell are you doing?" he asked.

"Keeping up appearances," she said, motioning toward the window where his coworkers were still watching. "We had a fight. Now you apologize. I accept."

She reached up on her toes and kissed him on the lips.

Son of a bitch.

"Just like that?" he said. "You turn it on and off just like that. You should have gone into counterfeiting instead of police work."

"Awww. Who said I was counterfeiting, Wesley?" She pulled him in tight.

"Wow. That's just fucked up."

He stood stiff as a board, resisting. But another part of his body was starting to do its own imitation of a board.

"You can fight it, Wes. Stand on principle. Then when we go to your friend Jules' place later, we'll look like a couple in the midst of a fight. Or." She drew even closer. "We can go home. Make up once or twice. And then Jules will think we're a happy couple that spent the afternoon fucking each other's brains out. I'm sure either will come off as realistic. But I know which one would be more fun."

"Can you let go of my ear?" he asked, trying for all the world to sound indignant, to be master of his body rather than the other way around. But his mind had been made up for him.

24

Excerpt from a letter to Wes Montgomery, signed, "Love, the Old Man" dated Nov. 25, 2025

I was giving you your very first Twinkie when everything went to hell. You're too young to remember this. You'd just turned two. We were in the back bedroom. Your mother was in the living room, watching her favorite show.

Earlier that day, I'd dropped 20 bucks on an individually wrapped Twinkie. Funny. My old man made a big deal about my first beer and here I was giving you your first taste of golden spongy goodness. I unwrapped it as quietly as I could and took a little tiny nibble to show you it was something to eat. I handed it to you with one hand and grabbed a wet nap with the other. I figured you didn't know shit—you were going to crumble it up, make a hell of a mess. That's part of life, you know. Hell, I don't want to live in a world where a kid can't bust up a Twinkie and mash it into his hair.

But no. You took it in your hands and studied the bright yellow cake before giving it the slightest little squeeze. Then you giggled. And did it again.

"Twinkie," I said. It was stupid, trying to teach you the word. It would lead to nothing but a month's worth of fighting with your mother. But you were my son, and you should know how to say the damn word. "Twinkie," I said again.

"Twinkie," you said. Goddamn, I remember it like it was yesterday. I should have videotaped it. Didn't have chips back then. And you didn't say it like a damn baby, either. You said it like you meant it. "Twinkie," you said again, and held it out to me.

"No," I said. "Take a bite."
And you gave it a go. A small one.
"Good?" I asked.
"Good!" you repeated.
"Take another." I wanted you to get to the cream filling. And when
you did hit it, you just stopped. Oh, the look on your face. I can close
my eyes and see it now. Priceless. Like you'd just lost your virginity
or something.
"Good," you said, a little louder this time. You put your finger in
the cream then offered it to me.
I licked it off. "Mmm. Good," I said.
You offered me more. "No, buddy, it's all yours."
You licked the cream off your own finger. "Mmm. Good, daddy."
Then I remember telling you to take a big bite, a real one, getting
the cake and cream at the same time.
Yeah, yeah, yeah. I knew you didn't know what the fuck I was
talking about. Then again, I kind of felt like you might. Either way,
you took a bite—a proper bite—and you dropped to the floor on your
diaper-padded ass and chewed that Twinkie and contemplated it and
beheld the wonders the world had to offer. I know you were only two,
but I guaran-god-damn-tee you, you were savoring that thing.
And then your mother screamed my name. "Miiikkkee."
I thought she'd somehow busted us. But she was still in the living
room. And her voice was all wrong.
Then my e-mail notification started dinging like crazy before the
whole computer locked up. My cellphone buzzed briefly, but when I
flipped it open to answer, a recording told me all circuits were busy—
something I hadn't heard since Sept. 11, 2001.
I left you alone with the Twinkie and shuffled out to the living room.
Your mother looked like she'd seen a ghost.
"Israel," she said.
"Now what?" I asked.
"Iran nuked it."
Three days later, the President of the U.S., God bless her soul,
ordered a tactical nuclear strike on Tehran and anything looking

remotely like a nuclear plant or military installation within Iran's borders.

"Let this serve as a message to the world," she said, then pointed our nukes at Pakistan, Saudi Arabia and Indonesia.

It was also a message to the rest of the country. She'd already brought the Oklahoma Tea Party Militia to its knees, and this was a way to put that chapter behind her, win back some love in the red states.

But this was too much for King Mike. He'd been contemplating a national run, and she had just basically declared herself the owner of the world's biggest pair of balls. And when the First Man or Husband or whatever the hell hit the TV circuits to make her case with that fiery aw-shucks nature of his? Forget it.

It was too much for the enlightened folks in the Northeast. She was supposed to be one of them. Now she'd gone and used nukes? Too much a red-state move for them to bear.

So King Mike and his minions launched a secession movement. Even I never saw that coming. You expect it from Texas. Georgia maybe. But New York? There was much chest-thumping and talk of the course of human events and beacons on a hill. Laughably, New York, Massachusetts, New Jersey, Connecticut, Vermont and Maine called up their National Guard units. Half of them didn't show. Not that it mattered. Despite what she'd done in Oklahoma, it was clear that no one outside the Northeast was going to fight for it. All it had going for it was New York and the only thing it manufactured was half-baked ideas. And I'd bet my testicles that the corporations helped grease this deal—it was a chance to build a wall around his crazy policy experiments, to quarantine his sin taxes.

Goodbye and good riddance—and while you're at it, take California, too. Otherwise, we'll just give it back to Mexico.

Within a year, King Mike found himself presiding over the Northeast Federation of States and impotently stamping his feet as companies decamped for the South. Houston became the new financial capital and Atlanta the new media capital.

And hell if I wasn't going with them.

But your mother was having none of it. She had a hatred of the

South that went well beyond the irrational. The rest of the country was a personal affront to her dignity.

I don't know what she's told you, but I want you to know that I fought like a dog to get you out of that place. It was my turn to cry and scream, rant and rave. She kept cool. This time her faith in the law would be well rewarded. As fast as they were throwing up obstacles to leave, it would have been hard enough for me to get out alone, much less with a child whose custody was in dispute. The laws were all in her favor. Even if I hadn't had a record, they would never have given me custody. And don't think I didn't think about kidnapping you. But they would have locked me up for life. The new Federation wasn't keen on letting anymore kids escape. As it was, large swaths of the Black and Hispanic populations were getting the hell out of Dodge (look it up). This was the last straw. Years of living in an increasingly bland world, an increasingly expensive world, one in which you could no longer take comfort in food—and now they weren't even living in the United States, but in some puppet regime set up by a rich white man for a society of gym-going, soy-milk drinking, yoga-bending whiny-ass white people? No thank you, Bob. Like me, they'd rather try their luck with the rednecks. At least the food would be better, the weather warmer.

But with that sort of exodus going on, the Federation wasn't going to let any more babies slip through its fingers if it could help it.

So I had no choice but to leave you behind.

Over the years, I forgave your mother many things—even ratting me out to the cops. But that one I never will.

25

By the time they pulled into Jules' driveway, Hillary was once again in a civil mood.

His shoulders should have been tensed up around his ears, his temples throbbing with stress and anger. But she'd explained, after she'd stopped transmitting, that her sinister threats were a word-for-word message from Blunt. Then she fucked him into a stupor. On some academic level, it crossed his mind that the government should have prohibited sex when it was crossing everything else off the list. Sex had the potential to do more harm than a can of soda or a carton of fried potatoes. Hell, there were less messy, more dignified ways of reproducing. At the least, there had to be some sort of law about using it during the course of an investigation. Maybe there was. Whatever the case, something needed to be done to protect people who couldn't protect themselves.

But after an afternoon in the bedroom, he couldn't even muster the energy to feel cheap.

Besides, he'd be leaving tonight, escaping her clutches, dignity mostly intact, head held high, freedom on the horizon.

Or so he kept telling himself.

Jules, when he was on the East End, lived in an old farmhouse between Bridgehampton and Sag Harbor. Situated on a hill, it was built for a large family and would have been too big for most single men. But it barely contained Jules. In fact, many of his parties were held in the massive barn halfway down the slope behind the house. The barn had long ago been converted to a studio by a previous owner, which is why Jules had bought the property in the first place.

The driveway leading up to the house had been cleared of snow, but there was only a small foot path between the dark lifeless house and the blazing windows and blaring music out in the barn.

"Let's not unload just yet," said Wes before they exited the vehicle and picked their way to the barn, trying to keep snow out of their shoes and their asses off the ice.

"What is he doing back there?" Hillary asked.

Wes stopped and turned to her. "Art," he said, describing a big circle in the air to capture the magnitude, the essence of what Jules did.

"Art," she repeated, not exactly impressed.

"No," said Wes, correcting her. "Art!" He moved his hands through the air again.

"Ohhh," she said. "Art." She half-assedly copied his motions, looking more like a kid trying to keep her balance in the snow than someone trying to catch the meaning of art in her arms.

"You've never heard of Jules?" he asked.

"What's his last name?"

"He doesn't have one. It's just Jules."

"He ever been arrested?"

Wes gave the question serious thought. "Not out here, I don't think. Maybe in the city."

She seemed to go into a trance. "Zwadinski," she said.

"What?"

"His last name's Zwadinski."

"What the hell?"

"Chip, Wes. We gave you one, you should try to use it. His last name. If you've been arrested, you have a last name—like it or not. So this guy is some famous hot shot?"

"Well, what passes for famous in his world."

She zoned out again.

"Seriously," she said, shaking her head.

"What?"

"Art," she said, moving her arms through the air and starting again toward the barn.

"Whatever," he said. "Just try not to act like a cop in there."

She patted a glove-covered hand on his cheek. "Aye-aye captain."

They pushed through a small side door and entered the blinding glow of the barn. The music died down. As their eyes adjusted, Wes took in what must have been hundreds of yards worth of yarn stretched from walls to rafters to floor. It looked like a spider web as dreamed up by a hallucinogenic three-year-old. It also looked like something that took all of thirty minutes to finish.

Hillary noticed something else.

"Look at those," she said, motioning to high-intensity lights set up on stands scattered around the room. "They look like old highway construction lights."

"So?"

"Those haven't been legal for twenty or thirty years. You know how much energy those things use?"

He shot her a look. "You're not a cop, remember?"

"Just saying."

"Don't you believe in global freezing?" he asked. "Wouldn't it help if he used *more* electricity?"

She started to say something else—probably "climate change"— but he stopped her.

"Just can you pay more attention to the art than the lights?"

"The art?"

"The stringy things."

She looked around the barn, noticing the installation for the first time.

"Art?" she asked.

"Art," he said.

Wes looked around, didn't see Jules lurking in any of the shadows of the cavernous space. Jules knew they were there. Wes was sure of that. What he was unsure of was how Jules would make his entrance. The man took the basic concept of art—artifice—to absurd levels, turning everything he did into a performance, a sham of sorts. Hell, the pieces were probably the least interesting aspect of it, so little thought went into them. No, the real art was the show Jules put on for an admiring public he had absolutely no respect for.

Jules would never be insulted by the comment, "My five-year-old could do better than this." Because Jules—the real one—would be the first to agree with the sentiment. Wes was pretty sure he was one of the few to see the real Jules, the guy behind the curtain, raking in thousands upon thousands of dollars of rich people's cash for ten dollars worth of craft-store supplies.

There were sincere artists out there, fumbling for life's meaning, trying to say something about the human condition. Jules had little but contempt for them. He saw the men as effete poseurs, the ugly women as bitter shrews in need of a shave and shower, and the attractive ones as prey.

At some point, Jules had given thought to becoming a serious artist. But, as he put it, he was too smart for that. After struggling with neo-neo-realist paintings, he dropped out of the scene to study it from afar, to figure out how the microcosm worked, how fame and notoriety and fortune were built. It had little to do with talent and everything to do with who the rich and the media crowned the next big thing.

There were attributes each next big thing needed to have, and Jules was delighted to learn he had them. He was ruggedly attractive—and his large frame would carry the bulk of a good life handsomely. He was loud. He was obnoxious. And he was happy to let go of whatever little bit of shame he'd been born with.

Beyond that, what the power brokers wanted wasn't someone who'd hold a mirror up to their corner of society and critique it, but rather someone who would affirm the worst parts of it, the idea that with enough talent, intellect or, failing those, money, a man could pretty much do what he damn well pleased. A genius could break the rules, hurl shit like an angry chimp and be rewarded with admiration and respect. Jules found that in art, especially, an inversion had occurred. Picasso, Van Gogh, Pollack had been talented lunatics, ground-breaking visionaries who happened to be crazy or abusive assholes. After enough of those guys, the art world came to expect the alpha artist to be a depraved ass. Misogyny, homophobia, racism, conspiracy theories, obsessions with Stalin or Hitler or Guevara, Hussein or Assad or Ahmadinejad. You had a free pass if you were an artistic genius—or convinced others that you were one.

Jules wasn't the first charlatan to hit the art scene, but he may have been the best. And Wes felt a grudging respect for that. It didn't hurt that Jules was his best client, the first, in fact, to call him when he took over the franchise from the previous guy. Jules appeared as if summoned from a magical lamp. "You and me are gonna get real close," he'd said.

Wes usually came out to Jules' alone and so typically found the real Jules slouching around, eating a sandwich, watching old action movies on video. But Wes knew the presence of a woman changed things.

"Jules," he called out, his voice drifting up into the rafters.

A loud orgasmic groan came from the bathroom. Then, "Ohhhhhh. Fuck yeah." This was followed by the sound of a flushing toilet. A minute later, Jules stepped out into the bright light, onto the stage, as it were. His brown hair fell in a curly mess to his shoulders. Stubble accentuated his chubby cheeks and a paint-splattered jumpsuit covered his impressive girth. It was the sort of heft only a rich man, someone above the law, could pull off. But he wasn't exactly obese—there was an athleticism about him. The uniform was completed by bright red vintage hightops.

Then he spoke.

"Hooooo!" He exclaimed. "Sorry to keep you waiting, but I just had to rub one out. Fine line for the artist. Too much sex, you lose your drive. Your spark. Not enough and semen backs up and starts fucking with your brain. Next thing you know you're trying to cut off your own ear or some shit."

He tossed a vintage magazine onto a small table. "Barely Legal. May 1995. They don't make 'em like that anymore. More innocent times back then."

He offered one of his big hands to Hillary. "Jules," he said.

Frozen in place, she looked down at his paw. This sort of behavior she expected from the criminal class, not the wealthy. But only because she hadn't spent much time with the latter.

"Don't worry," he said. "I washed it."

It was all Wes could do not to laugh. The Artist as Unrestrained

Sexual Appetite would be the evening's presentation.

Hillary took his hand, shook it.

"Nice grip," Jules said, looking into her eyes.

Squeamish as she may have been about shaking his hand, she wasn't going to lose a staring match.

"You got a nice one here, Wesley," he said. "I'm surprised at you. Can't see much of her figure through those winter clothes, but her face is something to behold. Those eyes. That nose. I could memorize that and paint it all day long."

Hillary smiled at him. "I'd bet a thousand dollars the only paint within a hundred yards of this barn in the stuff peeling off the walls."

Jules laughed and let go of her hand. "Damn it, Wes. You know I can't stand a woman who sees through me."

It was a capitulation of sorts, but also another level of flirting, a jujitsu move designed to use Hillary's own strengths against her. He'd just called her beautiful and smart, hadn't he? Still, Jules never tangled for long with smart women. Too much work, not enough reward, he said. And he honestly believed dumb girls gave better blowjobs.

But he wasn't done. Jules, Wes knew, would now shift into something a little closer to the real him. He'd make her feel privileged at how transparent he was. The Artist as Open Book.

"You two have a seat. Want a beer?"

They both accepted. Hillary motioned to the yarn. "Nice work," she said. "What were you going for?"

Jules waved his hands at it. "Five hundred thousand dollars is what I'm going for." He cracked his beer, tossed his feet up on a coffee table. "Not too bad for half an hour's work."

"Five hundred thousand?"

"Yup."

"Nice work if you can get it," Wes said. They looked at him as if he'd said something particularly clever—or stupid. It was hard to tell. He needed to quit watching 20th century video.

"The beauty is," continued Jules, "I didn't even think of it myself. Some rich guy saw a photo of something like this in an art history book. Wanted one for his own house."

"He couldn't do it himself?" Hillary asked.

Jules laughed. "You know what? I actually asked him that. I said, 'It can't be that hard. Why not just sling some yarn around your place?' Know what he said?"

He paused. They waited.

"He said, real slow, like to make sure I understood, 'Well, now, Jules, if I do it, it's just a bunch of string hanging from my ceiling. If you do it, it's art.' Ain't that some shit? He didn't have to tell me twice."

They all laughed.

"Customer is always right," Wes said.

"That's a good one," Jules said. "I'll have to steal that one." He went on to explain the real challenge of doing the piece at the guy's place would be to make it at least look a little bit hard.

"Figure I'll do it once. Have a fit because it's just not right. Maybe break some furniture, curse at the help. Or sleep with the help. Either way, someone's going to be crying. Then start over. You know, the whole show."

"So will Manhattan be covered in yarn by next month?" Hillary asked.

"Not by me, it won't," Jules said. "The deal on this one is exclusivity. Not even if someone offered me his virgin daughter."

"So it's not exactly a volume business?"

"Not the installations, no. That's why I don't like them. Have to go into these people's houses, spend all day there, put up with their shit. And these young strivers? The ones living in those awful micro-apartments? Don't even me started. But I do have some items that sell pretty good all year round at galleries."

"Like?"

"Like the Jarshit series."

"Which is?"

"My shit. In a jar."

She'd been in the process of bringing the beer can to her mouth, but froze. She looked from Wes to Jules and back, waiting for one of them to explain the joke.

All she got was a cheap shot from Wes. "And no, he's not shitting you."

"Real mature," she said. "Assholes."

"She's even better looking when she's mad," Jules said. "But yeah, sweetheart, it's shit in a jar. Another great unoriginal idea. First guy who did it, last century—his name was Piero Manzoni. Well, he put it in a can. But when I thought about stealing it—and I really wanted to, because it is the purest expression of how I feel about all of this— when I thought about it, I realized it must have been a messy ordeal. Little tiny cans he used. I may be an animal on many levels, but I handle shit with my hands as little as possible. No matter what you're paying me. And if I hired an Iranian or Venezuelan assistant, I'd have advocacy groups all over my ass. So I set up this rig in my studio toilet—I can show it to you if you want. It's a board with a hole in it. Hole's big enough to hold a glass jar. Jar goes in the hole. Turd goes in the jar. Lid on. Label with the date, what I'd eaten the previous three meals, consistency—because they start to fall apart after a while. And there you go. Art. If you ask me, this is one case where the copy is superior to the original, and I'm not saying it just because it came out of my backside. I say if you're going to be selling your shit to suckers, don't hide it in a metal can. If they want shit on their shelves, then make them look at it."

Hillary put the beer can down on the table. "And that sells?"

"Thousand bucks for run-of-the-mill mushy shit. Two thousand for small nuggets. Rabbit shit, I call that. And a full five if I can get one of them nice long coils going."

She pulled away from Wes—as if she suddenly found even the thought of the human body something too disgusting to tolerate.

"On that note," Jules said, standing up and brushing imaginary dust from his jumpsuit. "Let's go in the house, get something to eat."

They walked out into the cold. With dark approaching, the snow was turning from white to the bluish hue it took on at night. It stretched uninterrupted from the house until it ran into the woods surrounding the property. At the tree line, thirty or forty scraggly-looking deer were picking the bark off the trees.

"Vermin," Jules muttered to himself as he led them single-file down the rough trail between the barn and the house.

Snow was working its way into Wes' boots. "Why don't you get someone out here to clear out a path? Not like you can't afford it."

"It'll just get covered again in a week. Besides, snow makes it harder for the locals to sneak around out here. They've been sending their ankle-biters to throw rocks at the barn while I'm working. They break one more window, I might catch one of them and nail his carcass to the side of the barn as an example."

"Why are they throwing rocks at you?" Hillary asked.

"Jealousy, I suppose."

"You really are full of yourself," she said.

"No denying that," Jules answered without looking back. "But not that kind of jealousy. They've all been forced to convert their properties into working farms—to grow potatoes and other shit for the government."

"Why shouldn't they?" Hillary asked.

Both Jules and Wes stopped and turned to look at her.

"Guess she's not as smart as I thought she was," Jules said.

"Yeah, she's got a soft spot for King Mike."

"You obviously aren't getting enough meat into her diet, Wes."

"Look," said Hillary, "the land's just sitting here unused except to look at. The Federation needs vegetables. This is some of best land in the Northeast for potato farming. Why shouldn't the Fed step in and force them to convert their property? It's not like they do the work. It's not like they don't get paid."

"Listen, honey, I didn't buy this place so I could look out on fields of Iranians digging potatoes. As far as the payment goes, it's a joke. And they tax it. Fucking insulting is what that is. The locals? They're too chickenshit—or smart—to tangle with the government. Hell, if I was one of them, I'd be throwing rocks at my barn, too."

"What makes you so special?" she asked.

Jules started walking again. "Let's just say I've got connections."

"Like?"

"My network is vast and dangerous and top secret. Classified.

Need-to-know basis. But I can tell you that I decorated the north wing of the current King Mike's summer home. And he's got a jar of my shit sitting on the desk in his Manhattan office."

She stopped again, looking for all the world like she'd forgotten where she was, where she was going. Wes figured she was trying to do a deeper background check on Jules. He'd actually pay good money to see the results of that one, but doubted she'd come up with much of anything.

"Let's go eat," she finally said. She was done arguing with them. "I'm starving."

Whether it was the food and booze or she was acting for the benefit of Jules, Hillary—who'd been affectionate enough after their afternoon romp—behaved like a besotted school girl for the remainder of the evening.

They steered clear of politics, focusing instead on food and parties. She hung on their words, hung on Wes' arm. The more she had to drink and eat, the tighter she held on.

He loved her for it. And hated her, too. Here he was gearing up for his big escape and as fast as he reconstructed emotional barriers, she pulled them down. Rubbing his back. Kissing his neck. Talking about the first time they met as if it really was some spur-of-the-moment surprise. She squeezed his leg under the table and once, when she went to the bathroom, she rang through on his chip, activated the video and did a strip tease for him through the walls of Jules' house.

How much of it was acting? How much was woman's intuition— that ability to know when a man was up to something, to counter it before either of them really knew what was going on? How much was that desperate need of friendship brought on by all those years on the force keeping her colleagues at arm's length? How much was just booze flowing through her? Did the alcohol bring her closer to her true self or just make her a mess of indiscretion and bad judgment? If Wes walked out into the night, would she call Blunt and have him pick her up? Or would she simply throw herself into Jules' arms—after she got over the image of him crapping in glass jars?

Wes was sober as a church mouse. He'd been taking small sips and dumping the rest when he went to the kitchen for ice. Soon enough, the other two were stumbling drunk, laughing like they'd known each other their entire lives. It was only 9 o'clock; the early winter dark made it feel much later. As with any two drunks, they grew bored with the laughter and looked for something to fight about.

"So, sweet stuff, you got the hots for the government?" Jules asked, a smile on his face and a challenge in his eyes.

"Shit," Wes said. Last thing he needed was her getting riled up.

Hillary tried to blink her head clear. Took a sip of her drink. "You think you know the government," she said. "You don't know. You don't."

"Look, honey," Wes said, grabbing her arm. "We don't need to get into this right now."

She pushed his arm away, patted his cheek. "You're cute when you worry about me."

She turned back to Jules. "Let me let you in on a secret," she said.

Wes was certain she was going to tell Jules she was a cop.

"What's that?" Jules said.

"Fuck the government," she said, slapping the countertop. "Fuck the government," she said, raising her bottle.

Jules raised his glass. "Hear, hear."

Before Wes had time to even wonder where that sentiment had come from, she grabbed him by the collar and started dragging him toward the guest bedroom where Wes had set them up earlier. "And now you," she said, "fuck me."

"Hot damn!" Jules shouted after them.

26

He'd barely gotten the door to the room shut before she was on him.

"Come 'ere," she slurred. She pinned one arm behind his back, grabbed the back of his collar and pressed him up against the door. She whispered into his ear. "Oh, what I'm going to do to you." She bit his ear gently, then swung him around and flung him onto the bed where he landed face first with an audible "oof."

Wes turned over, bracing himself on his elbows, preparing for the onslaught. Excited as he was, he started to worry. The academy had taught her grappling skills, skills she might not be able to control in her current condition.

"Don't you fucking move," she said, struggling to take off her clothes. Satisfactorily naked, she crept toward the edge of the bed, then pounced on top of him. He wondered briefly how she didn't break his dick.

She kissed him, bit his bottom lip. Then, with one swift motion, she ripped his shirt open sending buttons flying. One hit him right under the eye.

"Ow, shit," he said, defensively covering his face, surprised more than hurt. "Damn, Hillary."

She froze, a fistful of shirt in each hand. As she eased him back down to the mattress, her bottom lip quivered and tears started to trickle.

"Oh, Wes," she said. "I'm." She stopped. "I'm so sorry."

Her head fell to his chest, and the crying had barely started in earnest before it stopped. She'd passed out on top of him.

"Shit," he said, not even sure what the word encompassed. Shit, a naked unconscious woman had him pinned to the bed. Shit, he'd fallen for that woman. Shit if it wasn't one of the best feelings he'd ever had in his life, her compact body nestled against his, burning like an ember, snoring like a little gas-powered engine.

Shit, she was a cop who'd involved him with some half-assed sting operation he wanted no part of.

The cellphone in his pocket—the old one Lou had given him—vibrated. Three times. A text. It started again then stopped. And again.

Shit, his former boss was frantically texting him to get the hell out. Shit, the voice of reason had to remotely dial into his pants pocket because his head was long gone.

He looked at his watch. Ten o'clock. Shit. If he was going to make his escape he didn't have time for this Hamlet foolishness.

His phone vibrated again.

Shit.

Or get off the pot.

Wes rolled Hillary off of him. She groaned. He pulled the phone out of his pocket and checked the texts.

"Time to get out."

"Better be on the road. No time for second thoughts."

"Goddamnit, you little cocksucker, you'd better be halfway to fucking Montauk by now, so help me."

And then.

"It's all a lie. She does not love you."

Shit. He flipped the phone closed and considered Hillary. He tried to seek out her physical imperfections—scars, hairy moles, weird bumps—the things that, in a bad relationship, would start to sicken him, drive him crazy. And wasn't this the very definition of a bad relationship?

But he found himself thinking the stray hair on her nipple was cute. Which wasn't like him at all. He had some stringent beliefs about where hair should and should not appear on a woman.

Shit. He was in too deep. It was time to go.

He took a deep breath and stood to leave.

She reached out and grabbed his shirt. "Don't leave," she said.

"It's cold."

Shit. "I'm just going to the bathroom," he said.

He covered her up, tucked her in, leaned into kiss her and stroked her hair.

"Love you," he whispered.

"Me too," she said.

"Shit." He said it out loud this time. He kicked and punched the air in frustration. What kind of shitting bullshit was this shit?

And in a second he made perhaps the stupidest decision he'd ever made in his life.

He whisked the covers off her.

"Hey," she mumbled.

"It's okay," he said. "We're gonna." He paused. What? What the hell were they going to do? "We're going for a ride. To the beach."

What did it matter? She was too drunk to sit up, much less argue with him about going anywhere.

He dressed her as best he could, no small feat as she'd gone all noodles on him. She burped once and, for one horrifying moment, he thought she'd projectile vomit all over the room.

He'd have to carry her. God knows what he'd say to Jules if he saw them. Hopefully, he was upstairs passed out drunk or masturbating himself into a coma.

Wes found the app for the car and got its heater started. Then he picked Hillary up and she instinctively wrapped an arm around his neck, the other one falling limp.

"Hey," she managed before her head fell back.

He started walking. Thunk. Her head had hit the door frame. Not very hard, but hard enough to leave a red spot.

"Owwwww," she moaned.

"Shit," he whispered.

Carefully, quietly he made his way out of the house with no further collisions. He opened the passenger side door and managed to put her in. After she was in, he paused to catch his breath. Was he really going to do this? How the hell was he going to get her down the hatch? Would she stay out the entire time? If not, how would she react? Hell, what would she do if she came to on a submarine making a straight line for the South?

Fuck it. He was already running out of time. Cross those bridges when he got to them. He climbed into the car and started down the drive. In his head, his chant was going full speed—shit, shit, shit, shit. Cram the neurosis, the indecision into a pocket and just act, Goddamnit. That was how he'd lived before all this started happening. If he could just get out of the drive and onto the highway without reconsidering his actions, changing his mind. That's all he needed to do. Through the stand of trees that hid Jules's property from the road. Almost there. Wes felt like his bones might jump out of his skin. He was going to do it. He was doing this. What was she going to do? Ask him to turn the sub around? Hell no. She'd get over it. She'd have to.

And then, impossibly, a black sedan materialized in the night. It pulled across the end of the drive, blocking his way. He stopped.

"Shit," he whispered, all the anxiety, all the excitement of escape, the hope and possibility and potential crashing around him. He put his head on the steering wheel. "Shit," he said, before resigning himself once again to fate and its fucked up wiles. He looked up. The sedan sat there like a turd on a dinner plate.

The implant spoke. "Going for a ride?" It was Blunt.

Wes said nothing.

"Why don't you get out of the car, Wes? Come over and let's have a little chat."

Wes wasn't sure, but it sounded as if Blunt was trying really hard to sound calm. The car's window slid down revealing the chief's face.

"I don't know," Wes said. "It's kind of cold out there."

"Get the fuck out of the car and get your ass over here," Blunt screamed into Wes's brain.

Wes looked over at Hillary. She snored, her head against the window, mouth open, a string of drool on her chin. He wiped it off.

"Fine," he said. He climbed out of the car and walked over to Blunt, who sat with his fingers in a white-knuckled grip around the steering wheel.

"The reason I'm still in this car," Blunt started. "The reason I'm strapped in and not beating you senseless in the driveway right his minute, is because I'm doing you another favor."

"Yeah, what's that?"

"Probably, she's so drunk right now, she won't remember any of this. And if she woke up to find your face all mangled. Well, then you—or me—one of us would have to explain that you tried to escape."

"What's it matter to her if I tried to escape?"

"You mean aside from breaking her trust?"

"Her trust? Are you shitting me?"

"Yes, Wes. Her trust. Partners need trust between them. We had a deal, no? We lay off of you and you help us. You. Help. Us. And you've been pretty good up to now. You're a train ride away from Manhattan's inner circle, Wes. You don't want to fuck things up now, do you? We're right where we wanted to be."

"What's all this 'we' shit?" Wes asked. "I didn't exactly volunteer for this."

"God fucking damnit, Wesley," Blunt said, releasing his seat belt. "You don't even know what—" He stopped, took a breath and put his hands back on the steering wheel. "Look. We had a fucking deal. Hell, it's only natural that you try to escape. But you failed. Game over. So that deal is still in place. I just don't want the two of you at each other's throats when you get into Manhattan. Your own friend there believed you were a couple, right? Then everyone else will. So, now, I suggest you turn around, get her back in bed and pray she doesn't remember any of this."

"Like I have a choice."

"No. You don't. And you try anything like this again, I may lose my temper."

It wasn't making any sense to Wes. Why did Blunt seem so on edge, so near panic? He had the full power of law on his side, no?

"How many people know about this case you're working on?" Wes asked.

"Get out of my face," Blunt said.

"Aye-aye cap'n," Wes said, offering him a salute.

Blunt rolled up the window, backed his car into his hiding spot on the side of the road. Wes considered mashing the accelerator and making a run for it, but knew he'd never make it.

He turned the car around and headed back down the drive. Halfway to the house, he gambled again. He fished out the old cellphone and texted Lou: "You up?"

"Better fucking be in Montauk, kid," Lou replied.

Slowly, silently, Wes explained that Blunt had caught him, conveniently leaving out the part that he had Hillary in the car with him.

"Shit," replied Lou.

"That about sums it up."

"Now what?"

"Don't know. Will figure something out."

"Anything I can do?"

Wes made a snap decision, one he'd toyed with earlier in the day.

"Yeah," he said, then gave Lou the exact location of his stash and the entry codes.

"What do I do with that?"

"Good scoop. Especially if you use my name."

"You sure?"

"Yes," Wes said.

Wes knew Lou would already have one foot out the door. His priority would always be to that fickle slut, the news cycle. His outdated dedication to the news was why the people who loved him loved him— and those who didn't, well, didn't. Lou, at that moment, was likely calling a photographer. He was so old-school, he refused to take photos himself. A reporter reported, a photographer shot. Taking six hundred shots and trying to find one that sort of worked showed a lack of respect for both trades. Old-fashioned and expensive? Sure. But Lou's silly little weekly paper out here on Long Island won awards every year for its photojournalism. So Lou would be rousting someone from bed or dragging someone from a party and then hauling ass to Montauk.

For his part, Wes started again toward the house, where he found Jules standing on the front porch, wrapped in a coat, smoking a cigar.

"Forget something?" he asked.

"She just had to go to the beach," he said. "Just had to go." How easily the lies were coming now.

"Bit cold for that, don't you think?"

"That's what I said," he said. "Didn't matter anyway. She passed out cold before we got to the end of the driveway. Want to help me get her out of the car?"

"How bad is it?"

Wes opened the passenger door. The interior light revealed a distinctly green tint to Hillary's face. Her breathing was shallow.

"Well hell," Jules said.

"I know."

"She's going to be a nightmare in the morning."

"You have anything to fix it?"

"I'm fresh out. We'll just have to get it out of her the old-fashioned way."

"Shit."

Jules brushed him aside, grabbed her by the shoulders and yanked her out of the car and on to her feet, trying to make her stand. He shook her. "Hillary! Doll! Hey!"

"Hunh," she said, her eyes opening. "Oh." It was as if she only then realized the state she was in. "I don't feel so good."

She burped.

"Jules," Wes asked. "What the hell are you doing?"

He didn't answer. Instead, he wrapped one of her arms around his shoulder and jogged her a bit down the driveway before giving her another good shake.

"Stop," she whined.

Jules jogged her back toward the car, bounced her up and down.

"Jules, come on. Stop it," Wes said.

"Oh, stop being a cunt," Jules said, shaking her again.

Her throat started to work. She made a couple of frog-like sounds.

"Here we go," Jules said, pushing her away from him and down onto her knees in the snow bank at the edge of the drive. There, she sprayed the white lawn with the contents of her stomach.

"Fucking hell," Wes said.

"Cure's worse than the disease," Jules said. "I'm going back in.

You should probably hold her hair or something."

Wes rushed to her side, but it was already too late. The lower reaches of her locks were already bathed in bits of barf. Still, he pulled her hair back as she puked. And puked. And puked some more.

"Wes," she cried. "Wesssss."

"It's okay," he said, rubbing her back. "Get it all out. You'll feel better for it."

"Wes."

He knew what she was going through, knew it was a different thing entirely from the bout of puking she'd experienced on her morning run. That had been a minor bit of cleaning house. This was chest-rattling, stomach-turning-inside-out vomiting that left you making deals with God, promising never to drink again.

"God," she whimpered. "Wes, I never want to drink again."

After a while, after moving her twice so she wasn't constantly staring into the same puddle, she emptied out. When she started to shiver, he stood her up and walked her back into the house. There, he stripped her down. Even in this wretched state, she was beautiful. He felt a tenderness for her, one immediately tested by another round of dry heaves.

Wes turned on the shower, got it nice and hot, took off his own clothes and climbed in with her, washing her hair, scrubbing her down and ignoring the erection prompted by the sight of her wet, naked body. The damn thing was like a clown at a funeral home.

He dried her off, wrapped her hair in a towel, and coaxed a piece of white bread into her mouth—evil, evil white bread shipped illegally from the South. He made her sip some water as well.

She tried to turn away.

"Trust me," he sighed. "You'll feel better in the morning. You'll thank me for it."

27

"What the fuck happened to my hair?" she wanted to know when confronted with the tangled mess resulting from being put to bed wet and unbrushed. "And why the fuck does my head hurt so much?" she asked, touching the side that Wes had rammed into the doorframe.

"You hit your head on the toilet while puking," he lied, pointing out how he'd taken care of her all night, that it was no picnic for him, either.

"And what about you?"

"What?"

"Why aren't you hungover?"

Then she argued with Jules when he suggested she drink a Bloody Mary to lessen her suffering.

"More alcohol to help a hangover? That's the stupidest fucking thing I've ever heard."

"Suit yourself," he said.

"You two are like animals," she said, storming back into the guest room.

Her mood was only the half of it. Wes spent the morning terrified that she'd start piecing together the previous night. Or that Blunt would tell her Wes had tried to kidnap her.

But by the time they left to catch the train to Manhattan, she'd said nothing of it. He began to feel a little more confident. At the station, Wes took small delight in watching her try to keep her anger in check during the ticketing process.

Jules had a yearly pass for the railroad allowing him to board with no hassle. Wes and Hillary had no such luck. So they stood in line, filled out paper work, showed proof of residence on the East End, proof of a place to stay in New York. And two thousand bucks a piece for a round-trip ticket.

Hillary was clearly annoyed that she couldn't just flash her badge to make it all go away. She was just some dude's girlfriend. And Wes made things worse.

In a fit of chivalry, he actually had his phone out of his pocket, credit code on screen, when he realized what he was about to do.

"Screw that," he said.

The ticket lady raised her eyebrows, whether at his statement or the fact she was going to have to process a payment with a phone rather than a chip, he wasn't sure.

Hillary grabbed him by the wrist and dragged him to a corner for a whisper fight.

"Why the hell should I pay?" she asked.

"Why the hell do you think?" he said. "This is your show. I don't want to be here. I don't want to go into the city and play narc for the weekend."

"You think I'm just made of money?"

"It's not like you're paying for it personally."

That brought her up short.

"Well," she said, casting about for an explanation. "It comes out of my account, then I have to file the paperwork and wait to be reimbursed. That's a lot of money."

"And that's not my problem."

They were glaring at each other when Jules walked over.

"Hey, lovebirds, train's a-coming. Get a move on."

"Sorry, Jules," Wes said. "My fault. Hillary was insisting that she pay for my ticket, too, and I got caught up in a moment of old-fashioned chauvinism." He knew how Jules would respond.

"That's not very gentlemanly of you, Wesley. Never second-guess a lady if she offers to pay."

The muscles in Hillary's jaw worked, the veins in her neck bulged as she faked a smile that succeeded only in giving her the appearance of a lunatic.

"I know, Jules," Wes said. "You're right. Sweetheart, you can pay for the tickets. But just this one time." He kissed Hillary on the cheek. "And I'll grab you a coffee. How about that? See you on the platform."

He walked off before she had a chance to take a swing at him.

"So what was that really all about?" Jules asked.

"Long story," Wes said.

"You two haven't been together long enough for long stories."

"On the contrary. We have at least a couple of novels' worth already."

Wes knew Jules wasn't necessarily concerned with their emotional well-being. There was probably some part of his predatory brain doing the calculations, checking to see if things were bad enough between Wes and Hillary that he could take a shot at her before the weekend was over—without jeopardizing his food source, of course. If Wes hadn't been his sole supplier, it wouldn't even be up for debate. Jules would do what Jules would do. But for the moment, he was likely only worried that he was going to be stuck with two miserable squabblers for a long weekend.

Wes tried to put him at ease. "Don't worry. She'll pass out on the train and wake up in a better mood. She's still not used to hangovers and heavy meals." He paused. "And no, you can't have her."

Jules put his hands up as if to say, "You got me."

"Can't blame a guy for considering his options," he said. "Good woman is hard to find. And she's dropping that kind of change on you? I hope you know how good you got it."

Wes laughed. "Oh, I know how good I got it. Trust me."

"Well, as good as you got it, you both have to go through security. See you on the train."

"What, you're better than security?" Wes asked.

"Like I said. Connections."

28

Excerpt from a letter to Wes Montgomery, signed, "Love, the Old Man" dated June 25, 2026.

Lord knows I shouldn't be the kind of parent who sets his kid on his mother, but I'm not going to lie. I will take some pleasure in doing this. Enclosed is a train-ticket voucher worth a thousand bucks. Should get you to Manhattan. She'll have to buy her own. She's likely to put up a hell of a fight. I don't think she's been anywhere near the city since you two split for Long Island when you were five.

You will have to fight with your mother. But that's part of growing up—standing your ground against your parents. Sure, I'm being a bit of a bastard for basically forcing her to spend two thousand of her own dollars to accompany you. But there are limits to my charity—and none, you see, to my baser urges for revenge. If she puts up too much of a fight, tell her you'll just go into the city alone and that I'll set you up with a hotel room. That'll shut her up.

Besides, I'm sure there's part of her that really wants to go, retrace her old steps, remember a time before the world fell apart. But be careful. She might get so nostalgic she'll want to go check out the old Brooklyn neighborhood. And her mushy-headed liberalism may even lead her to think that people are people, peace should be given a chance, and all sorts of other kumbaya bullshit. Whatever you do, don't let her hop a subway to Brooklyn. If she insists, let her go alone. Stay the hell out of Brooklyn. Trust me. Your old man knows what goes down in places like that.

By the way, you should also notice some credits appear on your phone in the next week or so—spending money for once you get to the city. But you don't need to tell your mom about that unless she asks. She'll probably get pissed all over again but, hey, it's less money out of her pocket. Maybe treat her to a nice dinner if there's still anything worth eating in the city—if you can get her to eat anything other than tofu and sprouts.

29

Wes tried to remember that first trip. His mother hadn't put up that much of a fight. "Your fucking father," she said, shaking her head. In fact, she'd seemed more than happy to go. "It'll do us good to get off the East End."

And when, on the train ride in, he asked her if all the other stuff in the old man's letter had been true—the bit about Manhattan being a walled community for the wealthy white, that Brooklyn and Queens had come under de facto Sharia law because King Mike opened the borders to Iranian refugees to spite the United States, that the $2,000 train tickets were there to keep the riff-raff off the East End—she didn't, as usual, offer a point-by-point evisceration of the old man's bullshit. "I guess he's got a point," was all she said.

The feeling of being overwhelmed was still clear as day. They'd taken the new Long Island Railroad spur into Grand Central. If he closed his eyes, he could still see the grand hall—the sunlight spilling in through those huge windows, the old spherical clock over the information booth, the tourists milling about looking at their watches and taking pictures, waiting for the rest of their parties to meet them. His mom had taken him to an alcove, stood him in one corner and gone to the other. She spoke into the wall, and her voice carried somehow through or over the marble, coming out clear as day next to his ear. Was that what the implants would be like? A disembodied voice landing somehow inside his head? He understood vaguely how communications technology worked—the data, the circuitry, the transmission. But how did a voice travel via marble and brick and land inside his head?

He remembered, too, the dark boarded up space just beyond that alcove—a haunted-looking place under an archway carved with the words "Oyster Bar."

"What was that?" he'd asked.

"Just an old restaurant that served dangerous food," she said. But even at 13, he noticed that she sighed when she said it.

They went out into the streets. It was a cool August day, sunlight blindingly bouncing off the glass and granite buildings. The buzz of people passing by. The wide open avenues with electric buses, cabs and police cars zipping silently along through fields of bike traffic. Every once in a while a gas-powered delivery truck—painted bright red and black, a warning that such things killed—trundled along, grumbling and growling down the street.

He remembered the swollen-headed Manhattanites, talking aloud to themselves, stopping short and slapping the sides of their heads. Lunatics they may have seemed, but they were the humpsters, they were the cool ones, the first to get chipsets implanted. The bulges on the right side of their heads were a badge of honor. External proof that they were something better than rich (though they were that as well): they were cutting edge.

She took him to the expansive pedestrian mall at Times Square, too. "We never would have been caught dead coming here when we lived in the City," she'd told him.

"Why? Was it dangerous?"

She laughed. "Oh, no. Probably the safest place in the world. It was crawling with tourists."

"Really?" He didn't see the attraction. Pretty much every building facing Times Square was covered in scaffolding as Iranian day laborers pulled down old signs signifying dead things called NBC, Reuters, Yahoo, or things that had left, such as Coca-Cola and Hershey. Another crew was lifting a Gawker sign into place, the monstrosity swinging from the end of a crane.

Still, there was always a tinge of electricity as he approached. It was even more powerful now because he'd be introducing it to Hillary.

He looked over at her, her face against the window, snoring. Thirty years old. A cop. Grew up on Long Island. And had never been to Manhattan.

"I don't know," she'd said, when it had come up back when he was under the impression that they were dating. "Dad couldn't afford it. My school never went. And I haven't had the time. Someday, I guess."

Someday had arrived and there she was, drooling herself through Queens.

A loud metallic clunk rang out on top of the train. Then another. Hillary's eyes opened and, as she was struggling to place herself, a large brick hit the window, bouncing off the plexiglass.

"What was that?" she said, jumping back, practically into Wes' lap, before remembering that she was pissed at him. She pulled away, sat up straight.

Jules, sitting in the seat in front of them, lifted his bulk on his knees and poked his head over the seat back. "Hey there, sleepy head. Welcome to beautiful Queens."

The thunks grew more frequent now, a veritable shower of bricks.

"The natives are restless," Jules said.

"What is it?" she asked again.

"The locals are making their displeasure with the system known," Wes said.

"Sharia savages," Jules said.

"Jules," Wes said.

Hillary looked out into the falling snow.

"It's nothing to worry about," Jules said. "The train's protected, and it doesn't even stop in Queens anymore. Zoom. Straight through. We'll be underground soon enough."

He turned around and sat back down.

Another brick hit the window. Hillary flinched.

Wes reached for her hand, but she snatched it back, shot him a look, then shook her head.

"Fine," he said.

They rode through the old platform in Jamaica, fenced in now with barbed wire, armed guards standing sentry. No Tasers for these. Old-fashioned semi-automatic weapons that pumped old-fashioned lead into a suspect's soon-to-be-dead carcass.

The snow grew steadily stronger.

"Looks like a blizzard," Wes said.

Jules stood up and marched off to the bathroom.

"You could at least try," Wes said.

"Try what?"

"We're supposed to be a couple, remember?"

"Real couples fight."

"Your first trip into the city and you're gonna be in a shit mood?"

"What? Like this is some kind of vacation for me? Some pleasure trip?"

Almost simultaneously, they both crossed their arms, sulking until Jules stepped out of the bathroom and made his way back to his seat.

"Fine," Wes said. "Like I want to be here anyway. It's a job, right? Then do your damn job. Shut up, quit being a bitch, smile and act like we like each other before Jules gets sick of us and sends us packing."

Jules was upon them. "What are you two lovebirds talking about?" He had a look in his eyes that suggested they'd better not be fighting again because he'd had just about enough.

Wes patted Hillary on the knee and smiled. "Oh, just talking about how much fun we're going to have in the city."

Hillary grabbed Wes' hand and squeezed it. Hard. Too hard. "Yeah. I can't wait! It's my first time, you know?"

"A virgin?" Jules said. "You didn't tell me that last night."

"Yup. A virgin." She turned on her flirtiest voice. "I hope I'm putting myself in the right hands, Jules."

Bitch.

Jules winked at her. "Trust me, honey. There aren't any better."

When he sat back down, Hillary turned to Wes, smiled, and stuck her tongue out at him. Then she let go of his hand.

30

Stepping off the train at Grand Central, Wes took her hand back. She tried to yank it away, but he held firm.

"Pretend," he hissed.

"Fine," she hissed back. "You want pretend?"

She took off at a jog, dragging him into the main hall.

"Wow!" she said, spinning around. "It's so beautiful." She oohed and ahhed, clasped her hands together. Wes hoped it was enough to fool Jules.

"Country come to town," was all he said.

She skipped over to him and playfully smacked him on the shoulder. "Oh, you stop," she said, looking directly at Wes as she did so.

Wes gasped as lines raced around the building, data started streaming before his eyes and blue targeting boxes sought places to land. One locked onto the clock in the center of the hall and the voice of a Gawkerpedia bot spoke softly into his ear.

"The main concourse clock of Grand Central is a perennial meeting place and is perhaps the most recognizable icon of the Terminal. Each of its faces is made from opal. Inside the information booth is a secret door that conceals a spiral staircase leading to the lower level information booth."

"Christ," he muttered.

"You okay?" Jules asked. "Looks like you've seen a ghost."

Wes felt more seasick than scared. He closed his eyes. "No. Stupid AR kicked in. Guess I'm not used to it."

"Turn that shit off," Jules said. "It's wrong half the time anyway. Garbage in, garbage out."

But Hillary, who hadn't activated this particular aspect of their chips back on Long Island and who was now seemed purposely trying to disorient Wes, didn't turn it off. Instead, she rushed outside. He followed. The sight of Lexington Avenue stopped her cold. The snow came down in blankets now. The streets were covered with fresh powder, the gutters piled high with five-foot drifts that the city had yet to clear. Across the street, the Chrysler Building rose, its top mostly lost in the snow and clouds, a bright white light hovering somewhere in the blizzard. The program superimposed an image of the building over or into or around the clouds and snow—it flickered like a ghost.

Smartly dressed people in long coats and hats hurried by, their collars turned up against the cold. Manhattan was in the midst of a 1950s fashion craze—not that the really rich had ever strayed very far in their choice of wardrobe. Fedoras. Mufflers. Vintage fur for the women. Extremely expensive and quite possibly illegal vintage fur. But with money, of course, came privileges.

An electric bus shooshed to a stop in front of them and disgorged about 100 hundred Persians—men first, women wearing head scarves second. They marched into a subway entrance for the Four Train.

"Getting back to Brooklyn in time for Friday evening prayers," Jules explained.

On either side of Lexington were clothing outlets offering hemp and linen, jewelry boutiques promising all-natural, Canadian-mined diamonds. The AR was rattling through the names and services offered. There were vegetarian burger shops, wheat-grass cafes, oxygen bars and two Starbucks. Signs in the latter two declared: "We have coffee any way you want it. As long as its black!" There was a massive indoor farmer's market, its stock of winter root vegetables supplemented with a full array of brightly colored fruit flown in from South America— with placards proclaiming that it was all on the up and up. No carbon dioxide produced. No rain forests cut down. No workers exploited. All bullshit, to be sure. But it allowed Manhattanites the food they so justly deserved without the guilt. And, too, it gave those of a contrarian, protesting mindset something to bitch about.

Hillary stood, mouth slightly agape, taking it all in. The streets may have been quiet, but the visual field generated by the chip and the accompanying voices were like rush hour in his head. Wes walked up next to her and took her hand. She didn't pull it away, didn't shoot him a look. He squeezed her hand.

"Can you please turn the AR off?"

Without answering, she acquiesced.

Jules hailed a cab and directed the driver to go through Times Square. Like a child, Hillary stared out the window. A massive Gawker video screen sat atop the north end. It cycled through news footage of the nuked-out remains of Pakistan, while comments from the Gawker staff and select readers scrolled along the bottom of the screen. "OMG. Disco inferno," read one. "Won't someone please think of the sad little goats," read another. "Note to self: Don't fuck with India."

Just to the left of the Gawker screen was a giant steaming Starbucks cup, the mermaid's nipples staring out like eyes at the Tonya's Tofu pyramid that dominated the southern end of the Times Square. Holographic images of Federation Airlines planes buzzed through the air advertising flights to Europe and San Francisco as snow passed through their fuselages. The massive Orgasmic Organics ad cycled through various faces of men and women who'd sent in photos of themselves in the height of passion. A giant ticker carried text messages from those milling about in Times Square, mostly teens inviting one another to "Fuck off" and to "Eat my hairy ass," the latter being the catch-phrase of the season so far.

"All that electricity," Hillary said.

"You got that right," Jules said. "They get special dispensation because it's a historical landmark. Then again, everything in Manhattan is. Conveniently enough."

They turned south, toward Jules' apartment in the West Village, a massive two-bedroom off Abingdon Square, where Bleecker ran into Hudson. He'd purchased two one-bedroom units on the top floor, knocked down the wall and consolidated the kitchen, living and dining areas into one massive space. If there were any doubt that the connections he always claimed to have were real, he'd put those aside as he broke all the zoning codes, building-department regulations and landmark provisions to blow out the exterior brick and replace it with sliding glass doors that led to a balcony. The neighbors had howled. They leaked gossip to the blogs about abusive work conditions and shoddy construction. But they never took Jules to court. Rich as they were, they knew that he must have friends in high places if he were doing something so ballsy in the first place. Wes had pressed him repeatedly on just what kind of connections he had, but all Jules ever said was "No comment."

Besides, the neighbors liked the drama, liked that they had a brash, womanizing artist in their building. Celebrities were a dime a dozen in Manhattan, but Alpha Male celebrities were a rare breed. And all that attention in the media—Gawker in particular—made their lives seem, if not worth living, then at least real.

In fact, the ones who leaked the gossip had been the first through the door at Jules' house-warming party. He held no grudges. He knew how the game was played. The only exception had been a couple of geriatric holdouts on the first floor, the sort who'd been in the building since "back in the day," before society went to hell, the kind of people who posted 1,000-word pen-on-paper notes in the hallway, notes accusing others of stealing their trash cans or taking socks out of the laundry or letting hookers into the building.

Just such a note, tacked to the bulletin board next to the elevator, was waiting for them when they arrived. It was written in bright green marker on orange paper, varying sizes of upper-case ranting interspersed with exclamation points and quotation marks.

"MICE!!!" it proclaimed in a headline.

We have found, on repeated and numerous occasions, mice in our apartment (1C)! It should be noted that we keep an extremely— EXTREMELY!!!—clean house. Any of you are welcome to come in and 'inspect' it for yourselves if you don't believe us. Yet we still have mice. Last week, we caught two mice—in a 'humane' trap, of course— and released them in the park across the street. Yet today we found another two mice in our apartment.

This has got to stop. We can't help but think this 'infestation' is due to improper garbage disposal (including illegal food), wasteful practices, and, yes, certain people and their massive parties. (Parties, we must add, which are both rude and mean.)

If this infestation continues, we will be forced to take action.

Jules ripped the note off the wall, turned it over and fished a pen out of his pocket.

"Who the hell carries a pen?" Hillary asked.

Jules didn't answer. Instead, he wrote:

Agnes, you crazy old bitch. Try killing the mice instead of letting them go. And maybe quit composting inside your damn apartment. It smells like shit in the lobby thanks to you.

As always, eat my hairy ass,

Jules.

He slid the note under the door of 1C.

"You did not," Hillary said.

"The fuck I didn't," Jules said. "Twenty million for this place. I don't have to put up with her shit. Besides," he added with a smile, "I think she really likes the attention."

They took the elevator up to Jules' apartment to find the twenty-million-dollar view obscured by snow. As they deposited bags and got situated, Jules began the disjointed speaking into the air that indicated he was fielding calls on his chip. While he dealt with his calls, he stood in front of the wall monitor tapping in texts.

"Okay, kids," he said, finally turning attention back to them. "Shower up, take a piss and let's get going."

31

Half an hour after walking two and a half blocks and climbing up the ratty stairs to a fourth-floor flat, Hillary found herself backed into a corner, a multiple-pierced meathead yakking on about the inferior sound quality of music played over implants.

"Really? Like, seriously, my cousin is a sound engineer and, like he says, you know, give me an MP3 file and a pair of ear buds. That's the way music is supposed to be heard. That's what most of those guys had in mind when they wrote it. You ever listen to music that way?"

"My God, no, I haven't," she said, offering a toothy smile. She'd already figured he wasn't going to be of much use leading them to the New York supplier. It took her all of thirty seconds to read that writing on the wall. But she'd let the conversation go on, knowing Wes would notice. She couldn't remember what happened the previous night—nothing after dinner. But she had a vague impression she'd humiliated herself somehow. She didn't know. She'd spent the waking moments on the train ride trying to remember, but she may as well have been chasing a mirage. Her head hurt all day, her stomach had been disagreeable. But it was the inability to shake the sense of shame that had fouled her mood. Even if it was cheap, fleeting and immature, revenge was the only thing providing relief.

"You've totally got to check it out. You hear things you didn't even know would be in the music. Boner. Really boner. Actually, I've got an old four-gig third-gen iPod Nano."

"Really? Wow," she said, glancing around the small room, spotting Jules—towering above a fawning audience, loudly talking about blowjobs—before finding Wes, who cut his eyes away from her at the last minute. He was sulking in a corner. She supposed if he were going to be of any use on this case, if she wanted to escape this particular hell in which she'd involved them both, she'd have to curb her baser urges for payback. Hell, if she were really honest with herself, it wasn't like she really was in a position to seek revenge.

"Yeah, back at my place," iPod man was saying, "you know, if you want to come over and check it out. You know, like after the party."

"Is that right?" she said, putting a hand on his chest.

"Totes," he said, offering that half smirk of victory that twitched up a guy's face when he thought he'd conquered a woman.

"So you have this pocket-sized player that you think the entire world should listen to, but you keep it back in your apartment?"

"Well. You know. It's a collector's item. I mean, I wouldn't want to just walk around with it."

"I bet," she said, pushing him away gently. "Look, I was supposed to be getting my boyfriend a drink."

She moved past him, inching her way through the crowd. Some party, she thought. This is what she'd imagined a rush-hour subway ride to be like. Shoulder to shoulder, bumps bordering on groping—with the bonus of spilled drinks. An old music system with external speakers—the sort that must have given iPod man a total boner or a total complex—brayed at full volume, forcing people to shout to be heard over Justin Bieber's Greatest Hits Volume Ten. It was an implant-off party, all the rage in the city apparently, the cool set trying to recapture a grittier time, an era when the city was "real"—whatever that meant—and a person talked, out loud, to the person in front of her.

She was enjoying that aspect of it—if only because it gave her a break from Blunt's increasingly unhinged rants. Still, the conversations bubbling up around her had all the appeal and weight of escaping steam. Implants, media, economy, the election. Jules was drawing a crowd because he was the only one talking about something that mattered, something any of them had any realistic chance of controlling. And she couldn't quite figure out if the millionaire hostess of the party was holding it in a 500-square-foot apartment to stay on theme or because real estate was that out of control in the city. Maybe it was a mix of both. At first glance, the apartment seemed as run down as it was small, but upon further investigation, Hillary noticed it was a studied sort of shabbiness, the wood rubbed down just so, curtain rods bent in the exact same place, the old three-pronged electrical outlets all in working order, no years of paint covering the screw heads or partially blocking the openings. The appliances, though, were the true give-away. Gleaming white enamel stove and refrigerator with oversized knobs. Hillary had the misfortune of renting an older home from one of the cheapest landlords on Long Island and she knew that a true period home would be furnished with finger-print smudged-stainless steel appliances, rather than this faux-mid-20th century setup.

And you didn't need to be a detective to see that the hostess, whoever she was, had hired a bar tender—a handle-bar mustachioed fellow in white shirt and suspenders shaking up classic cocktails like the Screaming Orgasm and Sex on the Beach.

"I mean, if you can't afford to hire a bartender, you shouldn't even be having a party," she overheard one of the guests saying.

Hillary grabbed two Flaming Balzacs from the bar and in the five minutes it took her to cross the room to Wes she managed to spill over half of both drinks.

She thrust one at him. "Is this how you report your stories?" she said.

"What?"

"I'm no reporter. And I know you didn't go to the Academy, but standing in the corner glaring at me doesn't seem like the best way to gather information, make connections."

"You seem to be doing a good enough job working the room for both of us," he said.

"Jesus."

"Sorry," he added hastily.

She waited. Would he have another outburst, get angry at himself for apologizing to her?

Instead, he offered a smile and a shrug. "Isn't this what I usually do at parties?"

She thought back to the first times she'd seen him, standing there apart from the party, somehow above the fray. Not having an implant had something to do with it, but there was a certain sense he didn't need anyone in the room. Much like her, he was content to observe.

"That's true, Wes, but people here don't know who you are. You have to get out there, snoop around, chat some people up. We might only have the weekend."

He banged the back of his head against the wall and blew a puff of air up through his hair. "Shit."

"Why don't we take turns," she offered. "I just got nowhere with one insufferable jerk. Now it's your turn. Make a round of the room. See what you can do."

"Okay," he sighed.

A sudden urge to reach up and kiss him gripped her, but she resisted. Instead, she smacked him on the butt. "Go get 'em, tiger."

It was enough to bring the hint of a smile to his lips, and he shouldered his way into the crowd.

The smile didn't last long.

He may have been aloof at parties out on the Island, but that aloofness came from a position of power. He was the dealer. Even in his professional life, he was spoiled by being a reporter. People knew him, came to him, working their angles.

Here, he was no one. Here, he was the one working an angle, working it poorly.

They'd been separated from Jules the second they'd walked through the door, so no one had made that connection. And he'd been seen in the corner with her, so he'd likely been written off by ninety percent of the room, single straight women and the gay men that could tell within a tenth of a second of looking at him that Wes was about as hetero as they came.

If he had any sense he'd make a beeline toward Jules, ride on his coattails. But no, she could see that he was going to try things on his own—a mistake with this crowd.

The coolest party in the coolest city in all the land was, in essence, a nerd herd. Not necessarily nerd as in smart and at somehow useful to society, but nerd as in picked on in high school, shut out from the cool cliques. Like their generations before them, they'd migrated to the big city and were delighted to find others of their tribe, to discover strength in numbers, to mine the possibilities of creating their own exclusive club with its own rules and language. And, of course, to get back at everyone else. They struck Hillary as a nasty lot, sneers on their faces, unable to ever completely let go of what had been done to them in high school, heaping scorn on what they held to be the power structure all the while unable to quite realize they were as much the power structure as anyone else, if not more. In reality, they sneered at those who did the maintenance for the power structure, low-level politicians, middle managers, cops.

But lowest of the low, in their eyes, were the non-nerds who tried to gain access to their club. Which is exactly what Wes was doing.

She could tell that part of him wanted in, that this may even have been his strata of society had his mother's death not called him back to Long Island, had he not become a dealer. From where she was standing, falling into a life of crime had made him a better person.

Comparing these people to the men she worked with put her in mind of cats and dogs. Dogs went about their business in generally well-meaning simple-minded way. Dogs were easy to negotiate. Feed them, pet them, talk to them and, from smallest dog to biggest, you'd be rewarded for your efforts. Sure, there were bad dogs—and when they were big and bad, things could get really out of control. But cats? Big or small, they were pointy at most ends. And a lifetime of nurturing, feeding and loving on your part was no guarantee that you'd be acknowledged with anything more than a scratch on your hand.

Perhaps she was being unfair to cats, but she didn't think so.

Whatever the case, Wes looked exactly like a dog sniffing around a cat and getting his nose swatted repeatedly. And unable to find a way in, he was getting more and more frustrated.

He'd hover at the edge of a conversation, hoping for an entry. One of two things happened. Someone, usually a man, gave Wes a once over, saw something about him—his clothes, his demeanor, his teeth—and drew the circle tighter, shutting him out. Or someone, usually a woman, smiled, said hi and thirty seconds after Wes started talking, cut him off in mid conversation and drew the circle tighter, shutting him out.

She was just about to wedge her way back into the crowd on a rescue mission when Jules sidled up to her.

"How we doing, hot stuff?"

"Having a blast," she said.

"With these miserable bastards? You didn't strike me as the type."

"Oh really? What type did I strike you as, Jules?"

"Still trying to figure that one out. How long you two been dating?"

"A few months more or less."

He did a bit of mental calculation. "Makes sense," he said. "That's about the time he dropped off the radar. Every thing going okay with you two?"

She didn't know where he was going with this line of questioning, but she was pretty sure nothing good would come of it.

"No complaints."

"Looked like a lot of complaining going on today. And here you are all alone and he's—well, it looks like he's making an ass of himself, mostly."

"It's a relationship, Jules. There are ups and downs."

"I wouldn't know," he said, smiling at her.

"That doesn't surprise me," she said.

"Well, now that's mean, Hillary. Hurtful almost."

"Nothing you haven't said yourself," she countered.

"You've got a point there." He paused. "I don't know what's going on between you two, but if there's a falling out, well, my door is open."

She took a step away from him. Everyone had an angle, but what was his? What was he? A customer only? A really bad friend? Something else? There had to be something else, she was sure of it.

"Lot of people would jump at the chance," he said.

"I'm not a lot of people," she said.

He looked into her eyes, like a cop searching for answers, trying to ferret out a truth. She knew the look well. "I'm glad to hear that," he said.

Now she searched his eyes. Was he being a smart-ass? Sincerity seemed so out of place in this room, like a naked man at a funeral. That more than Jules' come-on made her uncomfortable.

Before she could say anything else, Wes was on them.

"What's going on?" he said. There was an edge in his voice. He was pissed about being shut out of the party.

"Jules was just telling me what a good friend you were," she said. Wes considered both of them. "Yeah, okay," he said.

Jules put an arm around Wes's shoulder and said, louder than was necessary, "This guy? This guy's like the brother I never had. Love this guy." He looked out at the crowd, who'd turned to see who Jules was talking to or about. "Hell, I'd take one of him over the whole lot of these sick-o-phants and re-pro-bates."

Laughter rippled around the room, accompanied with confusion as it dawned on those who'd been shutting Wes out for the past half hour that they'd perhaps made a mistake in their social ranking algorithms.

Now, Hillary thought, maybe they'd be able to get some work done in this room.

But that wasn't meant to be. "It's getting late," Wes said. "I kinda want to blow out of here."

Jules considered him, then looked at Hillary. "Night's still young, Wesley."

"I know. But I'm exhausted, just not up for this."

"You sure, Wes?" she asked. He'd been through plenty—and being snubbed by the entire room likely didn't help. But he was squandering a perfect opportunity. "It is kind of early."

"Sorry," he said.

"Hillary, you're more than welcome to stay," Jules said.

Both men turned to her, as if the universe depended on the answer to this question. Left alone, she probably could work the room to her heart's content—and without wounding Wes with every smile and blush she offered to interested men. At the same time, he'd be up worrying all night. And she didn't know what to make of Jules. There'd been something hollow about his advance, but at this stage she'd rather play it safe.

"I think I'll head back with Wes," she said.

The tension went out of Wes' face and Jules' smile became a little less reptilian. "I like that. Stand by your man." He reached into his pocket and fished for a key card. "Here you go. You two don't get lost in the blizzard on the way home."

After a brief and silent walk through the snow, they were back in the apartment alone together.

"Want something to eat?" he asked.

"Yeah," she said, throwing herself onto the couch and staring out the window. "But no garbage. Not tonight."

He ordered soup and salad, which they ate in uncomfortable silence, both of them stewing. To an outsider, they looked for all the world like a typical couple caught in some sort of mid-life crisis, each sealed off in his or her own head, overcome by fear—fear of bad decisions, of being trapped, of futility and mortality.

After they were done eating, they flopped onto the couch, where Wes flipped through the channels. He settled on "So You Think You Can Hook," a show sponsored by the Sixth Wave Feminist Coalition and which involved young women using their sexuality to support themselves and advance in life by offering blowjobs to men in exchange for money or employment. Hillary couldn't quite keep up with the twisted logic, but neither she nor Wes were exactly watching for the philosophy of it all. They mostly ignored the screen, watching instead the snow pile up outside on the balcony, listening to the flakes flicking against the window panes.

"I'm going to bed," she finally said.

"That's fine," he said, his gaze fixed on the snow.

32

Wes felt a presence hovering over him and so woke. It was a slow ascent. He hadn't realized how exhausted the last few days had made him. When he'd called it a night and climbed into bed, Hillary turned her back to him and inched to the opposite edge. He could feel her body, her warmth still there beside him. He had no idea what time it was and hadn't figured out exactly where he was when his eyes fully opened and registered the silhouette standing in front of him, backlit by the blue glow of a snowy dawn.

"Extra, extra," said the figure, holding out a printed sheet of paper. "Read all about it. Stop the presses."

"Jules," Wes whispered, rubbing his eyes, still trying to get his bearings.

Hillary covered her head and mumbled for the two of them to shut up.

Jules rattled the paper again and swayed. He reeked of chemical stew—booze and lord knew what sort of designer drugs. There was another smell, one that Wes recognized but couldn't quite immediately place. As Wes' vision adjusted, he saw that Jules had a grin plastered to his face but that his eyes were having trouble focusing. Sweat sheeted off his forehead and dark splotches ran out from under the arms of his shirt and across his chest. His hair hung down in wet ropes.

"Christ, Jules. You okay?"

"Oh, I'm fine, buddy boy. Just fine." He burped. "You, on the other hand, are not. Not fine."

He stuck the paper at Wes again. Wes took it. It was a print-at-home version of the Suffolk News & Review.

"Massive Bacon & Egg Stash Found in Montauk," read the banner head over a photo of the snow-covered bunker. An inset photo showed the gleaming refrigerators, doors wide open. The Coke machine sat in the background.

The subhead line read: "Local Reporter Is Leading Suspect."

Wes' photo was halfway down the page.

"Crap in a bucket," Wes whispered. It was sweet of Lou to refer to him as a reporter rather than a journalist or blogger. And at least Lou got to the stash before Blunt changed his own mind and went after it. Wes knew it was coming, but hadn't mentally prepared himself for the fact of it.

"Crap in a bucket, indeed," Jules said.

"When did this come out?"

"It started coming over wireless about an hour ago. Guess your boss fed it immediately to the Manhattan bloggers."

That must have stuck in Lou's craw.

Jules swayed again, grabbed the edge of the bed and sat down heavily. He seemed to come in and out of lucidity, alternating between slow and stunned, and manic and racing.

"Whoo. Yeah. I was in the middle of a big ol' pile of pussy when it came over the wireless."

"What?"

"An orgy, man. A five-cooze pile-up." So that was the other smell. "You know. Tag-team oyster wrestling. Except I was the only guy."

Hillary's voice came out from under the blanket. "That's disgusting. And would you two shut the fuck up already? Christ."

Jules shook his head. "Well, looks like sunshine's going to grace us with another of her fabulous moods today."

Wes pulled the cover off her head. "Wake up. You need to see this." He stuck the paper in her face.

It took her all of thirty seconds to gather its meaning.

"Oh shit!" she groaned. "No! No! No!"

Jules jumped out of the bed and backed away.

"Blunt is going to go ballistic," she said. "This fucks up everything. Shit, shit, shit. Wes, now what are we supposed to do?"

Under the blankets, Wes grabbed a hunk of her thigh and pinched hard.

"Oww! Why did you do that?" she screamed.

"Who's Blunt?" Jules asked. "What's she mean, 'What are we supposed to do?' Holy shit, Wes. You didn't take her off some pimp, did you?"

It took every ounce of self-control not to say, "Something like that."

"Nothing," Wes said. "Nothing. She's just worried about me. Now calm down, honey. Please. And Jules, let me try to focus here. You said this broke about an hour ago?"

"Let's see. I'd already cum three times, so I had two of the girls just going to town, slurping away. Wait, no. I was doing this one girl in the ass, while another was fingering mine and another was licking—"

"Jules!" Wes screamed.

Jules shook his head, trying to clear it. "Yeah, an hour ago, I guess."

"Anything new since then?"

"Nah. Everyone's just repeating what's in the rag. So far."

Wes skimmed the story again. Lou had run it without contacting the police, it seemed. Most of the city was still asleep this early on Saturday morning. Hillary likely hadn't heard from Blunt yet, because Blunt likely hadn't heard about it.

"Why?" Hillary asked. "I don't get it. Why did Lou sell you out?"

"I asked him to."

"You did what?" Frustrated, unable to do anything, she threw the covers off and starting hunting for her clothes, stomping around the bedroom in her bra and panties.

Both men stared. Jules absentmindedly started rubbing himself.

"Would you cut that out?" Wes said to him.

"What?"

"That," he said, motioning with his head.

"Oh. Sorry. Didn't even notice."

"Christ. What are you on?"

"Don't know what it's called. Friend of mine invented it, so I'm giving it a test run."

"Jesus."

"Hey, you two. Frick and Frack," said Hillary. "Can we focus? Wes, think you can explain to me what the hell you were thinking?"

No, he couldn't. It was going to be hard enough to convince her he knew what he was doing. Now he had to come up with an explanation that was going to make sense to Jules as well.

"I gave Lou the location and told him to out me."

Jules swam into focus. "But why would you?" He started to sway again. "Hold on," he said, fumbling in his pocket and producing a white topical patch. He reached behind his head and pulled a purple patch off the back of his neck, putting the white one in its place. Closing his eyes, he held a hand up, motioning for them to wait. He opened his eyes finally. He took a deep breath and, as he did so, the bulge in his pants subsided.

"Better?" Hillary asked.

"Much. But I probably have about fifteen minutes before I pass the fuck out. So, Wes, spced up this tale of insanity."

"The cops were on to me," he said.

Hillary froze.

"So?" Jules said. "Not like it was your sixth offense or anything."

"Yeah, but you know the size of my stash. They bust me once— even if they don't find it. Then what? It fucks up my entire retirement plan. It spins out of my control. I started getting paranoid. Couldn't sleep. Always freaking out. Too scared to even go with my original escape plan. Just felt like they were watching me, would pinch me if I made a sudden move in that direction."

He had no idea if that sounded anything like believable. The look in Jules' eyes indicated that the story sounded like a heaping mound of Grade A compost. Wes was suddenly certain Jules was going to challenge him, demand a better explanation or, worse, the truth.

"So what's the new plan, Einstein?" Jules asked.

"Yeah, Wes," Hillary said. "What's your plan? I'm dying to hear it."

That was the easy part. It was really no different from the vague idiocy he and Hillary were already pursuing.

"I was hoping this would bring me to the attention of the city supplier. If I can get to him somehow, he can extract me. Sneak me out."

Jules looked confused, shook his head. "All of that, just to meet this guy?"

"Yeah," Wes said.

Jules laughed, mostly to himself. "You could have just asked." He was getting wobbly again, and shuffled slowly toward the bed. "Know people," he says. "Look. You stay out of sight for the rest of the day, your old pal Jules is going to make it happen."

Jules sat down on the edge of the bed, started taking off his shoes.

"How?" Wes asked, moving over to the side vacated by Hillary.

"We're going to party with the dude's number one customer tonight."

Like a cat, Jules stretched out onto the bed and closed his eyes.

"Who's that?" Wes asked.

Jules yawned. Hillary walked over to the bed, grabbed him by the collar and lifted him up. "Jules," she shouted into his face, shaking him. "Who are we partying with tonight? Jules?"

He cracked his eyes open, opened his mouth once, closed it, opened it again. "The Gawker," he whispered, his head lolling back on his neck. He found strength enough to swivel it back around one more time. "The. Gawker."

33

"Jesus fucking Christ," she said, before stomping out of the room.

Wes followed her out to the living room. "What?"

"What?" she said back.

"This couldn't have worked out any better," he said, realizing he might be right.

"You're just fucking lucky. That's all. Lucky. And I'm going to have to spend the entire day on the line with Blunt."

"I don't get it. You two come to me with almost no plan. None." If anything, she should be on her knees thanking him. He walked over to her, grabbed her arm and held tight as she struggled to pull away. "Every step forward so far has been thanks to me. My contacts. My sources. My plan."

She quit struggling. "Some plan," she pouted.

But a pout was less than fury. Maybe she was coming around.

"Look," he said, "I'll be the first to admit I'm getting lucky, flying by the seat of my pants. But we're one step closer. I got you one step closer. Not the force. Not Blunt. Me. And it's my name and face plastered everywhere now. My ass on the line. And don't think for a second I'm doing it for anyone other than you."

Oh, that was good. He hadn't intended that to come out, but there it was. For a moment, she searched his eyes. For what he couldn't tell. Then she blinked and it was gone.

"Fuck," she said, angry again. She shook free of his grasp.

"Now what?"

"Incoming from Blunt."

She walked off into Jules' bedroom and for the next hour alternated between soothing tones—"Yes. It's okay. I understand. It's under control"—to frustrated screaming—"Calm down. Why are you getting so worked up about this? I didn't hear any better ideas from your end!"

Meanwhile, Wes pulled up one of Jules' wall monitors and typed up a message. "To friends of the preservation fund: I have decided to retire. Your patronage and support over the years has been appreciated. It turns out our bookkeeper kept no books and the few records we had were lost in the recent fire. We apologize for this. Best of luck."

He then routed it through three anonymizers and hit send. That done, he expanded the wall monitor to full size, splitting it into multiple screens. On the three large panels, he put on Federated News, Gawker and, after figuring out Jules' system, Fox News from the South. Around those, he randomly selected video and blog channels. With the exception of Fox, the video on all the sites was the same—a shared feed from one dedicated video company that charged exorbitant rates to all the outlets. Sure, they all showed the same videos—but it was cheaper than hiring a full-time staff of videographers. Besides, it was how you packaged the video that mattered—the talking heads, anchors, analysts, bloggers, legal experts, psychiatrists, dieticians who clamored to tell you what it all meant.

To Federated News, which was for all intents and purposes a branch of the government, this was a tragedy averted, a public-health threat stopped in its tracks. They'd already tried him and found him guilty of murder. Of course, they conveniently ignored the fact that the government hadn't been the one to bust him. Also unmentioned was that heart disease and cancer had not sky-rocketed on the East End of Long Island due to his presence—and that he'd been operating for 15 years. And apparently it wasn't newsworthy that Wes supplied two of their anchors when they summered in the Hamptons. In fact, he figured one of the reasons Ernie Ignacio was so red-faced and worked up over this was that he was overcompensating—and pissed off that he'd have to find a new sausage supplier for his summer barbecues.

The most surreal moment was when Ernie looked down at his handheld and a look of relief came over him.

"This just in," he said, "from a source who wishes to remain anonymous. The suspect, who is on the run, seems to have notified his clients that all files and evidence that may have traced back to them have been destroyed." Then he looked straight into the camera and said, "They may rest easy now, but they'll have to do so with a guilty conscience, knowing that in escaping justice, they may have put others at risk."

Like most of Ernie's pronouncements, it made no sense, but also managed to sound important, the final word on the matter.

Fox, meanwhile, was delirious with glee over a story that made the Federation look bad. To them, Wes wasn't just a two-bit dealer with a big stash, looking to eat well, enjoy life and make a lot of money doing so. No, according to Fox News, he was a "latter-day revolutionary, a brave hero striking out against an oppressive nanny state." Their experts were worked into such a lather that they described the incident as a sure sign that the Federation was "teetering on the brink." They breathlessly reported rumors—or made them up themselves—that the Montauk base not only had a massive underground submarine dock, but aircraft hangers and a series of tunnels running the length of the island, that last bit a "fact" Wes immediately recognized as being lifted from "The Montauk Project" conspiracy theories.

Gawker was mocking both Fox and Federated, but focusing most of its attention on the News & Review. What was this print paper? Who was this reporter? What a strange ink-stained wretch—and a dealer to boot. They were in the process of turning Wes into a celebrity. That was what Gawker did best, that was why it was the highest rated news network in the Federation.

Wes had been dubbed "The Bacon & Egg Man." Bumper graphics, a theme song, decals and t-shirts had already been designed and put on sale by Gawker's sales side.

They tried to do the same with Lou. After all, he'd broken the story. He'd employed the dealer. He was an archetype, their Neanderthal man, a missing link still wandering the earth, smoking cigarettes and setting news stories into ink on paper. And he's fed the story to them even as his own press cranked out the first extra edition of a print newspaper since who knew when.

But the poor bastard they'd sent to stalk Lou was called a low-rent cocksucker and punched out cold before Lou holed himself up in his office. Still, Gawker had it on video, a running loop of Lou's fist making contact with the blogger's face, then the jerky fall as the blogger fell to the pavement, Lou's faux leather loafers storming off into his office. A still frame—showing a little of Lou's face and a lot of his oncoming fist—had been put onto shirts and posters above the words: "Lou in '62!"

Gawker was also conducting a classic debate: Was Wes "hot" or was he merely "journalist hot"? Would the average person find him attractive if she came across him in a club? Or did he seem attractive partly because of his new-found celebrity and partly because most journalists were unattractive?

"What do you think?" he asked as Hillary walked back into the living room and joined him on the couch, keeping her distance.

"I think this is full-on fucking retarded," she said.

34

Hours later, a bed-headed, red-eyed Jules shuffled out of the guest bedroom where they'd left him just in time to see that Gawker had dug up a photos of Wes and Hillary together, taken at one of the few East End parties they'd attended. The Gawker crowd, still debating the merits of Wes' appearance, declared Hillary objectively hot.

"There you go, hot stuff," Jules said, rubbing his belly and scratching his balls as he did a lap around the marble island separating the kitchen from the living room, looking like an old man who's forgotten what he's looking for. "Shower," he mumbled before heading toward the master bedroom.

Wes turned to Hillary. "Listen," he said, "I'm tired of fighting. I'm sorry for anything and everything. But can we reboot this job, try to finish it out with some civility?" He was hoping it resonated on some deeper level, but would be happy enough at this point with surface shine.

She looked down at her lap, seemingly sad herself. "Yeah. I guess you're right. I'll try."

He thought she might say more, but she stood up.

"I'm going to shower," she said, heading for the guest bathroom.

"Yeah?" he said, hopefully, a weak smile on his face.

"Wes." She didn't have to say no.

Jules walked out of his bedroom, towel around his waist. He poured himself a cup of coffee, washed down two pills and slapped another patch on the back of his neck. Two minutes later, he was bright-eyed, lucid and ready to operate heavy machinery.

"You two going to start getting ready?"

Wes had found spending an entire winter day glued to a couch watching video about himself exhausting. As was the idea of going out into a cold night, socializing with big-city strangers at a party. Never mind his emotional turmoil. There was also the inconvenient but real possibility that stepping out tonight could get him shot in the face.

"Yeah," Hillary said. "I was just heading for the shower."

"Good," Jules said. "And look, you wear something nice and elegant," he added.

"Elegant? Really?"

"You betcha. You think you can handle that?"

"What's that supposed to mean?"

"No offense, hon, but for someone so good-looking, you dress like a cop."

Wes knew that had to sting. "Okay," he said. "Let's not get carried away. Hillary dresses plenty fine. Judging by the ogling you've been doing all weekend, you don't seem to mind much what she wears."

Jules walked right up to her and, without a hint of irony or shame, looked her over from head to toe. "Yes. You're right. I'm just saying this party will be a big deal. Lots of celebrities. Lots of cameras. Lots of other women judging. I just wouldn't want you to feel out of place. Besides, there's no need to hide your lamp under a basket."

"My what? Under a what?" Hillary asked.

"Never mind," Jules said. "If you didn't bring anything, there's a closet full of designer shit in the guest room. Take anything you want. And call me if you need any help."

He winked.

"God," she said. Before she headed for the bathroom, she leaned over and kissed Wes on the cheek. Fake as it may have been, it was an unexpected peace offering that hit him with a little dart of sadness.

"And what about me?" he asked Jules.

"Just dress like you always do. You're tonight's celebrity guest, so you can do no wrong."

"Crap in a bucket," Wes said, his stomach turning, a wave of something resembling stage fright taking hold of him.

"Don't worry," Jules said. "Most of them will keep their distance, too cool to actually walk up and talk to you. Those who do so will kiss your ass. Your biggest problem will be the women. Half of them will just throw themselves at you. The real cool ones will mock you to your face, treat you like shit, tell you you're wrong about everything."

"Great."

"Then they'll corner you in the bathroom and beg you to fuck them right there."

They both laughed.

"I'm not joking," Jules said. "Mark my words. Either way, they'll all have knives out for Hillary."

"Great," Wes said.

"It's okay. She's a big girl. And we'll get you both loosened up before we get there."

Hillary was a long time in the guest room. But the reason became clear enough when she made her entrance. She wore a bright red dress that stopped just above her knees, a row of black buttons running its length. Her hair was piled on her head, loose tendrils hanging behind her ears. She'd gone light on the makeup except for a flash of bright red lipstick. She looked like she'd walked straight out of 1949.

"Holy fuck," Jules said. "Mommy, will you spank me?"

Wes couldn't think of much else to add. "Wow," he whispered.

"Too severe?" she asked, looking to Wes for guidance.

He could see she was a little insecure about the choice. It wasn't her usual style, and she likely felt like a girl playing dress-up. And whatever she said to the contrary, he knew she wanted to look good for the party.

"It's perfect," he said. "In fact, I'm afraid I might embarrass myself if I stand up at the moment."

Jules looked down at his crotch. "What he said," Jules said.

The truth was, just six months ago—when they'd met—the dress would have hung oddly on her, bunching up in places her body wouldn't have filled out. But now her boobs looked like two soldiers being held back from a fight. And her ass? What the dress did for her ass was a thing of beauty. Or the other way around.

Wes waited for the bulge in his pants to subside before making a break for the shower.

"Rub one out for me," Jules shouted after him.

"Only if you promise to keep your hands off of her," Wes shouted back.

35

There was only one reason Blunt hadn't stepped out of the car when he caught Wesley Montgomery at the end of Jules' driveway. With a clarity that at first made him think it was his AR acting up, he'd had a vision of raising his gun and emptying it into Wes. After a full night of being forced to listen to that reprobate artist flirt with Halstead, he was ready to pound his own head into the steering wheel until he blacked out. And then to have that little fuck try to sneak out—to sneak out with Hillary. It was too much. Too damn much. But he'd dug deep, found a reserve of self-control sufficient enough to stop himself from killing Wes.

And how had he been repaid for that small bit of mercy? What had he gotten for trying to keep this under the radar?

A full-scale media blast, humiliating both Blunt and the entire department.

If there was some small consolation to take away from this, it was that—to himself at least—he'd proven his purity of motive. Had he simply been some careerist cop angling for a promotion or publicity, he would have raided the bunker while Wes was in it. Underground lair, submarine dock, taking down the East End's biggest dealer. That was the sort of thing that launched political careers. But this was bigger than Blunt. Besides, he now had Wes in his grasp and the Montauk bunker was completely out of operation. Think of the lives that would save. And that was just a battle in the larger war. If this played out, he could knock out the other side's general, causing a ripple effect throughout the Federation. Victory once and for all. This wasn't cops and robbers. This was saving civilization.

After securing the site out at Montauk, he'd found that old fat-ass Lou and tried to get something out of him. He was a tough old bastard, though, and it was the sort of job that would take time or violence—neither of which Blunt had, especially once the Feds showed up and took control. So Blunt let Lou go back to his paper and handed the East End case over to the Feds without a peep of complaint. He was after bigger fish and didn't want to attract any more attention to himself than necessary.

Without a word to anyone in the department, he'd climbed into his car and headed west to Manhattan.

Halfway there, all of the alerts on his AR began flashing again and calls started coming in from his detectives. Cashing in on the years of loyalty he'd built up, he asked them to keep quiet until they couldn't any longer, to cover for him after that, to trust that he was working on something huge, something verging on personal with this Montgomery bastard. They all agreed. Most of them had their own grudge cases that haunted them. They knew how Blunt's old man had died, how it had scarred him. Some even had their own suspicions about his soft spot for Halstead. Blunt had been a tough mentor to all of them. If he didn't want internal affairs or the Feds hamstringing him on this case, they'd be happy—honored—to help.

The only one who didn't come through was Jimmy in tech. The AR was reasserting its authority, overriding the overrides. Jimmy managed to figure out a hack to get Blunt's data rerouted into a loop so that the alerts and warnings didn't show up on the wider Fed network—not for a couple of days, at any rate. Blunt had the weekend to wrap this up. It wasn't going to be tidy, but maybe it would be long enough.

But between the angry orange and red alerts cluttering up his field of vision and the occasional brick hitting the roof of his car despite doing 90 miles per hour through Queens, he was losing himself completely to rage with each passing mile. High-minded as his mission was, he knew that the next time he encountered Wes, he might not be able to restrain himself.

36

Jules led them on foot through the streets of the West Village, empty of all vehicular traffic save for the small fleet of extremely expensive cabs and, on the avenues, buses. Large swaths of the city were car-free zones on the weekends, and the snow kept the pedicabs off the streets. With the drifts now choking the sidewalks, the group walked in the middle of the street, going against traffic so they could see and avoid the silent electric cabs. The snow was just starting up again in small flurries; it looked like an old-fashioned Hollywood set.

The silence was broken at one point by the muffled shuffle of two-hundred feet. Wes and crew turned to see a battalion of clean-cut teens jogging their way—ten across, ten deep. They wore yellow sweat suits emblazoned with the logo of the Federated Youth Volunteer Corp. Wes, Hillary and Jules stepped aside, reliving their own memories of that year between high school and college when every Federation citizen was required to volunteer for a year of service.

Wes could practically see the rantings of his old man on this particular subject tracing themselves in all-caps across the snow. The references to Hitler Youth, Russian Reds and Cuba's Youth Pioneers.

It was that year that served as the final break between him and the old man. The old man had expected Wes, once he turned 18, to head South, go to college, and go to work for him—he was the plant manager at a Coca-Cola bottling plant in Birmingham. Wes had expected the same for himself. He'd promised his mom to keep his mind open about getting out of the Federation. But when the time came, he couldn't do it. Suddenly, the idea of working at a bottling plant had seemed crushingly depressing—a waste of his genius, whatever that turned out to be. And Birmingham? If he was going to live in a city—and that was a big if—he'd stick with New York. The heat, noise and confusion he'd seen of Birmingham on video made it look as alien as Bangkok, which it had practically become. After Thailand's new king—in an effort to cement his very tenuous grip on power, started purging the educated classes and picked a war with Burma (Cambodia refusing to take the bait once again), waves of refugees headed to the U.S. Along with them came a few invasive species that took root in northern Alabama and spread across the Southeast as the climate there inched away from subtropical to tropical. The kudzu never stood a chance.

Besides, everything Wes had known in life had been in the Northeast. He was a child of the Federation, a child of his mom. And while he didn't agree with a thing she believed in, there was no way he could bring himself to leave her all alone. Selfish, stupid teen he might have been, but even he knew she deserved more from him.

Wes' decision to stay prompted a flurry of letters from the old man, all of which alternated between pleading, heartbreak and fury—a man scorned, as it were. And finally there came a phone call very much like the letters except that it ended with the old man telling Wes, "You're fucking dead to me. You hear? Dead."

"What are you, the mafia?" Wes had snapped back, but the old man had already hung up.

Wes never heard from him again. He spent the next years furious. The bastard had never been there for him growing up, and now he was the indignant one? Fuck him. If Wes had to analyze it, the biggest reason he went into what passed for journalism was to get back at the old man. Oh yeah, that had showed him. Wes sometimes wondered what the old man would make of him now. Not this ridiculous sting operation. He knew how that would go over. But the idea of his son running an illegal food operation. Would he be proud that Wes was sticking it to King Mike? Or would he rant that a free man shouldn't have to sneak around breaking the law just to get his hand on a damn Twinkie, that such pleasures in life should be available to every man, woman and child—not just those who were willing to break the law or, worse, those rich enough never to have to worry about the law in the first place.

After four years in college in Manhattan, Wes was all set to take up blogging, perhaps work his way up to the top. But when his mom got sick, when the woman who'd gone above and beyond in her adherence to the dietary laws came down with cancer—one of the types they hadn't cracked yet—he moved back to the East End and took a job with Lou, figuring he'd move back to Manhattan after the situation worked itself out. She took three years to die, during which time he learned that she still carried a torch for the old man, that sometimes, late at night, one or the other would pick up the phone and call. Still holding on to the righteous indignation of youth, Wes refused to speak to him. But watching his mother die, watching someone attempt to tidy up the loose ends of life, mellowed him, as did the simple act of growing up, slowly but surely.

It was at her funeral that he'd fallen into dealing. Heartbroken as he was about her death, angry as he was still trying to be at his old man, he'd spent the entire mourning period half expecting him to show up. He never did. And Wes had been prepared to hold that against him as well. But Wes met plenty of their old friends, folks who must have evaporated when the marriage broke up. It just so happened that one of these guys supplied half the East End with illicit food. It just so happened that this same guy, Clark Butler, was getting a little old and looking to get out. It just so happened that this same guy felt that any son of the old man had to be good, trustworthy people with a healthy lack of respect for the regime.

Just like that, Wes had fallen into his second act in life.

37

Now he found himself in the middle of Manhattan, marching off through the snow to the second act's inevitable close. And just as he had little if anything to do with its beginning, he didn't seem to have any control over how it was going to end. Nothing to do but just march straight ahead. Would act three find him in jail for the rest of his life? Would it find him trapped along the border, trying to find a break through its defenses? Or would it be a short one, consisting of one scene of him bleeding to death, gut-shot by some New York City underworld sort—or Blunt—in a sting gone bad?

If he'd listened to the old man, he'd be sipping free Coke in the South instead of tromping through the snow on the way to what was all but certain doom. Hell, maybe he'd be fixated on his mother—turning into her more and more each day. Maybe he'd be a vegan.

"Hey, space cadet." It was Jules. He and Hillary were fifty yards ahead of him, waiting for Wes to snap back to reality.

"Sorry," he said, shuffling to catch up.

They walked until they arrived at what looked like a burned-out building. A rusted sign hanging over the door read "Hiroshima."

"What's your AR telling you?" Wes asked Hillary.

"Nothing," she said. "I turned it off. It was too much."

Once through the door, they marched single file down a claustrophobia-inducing hall, unadorned save for red lights, slowly spinning in little domes, casting eerie shadows as the bulbs made their revolutions. Through a set of double doors, they found a coat-check and changing room inhabited by a sullen Japanese-American woman wearing a period peasant costume minus the period peasant attitude.

She certainly wasn't going for Geisha. No bowing, no smiling. She made them feel as if they'd stepped into the department of motor vehicles two minutes before lunch break.

They gave up their coats. Hillary changed into high-heeled shoes. The coat-check girl put on a pair of rubber gloves before handling the snow-covered ones. Still, she gave Hillary's dress something approaching a look of approval.

Through the next set of doors was a small white room, similar to the waiting room in a doctor's office. Medical warnings were plastered all over the walls. They warned about the effects of animal protein and the health hazards of mercury in fish.

"Sushi?" Wes asked.

Almost as if anticipating where the questioning would end up, Jules answered, "Don't worry. This is on me. I insist."

Sushi was legal—despite it being from animals, despite the mercury silliness. It may have had something to do with fish not being cute and cuddly, not having any feet. Wes had only had it twice. He could afford it, but flashing the cash necessary to pay for a sushi dinner was the sort of thing to attract attention from the Federation. He'd planned to take Hillary for sushi—just the two of them—for their six-month anniversary, knock her socks off.

"Surprise, surprise, surprise," Wes muttered.

"What?" both Jules and Hillary asked.

"Nothing," he said. "Forget it."

They followed Jules to a receptionist's window. The woman on the other side stopped chewing her gum long enough to look at them and hand Jules three clipboards, which he distributed.

"Standard disclaimer," he explained to Hillary. "You understand the risks of eating sushi. You don't eat it more than once a month. You're not pregnant. You promise not to sue if you ever get whatever the hell it is they claim you get from eating too much of it."

"Right," Hillary said. "Because eating too much sushi is something I'll ever be able to afford."

"Excuse me," the receptionist cut in. She was chewing again, leaning back in her chair, her hands laced behind her head. "You can have a seat while you fill those out. It's going to be awhile anyway."

Jules turned to her and leaned on the sill separating them. "I have an appointment," he said.

She stopped chewing her gum. "Yeah?" she said. She wasn't impressed. Not yet. Assholes who thought they had an inside line were a dime a dozen. They all knew someone who knew someone. "With which doctor?"

"Doctor Imada," Jules said with a smirk.

That changed her demeanor. She snapped forward in her chair and spit out her gum.

"Of course," she said. "Name?"

"Jules."

"Last name?"

"That's it. Just Jules."

She picked up the receiver on the vintage phone and pressed a button—an honest-to-God button that moved from one position to another and lit up. It even made a clicking sound when pressed.

"I've got a Mr. Jules here to see Dr. Imada," she said into the phone, now looking at the three of them in a new light, trying to place their faces. Apparently, she was neither a patron of the arts nor the sort who stayed on top of the news cycle. "I'm sorry, Mr. Jules," she said. "We usually don't get appointments through this entrance."

"What's the point of VIP access if I can't rub it in other people's faces?" he asked before turning his back to her. He winked at Wes and Hillary.

A smiling woman in a nurse's scrubs came hustling from somewhere in the back. Popping her head through the door next to the receptionist's station, she said, "Right this way. Sorry for the delay."

Every other head in the waiting room snapped up to gauge whether this trio was important enough to jump the line, but all they got was a parting vision of Hillary's ass swishing away in its red dress. That was answer enough for most of them.

The nurse led them through a hall to another set of double doors, which she pushed through with no hesitation, no warning. Both Hillary and Wes stopped dead in their tracks, struck by the vision—

and noise—of 500 New Yorkers sitting in a cavernous room designed to look like a bombed-out city. Waiters ran about in old-fashioned chemical warfare suits. Fake smoke drifted through the room. Holographic B-29s thundered overhead, dropping holographic bombs that sent up holographic mushroom clouds.

Jules and the nurse were ten steps ahead before noticing they'd lost Hillary and Wes.

Jules turned back. "What say we don't stand here and gawk like slack-jawed yokels."

They started walking again, straight through the room. As it became clear that they were headed for yet another door on the far side of this room, conversation dropped to a lull at the tables alongside the aisles—a little wave of hush following in their wake.

"It's just killing them," Jules said. "Killing them. They've seen you on video all day, but they're not supposed to react to celebrity. It's not cool. But they just can't help themselves."

In fact, a young man walked right up to Hillary and thrust a cloth napkin at her.

"Can you sign it? Please?"

He was running a simultaneous dialogue with someone on the other end of his chip. "I'm totally asking her. Yeah. I'm standing right in front of her. Dude. So hot."

Caught off guard, she didn't think to ask who he thought she was. Instead, she said, "I don't have a pen."

When no one produced a pen, he rolled up a sleeve and offered her a knife. "Here. You can carve your initials into my arm."

At which point her inner cop took over.

"Get the fuck out of my face."

"Oh my God, did you see that?" he said to the chip friend. "Awesome."

With that, he was gone, and they were out of the room, the cacophony receding behind them. They climbed a set of stairs, and the light changed to something resembling twilight. Through a door at the top of the stairs, they found themselves on a mezzanine level looking down onto a forest of bamboo arranged around a pool of water fed by a waterfall pouring through the far wall—enough water, Wes figured, to broker a peace deal between Texas and Arizona for at least a month. Along the right wall was a sushi bar, the seats filled by very fat men in suits, each accompanied by a strikingly beautiful, yet plump, Asian woman.

The nurse led them to the left side of the room, walking by a number of easily recognizable celebrities: Nevin Levy, lead singer of Polanski, sitting with a couple of girls surgically altered to look like they were 13; Vanderbilt Johnson, second-baseman for the Jersey City Mets; and Jemma Jenner, board member of Sixth Wave Feminists and queen of an empire founded on her sole talent of being able to talk the daughters of politicians and business leaders into filming themselves having sex.

They stopped at a massive booth in the corner.

"Best seat in the house," Jules said. "We can stare at everyone while pretending to ignore them."

After the nurse left, a Geisha tip-toed over and poured them tea, put out hot towels. Shortly after that, a young Japanese man arrived.

"The usual, Mr. Jules?" He looked severe, professional. The ninja of waiters.

"The usual on the fish, yes." He turned to Wes and Hillary. "Hot or cold sake?"

"What's the difference?" Hillary asked.

"Well," Jules started, a pensive look on his face. "One's hot and one's cold."

"If I may," said the waiter. "Cold is usually of a higher quality, with a clean, crisp taste. Hot, while of a lower quality, can be more soothing."

"Oh," Hillary said.

"Cold," the waiter said, suddenly changing his demeanor, "makes you want to party, makes you go 'Wooooooo!'" He put his hands up in the air and waved them. As if he just didn't care. "Hot, on the other hand, makes you go, 'Ahhhhhhhhh.'" His body went limp as overcooked spinach and his shoulders slumped.

They all laughed.

"I think these kids could go for some 'Ahhhhhhh' before heading into the rest of the night," Jules said.

"Very well," the waiter said, straightening up and removing any hint of human emotion from his face.

"So they serve real sake here?" Wes asked.

"Not up front," Jules said. "Not to the proles."

"How do they get away with it?"

"See those guys over there, at the sushi bar?"

"Which ones?" Wes asked.

"Don't stare," Jules said. "All of them. Don't waste your time trying to figure out who they are. I know a couple of them, but for the most part, those guys are too rich and powerful to be recognized."

"What do they do?" Hillary asked.

"They run things," he said.

"Like what?"

"Like everything. They're the men behind the men behind the men. The two on the left picked the next King Mike."

"What do you mean, 'picked'?" Hillary demanded. "We have an election in two weeks."

"Yes. And in December, Santa Claus will bring you a pony. They plucked him from the midlevel ranks years ago, groomed him, put his campaign together and made sure no viable contenders accidentally landed on the ballot. Lot of responsibility, that. So they're here to blow off steam by getting drunk, eating poisonous fish—real poisonous fish—and letting these little Japanese women step on their balls with high-heel shoes."

Hillary rolled her eyes.

"I'm telling you, Red. I've been with every kind of woman in every kind of situation and the Japanese take the prize for deviant sexual behavior. It's the kind of shit even I don't get involved with." He paused long enough to wink. "Not anymore."

To a man, they were fat. In an earlier time, they would have been seen as running the gamut from pleasantly plump to morbidly obese, from someone to be tolerated to someone to be shunned and laughed at. Now, in the Federation, scarcity had made them something else entirely. Even the thinnest of them stood out in a crowd—not as a loser or the butt of a joke or even some sap who struggled with self control, but rather someone who could afford to eat enough to get that fat. Someone who could afford to get away with it, to blatantly disregard the laws of the land. Plenty of people could scrape up money enough to buy black-market Twinkies or eggs. And there was no shortage of people who could do so on a regular basis. But those people had to exercise twice as much—or start a binge and purge cycle—so as not to attract the attention of the law.

Fat was a sign of wealth and power, and at Hiroshima's sushi bar, the fattest man there that evening sat alone at the end, eating. And eating some more. If one were to ask how a person could get fat on sushi, one had only to watch this man as he devoured sushi rolls—the sort that were less fish and mostly tempura batter rolled in cream cheese and mayonnaise. He ate with his hands, his thick fingers continually moving food into his face, yellow-gold rings glinting in the light. The sushi chefs behind the bar kept feeding him. Though he was a regular customer, they still seemed to regard him with a mixture of horror and amazement, as if he were their own personal monster, a trained freak and, to their delight, a useful test subject, someone who would put anything in his face.

The man stopped eating only when one of the other fat cats stopped by his seat—and they all did—to say hello or goodbye, at which point he'd dab each corner of his mouth, then wipe his fingers before setting them free in a flurry of hand shaking and arm patting, all accompanied by one of the most insincere smiles Wes had ever seen.

"Who the hell is that?" Wes said.

"You don't recognize him?" Jules asked.

"Yeah, but I figured I'd ask anyway. Just to practice my communication skills."

"Just for that, I'm not telling you."

"Oh, c'mon."

"Nope," Jules said. "Oh, look. Our drinks are here."

The waiter placed a porcelain pitcher and three matching cups on the table.

"Who is it?" Hillary asked.

"Don't worry about it. I'll introduce you at the party later. It'll give you something to look forward to." Jules raised his glass. "To the outlaws," he said.

"To outlaws," they answered. Hillary and Wes smirked at each other when their eyes met.

Wes took a sip, the acidic steam hitting his nose seconds before the tang coated his tongue, leaving behind an aftertaste that reminded him of bananas. He felt a warmth creep through him, a sensation similar to that delivered by bourbon, but less violent. It left him feeling like someone had given his shoulders a firm squeeze, a promise of a massage.

They sank back into the booth, listening to the waterfall and surrounding conversations. There was a hush in the room, the result of chips being blocked from sending within these four walls. It was an enchanted forest where decisions and plans could be put off indefinitely.

Wes found himself reaching along the seat for Hillary's hand. She looked down at the two hands—as if one of them wasn't hers, and the other hadn't been on or in every part of her body. She shrugged and let them remain entwined, a gesture more cruel perhaps than if she'd simply withdrawn it and folded her arms across her chest. It made him want to snatch his own hand back out of pride. But it felt nice.

When the food arrived, it took effort to sit up again in order to eat.

Confronted with a rainbow of raw fish, Hillary had one question. "Where's all that fried-looking stuff that guy was eating?"

"No offense to our fat friend, but he doesn't know shit about sushi," Jules said. He talked them through the pieces, explaining the difference between sushi, sashimi, rolls and the different types of fish.

Hillary fumbled with her chopsticks but Jules told her to forget them and eat with her hands. "It's sort of like using a fork and knife to eat fried chicken," he said.

She answered him with a blank look.

"I haven't worked her up to fried chicken," Wes said.

"Saving yourselves for the wedding?" Jules laughed.

Wes felt himself blush and thanked God for the dark room. But he could tell by the look in her eyes that Hillary had noticed.

They sat for four hours, eating slowly as the food was brought out. They'd reached a pleasantly odd state of equilibrium—sated but not full, inebriated but not drunk.

Eventually, the check was called for and paid. Someone fetched their coats from the front, and they were sent through a back door so as not to have their mood ruined by the cacophony of the main dining hall. They found themselves on a deserted side street. On their left, blocked by a ten-foot pile of plowed snow, they could hear the few revelers out on Bleecker Street, braving the cold on the way to some speakeasy. To their right, a path had been cut leading through the tangle of streets that crossed the West Village. Eventually, they found themselves on Seventh Avenue, where a black car slid up to the curb in front of them.

"Our chariot," Jules said, opening the door.

"Pays to know the right people," Hillary said.

"Pays more to know things about the right people," he answered.

38

The car slid south in silence. Ahead of them, the skyline was dominated by the city's shame, a structure that looked like a splintered post broken off at the base.

They drew closer to it.

"Where are we going?" Wes asked, unable to take his eyes off the structure.

"The old FT"

"What are we doing there?" Hillary asked.

"That's where The Gawker's secret lair is," Jules said. "That's where he holds his monthly bacchanalia. You two are privileged. Not just anyone gets to go to these things. There are people worth twice what we are put together who can't get in. You're going to see things… Well, let's just say that even I blush at some of the shit that goes down in there."

"How appropriate," Wes said.

"What was that?" Jules said.

"Nothing," Wes said.

"Now's not a good time to be developing moral aversions," Jules said. "You're the flavor of the month, and they're not going to want it soured by a scold."

The car dropped them at the foot of what was once the Freedom Tower—and would have been again, after the 2028 incident. But FT2 was never finished. Such things had become beyond the imagination, will and taste of the Federation. A ramp led down to what seemed like a finished structure, a concrete bunker about four floors beneath street level. Jules stopped halfway down the ramp and held up a hand.

"You hear that?"

There didn't seem to be anything to hear.

"No," said Wes.

"Didn't think so," Jules said, but stopped again after another hundred yards. "How about now?"

Wes started to say no, but before opening his mouth he noticed it. It wasn't so much a sound as a sensation, a hum almost, a slight vibration coming up through his feet.

"What is that?" Hillary asked.

"Wait," Jules said, jogging another 50 yards.

The hum there was louder.

"Is there a power plant down there?"

"No," Jules replied. "That's the party. Tonight is going to be a rager."

Wes and Hillary looked at the concrete structure, then at each other, not sure they were ready for such a scene.

"Well, come on," Jules said.

They hesitated, something about the situation touching them on a primal level. The hum struck Wes as a warning sound.

"That's got to be what a beehive sounds like," Hillary said.

"That's just what I was thinking."

Finally, she shrugged. "It's just a bunch of drunk assholes, I guess." She started walking down to meet Jules.

Wes followed, but he couldn't quite shake the fear. He'd been around drunk assholes, plenty of them. This was something else entirely. Whatever it was seemed angry. It was irrational, he knew. It was just the result of loud music and loud people—lots of them. Still, there seemed a hostile note to the buzz. And the closer they got to the building, the more panic took hold of him. He could feel it starting in the base of his neck, pushing aside whatever soothing effects remained from the sake and spreading from there and enveloping his brain until he felt a different electric buzz, this one in his head and chest, squeezing, making it hard to breathe and giving him tunnel vision.

He stopped 25 yards shy of the unmarked door where Jules and Hillary waited under the glow of a red LED array. They turned to him.

"Come on, stud," Jules said. "The world awaits."

Wes looked at Hillary, hoping for some sort of lifeline but was given only a confused grin. "You okay?" she asked.

"I," he said, then stopped. He tried to take a step, but couldn't. Instead, he put his hands on his knees and tried to take a deep breath. He found himself fighting an urge to vomit even as his bowels threatened to let loose.

"I don't know," he finally managed. "Maybe it was bad sushi," he lied.

"Horseshit," Jules said, walking over to him. "I know what this is. You got yourself a case of the nerves."

"That's ridiculous," he said, but knew there was really no other explanation for it. What made it worse was that he was embarrassed. Panic attacks and nervous fits happened to other people, not to him. He wasn't the type. He couldn't bring himself to look at Hillary, afraid he'd see nothing but scorn in her eyes.

"Perfectly understandable," Jules said. "Anyone with half a brain wouldn't want to go into that viper's nest. Nothing to be ashamed of." He rubbed Wes' back. It was a touching, almost feminine gesture. "There you go. Breathe." Jules breathed along with Wes. After a few deep breaths, Jules pulled Wes back to an upright position.

"Look at me," he said, clasping Wes by the neck. "Look me in the eyes. Breathe in. Out. In. Out."

Wes looked Jules in the eyes and did as he was told.

"Feeling better?" Jules asked.

He was. Miraculously. By the second, he was feeling better. At peace, almost. That "ahhhh" from the sake seemed to be taking hold once again.

"Yeah," he said. "I am feeling better. I don't know what came over me."

Jules smiled. "Like I said, a little panic attack is all. Nothing a wee patch of At-Ease can't take care of." Like a magician, Jules pulled his left hand from behind Wes' head and showed him the patch he'd been pressing against Wes' neck.

"You drugged me?" Wes asked, trying to feel outraged about it.

"But you don't care," Jules said.

Wes thought about it. "No. You're right. I don't."

"Then it's working. Like I said, nothing to be embarrassed about. I used one myself. Now, we good to go?"

"Yup," Wes said, feeling much better about things. For the moment.

"Excellent. Red Riding Hood? You want a dose?"

"I think I'll pass," she said, giving Wes a look that registered on some level as disappointment bordering on disgust.

"Suit yourself," said Jules. "Let's get in there and get a couple of drinks in us before this wears off completely."

He leaned over a keypad next to the door and punched in a ten-digit code. The locks clunked free and he grabbed the knob.

"Ready or not, here we go," he said, tugging the door—a good two feet of concrete and steel—open along its tracks.

A fist of sound escaped into the night and punched Wes in the chest. He took a step back.

"Crap in a bucket," he said.

"Yes, indeed," Jules said, shoving first Wes then Hillary into the darkness of the hall. "Get in there. You're letting the cold in." He pulled the door shut behind them, and they were assaulted by the thumping bass of the music, which now had nowhere else to go.

And then there was the murmur. That's what the buzz had been, a murmur. Or, to be more accurate, a babble, a din of human noise, what sounded like a million schizophrenics talking angrily to the voices in their heads. Which, as it turned out, wasn't necessarily that far from the truth.

They walked the dark hall to its end, where they were met by a bouncer sitting at the top of a set of stairs. Beyond him was a cavern of a room, a pit in which what seemed like thousands of people milled about talking over the music, talking at each other, beyond each other, to the chips in their heads, to the screens on the walls. They were multitasking, all of them, conducting no fewer than three conversations at once. Not content with that level of interaction, they were posting comments to the wall.

Jules shook the bouncer's hand, patted him on the back and introduced Hillary and Wes. The bouncer seemed unimpressed.

"Let's get some drinks," Jules said, starting to make his way down the stairs.

The bouncer shook his head. "Nuh-uh, man. Mr. Sulzberger wants to see him first." He pointed at Wes with his chin. It took Wes a moment to realize they were talking through their chips since it was the easiest way to be heard over the noise.

"Who's Sulzberger?" Hillary asked.

"A man behind the man," Jules answered. "Someone we need to see if this is going to work."

The bouncer turned toward her. "You can go down to the bar," he said.

"Wait," Wes said. "She's with me."

"No skanks allowed," the bouncer said.

"Excuse me?" Wes could feel the tranquilizer wearing off a bit.

"No. Skanks."

"Now wait just a fucking minute," Wes started. "She's not a skank. If she doesn't go, then I—"

He felt a sharp pinch and twist to his lower back.

"Owww. Fuck!"

He turned to Hillary, who went off chip, leaned in and shouted into his ear. "Just go. This is our chance, idiot. Don't blow it because you caught a case of misplaced chivalry."

"We have a problem?" the bouncer asked.

"No," Hillary said.

"Good," he said, handing her a wrist band and sending her down into the crowd, the three men watching in silence as her ass worked its way down the stairs.

A pang of worry hit Wes, not so much for her safety or dignity, but for himself, that she'd definitely put him out of mind now. There were thousands of men down there, richer, better looking, more powerful. And there was no way they weren't going to make a play for her. He could see the heads turning, the guys excusing themselves from conversation as they followed her toward the bar. He took a deep breath and tried to tell himself he had nothing to worry about.

But it was futile. He knew that such optimism was useless against primal urges of jealousy and territoriality. And of course, he had plenty to worry about. She wasn't his. She was a cop, doing a job.

Wes felt a hand on his shoulder. "Let's not keep Mr. Sulzberger waiting," Jules said. "She'll be fine."

"That's reassuring."

"You want another patch?"

Wes remembered the look on Hillary's face. Then he heard her voice in his chip. "It's probably better if you're conscious," she said, notes of disdain loud and clear. Also loud and clear was the voice of some guy standing next to her. "You've got a great ass, baby. Anyone ever tell you that? I mean, perfection."

"I don't know," Wes said to Jules.

"Look," Jules said, going off the chip and leaning in to shout into Wes' ear. "It'll do you no good to be nervous. It might make Sulzberger nervous. And no one wants that. We get in there, you follow my lead. There'll be some drinking, some patches. Things you probably haven't done before. Just keep it together. Go along. It's nothing that can't be undone with a Clear Patch if we need it."

"You're not exactly setting me at ease," Wes said.

Jules grabbed him by the neck. "How about now?"

This time, Wes noticed it almost immediately. "Yeah. That's better. Much better," he said.

"Perfect," Hillary said. "Just perfect."

"Oh relax," Wes told her.

"What?" Jules said.

"Sorry. Just talking to Hillary."

"You two cut that shit out. All of the communication channels in here are being monitored. They can and will be used against you on the big screen."

"Oh," Wes said.

"Did she get that?" Jules asked.

"Did you get that?"

"Just fucking great," she said.

"Yeah, she got it," Wes said.

He assumed he didn't need to tell her to stay off the damn thing with Blunt. Imagining Blunt having another red-faced hissy fit because she'd dropped out of contact had an effect on Wes that was almost as soothing as the patch Jules had just given him.

"What are you smiling at?" Jules asked.

"Nothing," he answered. "Let's get it on."

39

It took Wes a moment to adjust to the new environment. It was brown. Very brown. The floors were hard wood, overlaid with earth-colored rugs. The ceiling, though white, was carved into rectangular panels by heavy wooden beams. The walls were paneled with a dark wood of the sort he'd never seen. Wes reached out and touched one.

"It's real," said a voice. "Mahogany on the walls, teak floors, oak beams. I tell people it's recovered from an old yacht so we don't feel guilty about all the little rainforest animals who died for our sins."

Wes turned to find an incredibly fat man standing in the doorway of a bathroom drying his hands on a towel. He wore an alligator's smile and the same dark suit he'd been wearing in the sushi restaurant.

"Jules," the man said, nodding in the artist's direction.

"Mister Sulzberger," Jules said, with a curious, almost sarcastic emphasis on the Mister, as if he had no choice but to use it but couldn't quite bring himself to do so seriously.

"And this must be Wesley," he said, dabbing sweat off his brow with the towel. He hadn't moved from the spot in the bathroom door.

"Yes," Wes said. "That's me."

"Excellent," said Sulzberger, though Wes couldn't tell if he meant anything by it. The man seemed as inert and emotional as a mountain. But the mountain did begin to move. Slowly, he made his way to the chair stationed behind an oak desk. He pushed a button—another of those proper buttons that clicked. Funny what the rich spent their money on. The chair rose to meet him. Situated to his satisfaction, he pressed another button and the chair lowered.

"Have a seat," he said, motioning to a pair of leather club chairs.

They sat.

A waiter or waitress—Wes couldn't tell which gender the androgynous thing belonged to, though it disturbed him that he found it sexually appealing—walked in with a tray, leaving them each with a tumbler half full of bourbon poured over a hefty cube of solid ice and a little dish containing three pork cracklins.

Sulzberger popped a cracklin into his mouth, savoring it for a full thirty seconds before following it with a swallow of bourbon. Jules did the same. Wes picked one up and stared at it. He'd never seen one that he hadn't personally ordered into the country. What little competition he had on Long Island didn't supply them.

"I suppose I have you to thank—or to blame—for this little addiction, Wesley." The man's voice sounded like it was drenched in butter. "I first had these at a party at Jules' home. I simply had to have more. His stays on Long Island—and wherever else it is he disappears to—are tragically long, and I'm an impatient man so I inquired with my supplier. The good news is he has them. The bad news is he charges entirely too much. But such is life."

He popped the second cracklin into his mouth. Jules and Wes followed suit. Not until he finished the third one did Sulzberger speak again.

"So, gentlemen. I suppose we should attend to business before we get on with the evening's festivities."

Wes was pretty sure if he was subjected to any more of Sulzberger's festivities, he'd fall asleep.

Sulzberger turned to Wes and focused so intently on him that Wes thought for a second the man meant to eat him.

"Now, Wesley, what is it that you need?"

"What?" The question had caught him off guard.

"It's not a difficult question. What you do most need and/or desire at this moment?"

It was an absurd and open-ended question. What did he need? What did he desire? To rewind his life a week, before he was arrested? Farther than that, back to when he and Hillary were at least pretending to be a real couple, a happy couple? Or back to the party where they met, so that he could undo all of it and tonight he'd be sitting in his house in Hampton Bays reading a book, his eventual escape to the South nothing but some distant, intangible daydream? Hell, while he was considering the impossible, why not just ask for the key to Hillary's heart? Staring into the fat man's eyes, Wes was half-convinced Sulzberger could deliver these things and more.

"Wes," Jules said, breaking the reverie.

Wes broke from Sulzberger's gaze. "Huh?"

"The man asked you a question. Didn't you have something specific in mind?"

Yeah, sure he did. What was it?

"The Gawker's dealer," Wes finally said.

Sulzberger raised an eyebrow. "But The Gawker already has a dealer, Wesley."

The response didn't make sense to Wes at first. "Oh, no. Not that. I want you to take me to his dealer. I need to get out of the country."

"But Wesley," Sulzberger said, "You've just begun."

"Begun what?"

"Why your story, of course. You're in the press. You're almost famous. The people need a new hero. And here you are. We build you up, hold you up. We put your face on our t-shirts, your name in lights. Women throw themselves at you."

"They going to throw themselves through the walls of a jail?" Wes asked, while trying to picture Sulzberger in a t-shirt.

"Jail?" Sulzberger said. For a moment, it seemed he wanted to append a "Ha!" to the question, but found it required too much energy.

"They don't just have me with possession," Wes explained. "They have me with intent to distribute a stash big enough to give the entire East End a heart attack. And God only knows what the sentence is for an illegal nuclear reactor."

"That may be true. But also true is that our sort don't do jail, Wesley. You cover the news. Surely you know that."

"Our sort? I don't know if I'm your sort—not in the eyes of the police."

"Yes, Wesley. Our sort. The celebrity class. You stick with me, even for one weekend, and you won't be just some random dealer out to corrupt mankind. You'll be a Robin Hood, a Batman. Everything Fox News claimed you to be. We'll make that true two times over. Hell, you're an old-fashioned print journalist and a rogue. Maybe we can make a Rhett Butler out of you."

"Who?"

"Never mind that. The thing is they won't keep a man of the people—my people—down and out for long."

This was insanity. The world didn't work like this.

Except for the fact that it did. And Wes knew that it did. Jules was a perfect example. Some men were above the law. Still. Even so. It didn't make any sense to him. *He* wasn't part of that world. And one didn't simply stumble into it. Even if one did, he was too old for this shit. Had he been a few years younger and single—even, though, he had to remind himself he was technically single—he might have gone for it. But now? He'd already had enough excitement for one week.

"I appreciate the offer," Wes said, trying to sound like he really did appreciate it. "But I don't know if it's for me."

"Interesting," Sulzberger said. "Most people would jump at the chance. If I had to guess, I'd have to say there's a woman at the bottom of this."

He poked at the desk and a vid screen lit up the wall behind Wes and Jules. They turned to look. On the screen was Hillary standing at the bar, wedged between two men. The three of them were facing out toward the crowd.

"She is a fine piece of woman," Sulzberger said. "I don't go in much for ladies, but that ass in that dress is almost enough to make me reconsider."

Wes wasn't sure he liked Sulzberger's tone, but he held his tongue. Hillary turned back toward the bar and motioned for a drink. As she did so, the man to her right spun around and tried to force her hand down, as if trying to stop her from ordering.

"But what have we here?" Sulzberger asked. "He does seem awfully familiar with her."

"Blunt," Wes said aloud, unable to stop himself.

"Blunt?" Jules asked.

"What a charming name," Sulzberger said.

"Her boss," Wes said.

"Really?" Jules asked. "And he just happened to find his way in here?"

"That is an interesting coincidence," Sulzberger said. "He must be a particularly sleazy fellow, too. He gained entrance as a guest of the Manhattan Vice Squad."

Wes realized he needed to make something up immediately. "Cigarettes," he said. "Out on the island, he's into tobacco."

Jules eyebrows went up like inch worms, undoubtedly convinced now that Wes had gotten Hillary off of a pimp.

"Filthy habit," said Sulzberger.

On screen, Hillary and Blunt started arguing, presumably over the drink.

"It's a pity they're not using their com chips," Sulzberger noted. "And curious as well." He shrugged and shut the feed off.

Wes turned away from the screen, grabbed the glass of bourbon and finished it. What the hell had that been about? He figured Blunt had been following them, but didn't think he was so close. But that wasn't what bothered him. It was the familiarity of the fight. It didn't look like an employer-employee sort of argument. He felt a sickness rising in his stomach and suddenly just wanted to be done with it all. Get to the dealer and either he'd finish the mission and get his amnesty or he'd give them the slip and actually make his escape. Hell, at this point he'd even settle for being gunned down in crossfire.

"My request remains the same," Wes said. "I'd like to be taken to The Gawker's dealer, so I can get the fuck out of this country."

"Really?" Sulzberger asked.

"Can you do it or not?"

Both of Sulzberger's eyebrows went up. "No need to get testy, Wesley."

"Sorry."

"Apology accepted. Now, as to your demand. That's a pretty tall order. You are aware that he may not agree to such a meeting.

Especially now that you've been compromised."

"Yes," said Wes, though in truth the possibility, obvious as it was, hadn't occurred to him. The realization was almost enough to deflate him completely.

Sulzberger reached into a desk drawer and pulled out a red phone attached to a land line. He kept his eyes on Wes as he dialed a number and waited for someone to pick up.

"Hello. Yes. It's me. We have an urgent delivery request. Call back as soon as possible."

He returned the phone to his cradle and shrugged. "Best I can do for now," he said.

"Shit," Wes said.

"Listen, he'll get back to me tonight. No need to mope around."

"Thanks."

"Now, on to reciprocation. I do you a solid, you do me one."

"How much do you want?" Wes asked, "I can have the funds forwarded."

"Please," Sulzberger said, putting up a hand. "Money? Look around you."

"Then what?"

"You'll be part of tonight's show."

"Which entails?"

"Nothing to get worked up about," said Sulzberger. "You just sit there and look pretty. You may even find you enjoy it. Who knows? You may change your mind about staying. After all, there's still time to change the road you're on."

Wes turned to Jules. Jules looked back at him and shrugged.

"You ain't got much of a choice," Jules said, slapping Wes on the knee. "Besides, nothing like a little fame and popularity to get her attention."

"Or to get over her," Sulzberger added as his chair raised him into a standing position. "Now, gentlemen, let's get a move on, shall we?"

40

Move was a generous term for what The Gawker was doing. His pace suggested he was storing up energy rather than struggling to carry his incredible bulk across the room.

They entered a second chamber, this one white and antiseptic, similar to the waiting room at Hiroshima except it had only one seat, a swiveling barbershop chair in front of a wall of mirrors. Next to the chair was a makeup artist's table. The opposite wall was taken up by closets.

Two young men entered the room from another door. One carried a black satchel, which he opened on the counter that ran along the mirrors. The other carried a tray of shot glasses, pills and tabs. Sulzberger washed down a pill with a shot. Whether he closed his eyes to savor the experience or to suppress a gag reflex, Wes couldn't tell.

"Tequila, gentleman?" It was more command than questions as he waved the tray toward them. "Jules, try a pill. Wesley, don't. I gather your vices don't encompass many pharmaceuticals, and it wouldn't do to have the guest of honor slumped over on stage drooling all over his shirt."

The word "shirt" tripped something in Sulzberger. "Yes," he said to himself. "Lawson, quit playing with your tools. Before we get started with me, why don't we"—Sulzberger motioned to Wes and paused for theatric effect—"*redress* this grievance?" He spoke slowly, his facing moving into an actual expression for the first time—one suggesting he was partly pleased yet partly ashamed he'd made such a bad pun.

Lawson, who'd quit messing about in the satchel, emitted one short "Ha!" before scampering across to the closet.

"Something from the 2012 Dov Collection," Sulzberger said.

Jules and Wes did their shots. Jules took a pill from the tray and dug through the patches before finding what he was looking for and offering it to Wes.

"Here. Deadens the nerves but heightens the senses."

"What?" Wes asked.

"Just trust me."

Within seconds, Wes felt something come over him. Whether it was the tequila, the patch, or Lawson helping him out of his clothes, he wasn't sure. But there was the fact that Lawson was helping him out of his clothes, and he didn't mind much at all. It was pleasant in its own way. And, though it made no sense at all, he was pretty sure he could smell the color of the fabric being pulled over his skin. The thin blue v-neck t-shirt smelled blue. The skinny-legged black jeans smelled black. He couldn't smell the white high-top sneakers, but was pretty sure if they had to pick a favorite song it would be something by Led Zeppelin.

"Perfect," said Sulzberger. "You now look like a proper throwback, the last of the print journalists."

Wes looked into the mirror. "Funny. I kinda think I look like a pedophile."

"Ha!" Lawson said.

Sulzberger smiled. "Wesley, I do believe the designer would have appreciated that remark," he said.

Wes shrugged and did another shot of tequila. He heard the taste burning at the back of his throat.

Lawson turned his attention to Sulzberger, removing the suit jacket, tie and dress shirt, freeing the folds of fat hidden underneath a white t-shirt. The businessman walked over to the barber chair and practically hopped into it—as much as a 350-pound man could hop into a chair.

For a brief moment, Wes wanted to ask for some of what Sulzberger was having, but then noticed Jules pacing the room like a caged tiger, doing pop-squats when he reached a corner. After Jules lowered himself then jumped into the air ten times, he'd exclaim, "Hoo boy!"

and then drag a sweaty palm across his face, then set off pacing again.

Wes decided against the pill and decided just to watch Lawson work on Sulzberger, whose bulk was now covered by a barber's cloth. He'd never understand the very rich. All this trouble for a haircut and shave and for what? To go sit in a skybox above the party, where no one except the staff would see him. Surely someone of Sulzberger's apparent status wasn't going to submit to paparazzi photos and couldn't really care what The Gawker's minions would think of him. But who knew, really, the minds of such people?

The door opened and a third young man entered.

"The gang all here, Corey?" Sulzberger asked as Lawson started applying what looked like white makeup to the man's face.

"Most of them are. Politicunt, Tim-Z, Eye-O, Deadspin, and all the skanks except one."

"Which one?"

"The J.A.," answered Corey. "But Jezzie and Belle are here."

"And where is J.A.?"

Corey paused. "She said she was sick. I think we're losing her. Said something about getting too old for this. Said it might be time to lose some weight and lay off the booze."

Sulzberger sighed. "She was too old five years ago. And here we were doing her a favor, keeping her scrawny ass around even after she'd grown out of the role. So be it."

"Can't we just give her," Corey started, but stopped when Sulzberger pushed Lawson's makeup brush away from his face and shot a glance toward Corey's reflection in the mirror, a glance that Wes could hear from clear across the room. "Sorry," Corey said quietly.

"I know she's your friend. But you all know why you're here."

"I know," Corey said again, his voice a quivering whisper. "Jezzie and Belle are pretty upset about it as well. Jezzie's been crying and Belle—."

"Stop," Sulzberger said. "Stop it right there. After you're done here, you get your ass back there and tell them if I see so much as a tear drop or a puffy eye, you're all going to get your pay docked tonight? You hear me? Am I clear?"

"Okay," Corey answered.

"Now, what else?" Sulzberger asked as Lawson went back to work. Were those fake eyebrows being glued to the big man's head? Wes wondered.

"Slow night. Governor of Rhode Island is here with one of her boy toys. They're in the next room, but we might have to boot them soon. They've been groping each other so much, the paps have grown bored already. The owner of Tofu Nation and his 17-year-old assistant. The LOLcat guy. The lead singer of CumSpunk. The entire cast of 'I Won't Do Anal'—one of whom is walking as if she just has. And that goofy guy from New York 1."

"I love that dude," Wes found himself saying. And he did. He really did love that dude. Further, he felt a need to explain. "Standing out in the cold, freezing his ass off and filing reports about the stupidest shit in the world and never a complaint. Hell, if someone decided to hold a rat rodeo in Bryant Park in the middle of a blizzard, that dude would go there and cover the *shit* out of it."

"See, Corey? Celebrity takes all forms," Sulzberger said as if imparting a very important lesson to a head-strong student.

"If you say so," Corey answered. "And, finally, we have Jules and Mr. Man, here."

His report done, Corey slipped out of the room. Wes and Jules did another shot, clinking glasses together before and after.

"Having fun yet?" Jules asked.

"Having fun? I'm tasting fun," Wes answered, his cares—and many of his faculties—somewhere off in the distance. He pictured them frolicking in a field of clover, like puppies, maybe.

"Enjoy it while it lasts," Jules laughed.

He gestured toward Lawson, who had just affixed a bright blue spikey-haired wig to Sulzberger's head. Stepping back to admire his work, Lawson revealed in its entirety the shiny white face, the bushy fake eyebrows and a bright red stripe that ran from ear to ear across the eyes, like a painted-on visor. Bright red lipstick completed the picture.

"Wow," Wes said. "He looks just like The Gawker."

"Ya think?" said Jules.

"Yeah," Wes said. "I mean, JUST like him."

Jules gave Wes a soft slap to the back of his head.

"Hey! What was that for?"

"It is The Gawker, dumb ass."

Wes looked again.

"Ooohhhhhhhh. Shit." He tasted and smelled fear. It was as if he were casting eyes on a monster in the closet. Or God. He'd seen The Gawker on video for so long, conducting his shows, larger than life, ranting and railing, that in some way he'd ceased to be something real. He was something that lived IN the video ether, in the nets, above with the satellites.

And now they were locked in a room together.

"What if he eats me?" Wes whispered to Jules. He didn't know exactly where the thought came from, but it was there, impossible to stifle.

"Ha!" said Lawson.

Jules laughed.

"I think your whisper setting is broken," Sulzberger said.

"Sorry," Wes said.

"No apologies necessary," said the fat man, popping out of the chair.

Lawson ran across the room to fetch a glowing silver Slanket, which he wrestled over Sulzberger. He then handed over what looked like an old-fashioned hearing aid.

"What's that?" Wes asked.

"It's an external chip unit."

"You don't have an implant?" Wes asked.

"Of course not," said The Gawker, with no further explanation.

The Gawker. With the Slanket and headset in place, Wes couldn't think of him as Sulzberger any longer. He was The Gawker.

41

The transformation complete, The Gawker raised one last shot glass of tequila, drained it and turned to the door Corey had come in and gone out through earlier. He swiveled his neck around a few times and did what passed for squats.

"God," he sighed. "This might actually be the worst part of the night."

"Why's that?" Wes asked.

"You'll see," said The Gawker, swinging open the door and entering the room.

"Bitches!" he called out in a loud, almost womanly voice. He threw his arms open wide.

Everyone in the room—staff, dignitaries, guests of honor—stood and faced The Gawker. "Hey-hey!" they shouted in response, then froze, waiting for further instructions.

"At ease, assholes," he shouted.

They all laughed.

A waiter ran up to The Gawker, offered him another pill, another shot.

"Oh my!" The Gawker said, putting a hand to his throat after finishing the shot.

He waved to someone in the darkness. "Okay. Grab a pic of Mr. Man, here. Flash it on the screen a bit, then leave us alone while we unwind."

Just as Wes was wondering if he could unwind any further, one of the women in the room sauntered up to him. She was shaped like a pear. A pear with huge tits. For a moment Wes was afraid he'd be unable to control his hands, that one or the other would reach out and touch her. He averted his eyes, looking down. But the shape of her hips was just as tempting. And the love handles poking out on either side of the jeans. The bit of muffin top at front. He was a sucker for muffin tops—whether it was biological or something ingrained in him by the media, he didn't care. He'd been hoping for the day when Hillary grew one. He wondered if it tasted like a muffin.

"Eyes on my face," the woman said.

He looked up. She had spiky red hair, an aggressive nose and lips that complemented the rest of her body.

"Smile," she said, then turned away and walked off to a vid screen.

She poked at it, and Wes saw his face appear and with it the sound of a roaring crowd. It wasn't an aural hallucination. Of that, he was pretty sure. He looked across the room—it was set up as an old-fashioned bar, with stools and booths and everything—and saw through the darkness that the far wall was tinted glass. Beyond the glass, vid screens looked down on the masses partying below. And on the screens was his face, under which was written the words, "In tha house."

The redhead walked back over, her eyes locked on Wes the whole time.

"Now what?" she said to The Gawker.

"Ugh," he said. "Beat it, skank. You'll get your turn."

"Whatever," she said, walking away, her ass beckoning to Wes.

Jules grabbed him by the back of the collar. "Boy, that didn't take you long," he said.

Wes tried to defend himself. "I don't know that I'm exactly in control at the moment."

"Good point," Jules said. "Whatever the case, you don't want to get involved with that."

They retired to a booth and were brought another tray of drinks, pills and patches. And then the food started coming—candy, potato chips, pigs in blankets, fried chicken wings, Twinkies. The Gawker began eating as if it were his job.

Wes helped himself as well, recognizing that he needed to sober up a little, regain some control over his faculties, preferably without the help of more pharmaceutical miracles. A stew of emotions bubbled within him. Cutting through the funk brought upon by the betrayal was a new insecurity, the remnant of the previous night's party. Like a high school kid, he couldn't get over being snubbed, shut out of conversation after conversation. Last night, he was nothing. But now? Every time Wes looked up, he caught them sneaking glances. Some were pushing their peripheral vision so hard he wondered if their eyeballs might roll sideways out of their sockets. He felt bitter, elated, unworthy, lucky, in too deep, in love, on the verge of death. So he drank.

"Look at them," The Gawker said. "IQs off the charts. Aced all the standardized tests in the Federation. Best schools. Graduate degrees. They get paid to create and destroy fame. But they're still awed by raw, untapped celebrity."

"Who's a raw celebrity?" Wes asked.

"He can be a little dense," The Gawker said to Jules, who shrugged. The Gawker continued. "It's okay. That sort of naiveté only helps. It's like he doesn't even care."

Were they talking about him? Because if they were, he felt he did care about that. Sort of.

"It's their currency, and it's as if he's taking stacks of thousand-dollar bills and wiping his ass with it. They can't resist that. It's going to drive them fucking crazy."

And with that, The Gawker started calling them over, starting with Politicunt. Wes had read and watched a bit of his stuff—typically asinine twaddle that did little more than preach to the converted. But a job was a job, right? Hell, the guy seemed nice enough at first— just a young man hanging out before heading off to work. Until he started talking politics as if he actually believed the stuff he wrote for public consumption. Working himself into a minor frenzy, Politicunt ranted about how backwards the U.S. was, the inequities there, the superiority of the Federation and the wisdom of its laws.

Wes had never commented on any Politicunt stories—on any of the Gawker properties for that matter. He was the type to obsess over replies, to get into flame wars and fight the unwinnable fight for the last word. And also because he suspected he'd never write anything quite witty enough to get their attention. But now he couldn't help himself.

"That's big talk coming from someone sitting in a VIP room at an illegal party shoving a Twinkie in his face," Wes said.

"Excuse me?" Politicunt said.

"Well, the government's so wise and all, why are you breaking all its laws?"

"Me? You're a dealer."

"Yes. But I'm not on my knees giving a virtual blowjob to King Mike, am I?"

Wes noted a glimmer in The Gawker's eyes. The man liked a good fight, liked someone taken down a peg. For some reason Wes suddenly felt a need to please him. Perhaps that was part of the big man's magic.

The rest of the staff, which had been hovering near by, stopped pretending to work and listened for Politicunt's reply. "Listen," he said. "We all know the Federation has its issues, but the laws are there for a reason, to save the people from themselves."

Wes pounded another shot. "And by 'the people' you mean that mass of stupidity in the rest of the Federation that doesn't include high-powered intellectuals such as yourself." He felt the alcohol asserting itself in his system, overriding whatever weird vibes the patches had been giving him.

"As a political journalist, part of my job is explaining the government's intentions to the people, helping them make sense of it."

"Only someone who went to a Federation-approved J-school could say something that fucking stupid," Wes said. He had a very clear vision of Lou launching his bulk across the table and choking the life out of Politicunt. It wasn't just that he was wrong, it was that he delivered his line with such contempt for any other possibility, as if he were not arguing from reason but reciting from faith.

"Whatever, fascist," Politicunt said, the signal that as far as he was concerned the argument was over.

The spiky redhead slid into the booth, pushing her bulk against Wes. "Don't worry about Politicunt," she said. "He might win his arguments out in public, but he's used to getting his ass kicked back here. And I think he's always been a bit touchy about that name."

Wes felt like he'd been crowned a champion. Of what, he didn't know, but it was enough to make him feel a little more welcome.

"Fuck you, skank," Politicunt said.

"Whatever," she answered. "Now you," she turned to Wes. "Who was that fox you came in with? She your girlfriend?"

Wes had to think about it. "Yes," he found himself saying.

"That's nice," she said, sliding a hand onto his crotch and massaging it. Her breath was on his ears and neck. Heat emanated from her thighs and exposed midsection. Wes glanced down at the little roll of belly fat hanging over her waistband, wanting so badly to touch it. "Your girlfriend's pretty fucking hot. Her ass looks great in that dress."

Wes didn't know quite what to do about the erection she was now fondling. Between the rubbing and her talking about Hillary's ass, he figured it might resolve itself sooner rather than later.

"Jezzie," The Gawker said, "get both your hands on the table where I can see them."

"Why? I can do what I want. I'm a grown woman."

"Yes. You are. I'm not trying to oppress you or deprive you of your God-given rights to feel up a complete stranger and thus emasculate him." He said it as if it was part of a speech he delivered often. "But he's part of the show tonight. And I don't need him drained before he goes out there."

Goes out there? Wes still didn't have a clue what he was expected to do. And did she really have to stop rubbing? It wasn't that bad. How much energy was he going to need, anyway?

"Whatever," Jezzie said. "Just wanted to give him a proper welcome." She turned to Wes. "Admit it. You think I'm fucking hot, don't you?"

It didn't even occur to him to play it cool. "Oh, yeah. Absolutely."

Her hand slid back under the table.

"God damn it," Jules said, sliding over Wes. "Watch your boner, pal," he said. "Look, if you absolutely need to rub a cock, rub mine."

"That's yesterday's news," she said, sulking now. "Besides, I'm not just some slut out to rub any guy's crotch." She crossed her arms.

Faced with a challenge to his manhood, Jules took over the table.

"Now, come on, sweetheart. I'm not just any old guy. Besides, you know how hot I think you are."

"Yeah, whatever," she said, still pouting, but already coming around.

"You're the best kind of hot," he said, then turned to the rest of the table. "Wes, I ever tell you about the best kind of hot?"

Jules grabbed Wes by the back of the neck and gave him a friendly shake. Wes felt the new patch almost immediately, a sense of clear surrealism—if such a thing existed—nudging the aggression and confusion of the alcohol to the side.

"No," Wes said. "You have not told me about the best kind of hot." He enunciated each word as if hearing it—really understanding it— for the first time in his life.

"Well, it's like this. You've got your normal range of beauty. You got your cute. You got your knock-out bodies. You got your pretty eyes, your button nose. The nice tits and ass. You got your old-fashioned scrawny hot like they favor down South. And your plump, curvy, dive-right-in girls that are all the rage up here. Sometimes, you somehow get a mix of all that. Now, Hillary is a bona fide fox. No doubt about it. I guaran-god-damn-tee you there are skeezers passing themselves off as modeling agents chasing her around downstairs right this minute."

Minutes earlier, under the influence of tequila, that statement would have sent Wes into a jealous fit of paranoia. Now, all he could muster was, "Good for her."

"And Jezzie, here, she's a sexy something else, too. But the true nature of a woman's beauty can only be judged by what her face looks like." Here, Jules paused for effect, and to down a shot. "By what her face looks like when your cock is in her mouth."

"Ha!" Lawson said from over at the bar.

Even Politicunt and The Gawker chuckled.

Oh Jules, Jules, Jules, Jules, Jules. Big hairy sasquatch-looking Jules. Wes' head swiveled on its base, and he grinned at the closest thing he had to a friend in his life. He wanted to reach over and kiss the man on his forehead.

Jezzie punched Jules in the arm with her left hand, but then leaned into him and put her head on his shoulder. Her right hand was no longer on the table.

He continued. "Some girls, their eyes don't look right from that angle. Some, their nose doesn't. Some look like deranged lunatics—which some guys like. Some pretty girls turn ugly—whether from the angle or because they look like they're having no fun. On the other hand, you can take the ugliest girl in the world and she's suddenly a vision of beauty, and you think to yourself it's too damn bad she can't walk around with a cock in her mouth all the time."

"And then you have someone like Jezzie. She's a beauty out in the bright glaring light of day, but she is something to behold, I tell you, when your cock is in her mouth."

By now, the entire booth was in hysterics, as was the booth behind them.

"Jules, you are a disgusting lech," said a new voice.

Wes immediately recognized her as Belle—the pepper to Jezzie's salt, the yang to her yin. Or was it the yin to her yang? Wes couldn't remember.

She was dressed in the style of the feminist. Which was to say she looked like she'd just woken up. Under the bed. Then dressed hurriedly in whatever clothes she'd found down there among the dust bunnies—brown, black and more brown. But even a fashion-backward idiot like Wes—drugged and drunk as he was—could tell it was a sham. The corduroy pants looked expensive and hugged her thighs and ass just so. And while her blouse and wrap seemed frumpy at first glance, thirty seconds of closer observation was enough to see the curves of her underboob and the rich mahogany color of her pudgy and flawless arms. She wore a pair of wire-frame glasses—Wes noticed the data scrolling through the left lens. Her black head was shaved to the scalp, and Wes suddenly wanted to lick it.

Her brown eyes flamed. "And Jezzie, you're a fucking embarrassment to women everywhere. The original Jezzies would puke if they could see you now."

"No they wouldn't," Jezzie said. "You know damn well they were sluts and proud of it. If I feel like being every bit the horndog and lech that Jules is, that's my choice."

Around the table, eyes rolled.

"Here we fucking go," said Politicunt.

Lawson, somewhere in the darkness of the bar, said something other than "Ha!" for the first time that night. "Oh for fuck's sake," he said.

Belle ignored them. "There's a difference between getting yours and debasing yourself in public, acting like a brain-dead 17-year-old all atwitter over some perv because he throws a few compliments your way."

"Is that it?" Jezzie said with a laugh. "You're jealous!"

"As if."

"Now wait a minute," Jules cut in. "If that's what this is about, then Belle, you know damn well I think you're beautiful—with and without my cock in your mouth."

The men at the table broke into peals of laughter. Jezzie tilted her head and smirked at Belle.

But Jules wasn't done. "Though I don't know about that shaved head thing you got going on these days. That could make a guy think he was fucking a bowling ball."

Her eyes flamed. "You disgusting piece of shit, you. You're nothing more than a has-been, a never-shoulda-been, repackaging other people's ideas, coasting on their work, pretending to be an artist and wallowing in your fame."

"Whoa," Wes said.

"Hello?" said Jules. "Hello? Pot? This is kettle? You're black."

"Oh, no now you have to bring race into it," she said.

"Jesus. Fucking. Christ," Jezzie chimed in. "Are you that stupid or do you need to fight so bad you're just making shit up?"

"Shut up, white girl," Belle answered. "Shouldn't you be sucking a dick somewhere?"

"Like your tank isn't three-quarters full with jizz right this minute. That's probably why you're so cranky. You just need to top off."

"You. Little," Belle started, but was cut off.

"STOP IT!" The Gawker said, bringing his hand down on the table with a crash, rattling shot glasses and causing a Twinkie avalanche. "Both of you fucking stop it. Stop it. Stop it."

Everyone fell quiet.

"Every fucking time," he muttered to himself. "Now, if you two skanks can't play nice, you're going to get the hell out of here. The both of you. We are not backstage. We are in the VIP room. There's only so much of this routine people will get off on before they start leaving."

"God," Belle started. "You're just as sexist as—"

"Shut up," he interjected. "And no, I'm not just as anything as anyone else. I'm probably more sexist, thanks in large part to you two twats. You see the guys in here going after each other like two cats? No. And most of us are gay."

"Ha!" Lawson shouted from the bar.

"Besides," The Gawker continued. "As much as I pay you two, I should be able to have you carry my fat ass around on a litter without complaint. Now sit down and play nice."

Belle slid into the booth, muttering. "Eight years at Columbia and a doctorate and this is the shit I have to put up with."

The Gawker got in one last jab. "Hey, don't blame me because you wasted all daddy's money on J-school. You wanted to do something useful or dignified, you should have become a nurse or a plumber."

"Ha!"

Wes wasn't exactly sure why, but all eyes turned to him. Eventually, he realized that it was he rather than Lawson who'd unleashed the "Ha!"

Belle put a popsicle into her mouth. She tossed back a shot. "You think that's funny, huh?"

He froze. How many times had he seen her on video? How long had he carried the shame of a celebrity crush—worse yet, a media-celebrity crush? Though he was starting to suspect Lawson—whatever his real name was, wherever he'd come from—was the only one with any damn sense, Wes had always felt Belle was the smartest of the crew, the one wasting whatever potential she had. And now there she was, sitting across the table from him.

Jules nudged him under the table, slapped yet another patch on Wes and put a shot glass in his hand.

Fired with liquid courage, Wes found his voice. "What I think is funny is that anyone who can string three sentences together, speak clearly and ask simple questions would have to go to school for journalism."

She did another shot and started unwrapping a Twinkie. "So you know from journalism, huh? Oh, that's right. When you're not clogging the arteries of dim-witted East Enders, you're supposed to be some kind of journalist your own self."

"If you say so," he said, his mind running away from him again. He wanted to channel Lou. He wanted to pound the table, call them all cocksuckers, tell them no self-respecting man would call himself a journalist anymore. What was journalism, anyway? What they did? Ranting and raving, whipping an audience into a lather? The only difference between what they did and what Fox did down South was that The Gawker's people dressed better and had bigger parties. All he managed to get out of his mouth was, "Me? All I am is a reporter."

It didn't seem a very convincing argument.

"Is that so?" she said. "And what exactly is it that you report? Please—pretty please with a cherry on top—let your answer be 'the Truth.'"

"The Truth?" He blinked a couple of times. The thoughts were there, damn it. They were. But he just couldn't catch them. "No. Just the facts. Just the facts, ma'am. Facts for the people. Report. Decide."

Belle rolled her eyes. "God. You mean the sheeple who walk around in a fog every day, going about their lives, taking what the government gives them at face value?"

"Don't fucking roll your eyes at me," he said, keeping his voice flat.

"Oooooohhhh," she said.

"Seriously," Wes said, pointing at her. He had more to say. About how she'd never change her opinion, the one installed by her parents, reinforced by her education and calcified by her job. There's no debate here, he'd tell her, only preaching and reinforcement.

But again, he came up with nothing. "Fuck it," he said. "No sense opening my mouth when I'm neck deep in bullshit."

"Well then!" Jules said, offering a broad fake smile and scratching at the table top. "Better get a different patch on the kid."

The rest of them stared at Wes. "Den of vipers," he mumbled, random phrases from some old reading assignment surfacing now. "Money changers in the temple."

And The Gawker? Wes couldn't quite decipher the sphinx-like expression, the eyes that were now considering him.

For a moment, Wes wanted Blunt's stupid mission to succeed if for no other reason than to deprive this lot of food and booze. On some level, he blamed Belle for being shut out of all those conversations last night. Or maybe he was just pissed for getting his ass handed to him in an argument. He looked at her. She looked back at him. He blinked first, and she offered him a sly smile. She wasn't so bad, was she? She'd beat him in a fight, that was all. It wasn't like she'd betrayed his trust and had him arrested.

"Anyway," The Gawker finally said. "I think we've had enough pre-game. Now all of you kids make nice so we can put on a good show for our guests."

His employees started to climb out of the booth.

After allowing a minute or two for the latest patch to work, The Gawker grabbed Wes' shoulder. "Are you ready for primetime, Wesley?"

"What am I supposed to do?"

"You just stand there, look pretty and, for God's sake keep your thoughts to yourself."

The Gawker washed down two more pills with a shot of vodka. They slid out of the booth, and lined up behind the rest of the staff at a door leading to the main hall, The Gawker standing immediately behind Wes.

The fat man tugged on Wes' shirt, leaned in and whispered. "Now you listen to me. If you want my help, while you're on my stage, don't you so much as think a word of that shit you were saying back here. You do and I will destroy you. Prison will be only the beginning of your travails."

Wes turned to look at him. There was no laughter in the man's eyes—only a cold, reptilian threat. "Yeah, sure," Wes said. "Okay." He was nervous all over again.

The Gawker smiled and clapped Wes on the back. "Lawson!" he

shouted. "Get this man a flask, a blue pill and his sack of goodies."

Wes took the pill without asking and put the flask in his back pocket. He looked into the sack. Twinkies. More damn Twinkies. And candy. And cigarettes. As well as plastic-wrapped hot dogs and hamburgers and chicken legs wrapped in foil.

"Like I said," The Gawker told him. "Smile, keep quiet, and just throw this at the crowd at the appropriate time. It will all be over soon enough."

"Okay," Wes answered.

"Let's do this," The Gawker said.

And with that, the metal doors in front of them slid open. They ran out through a wall of sound, into calamity, onto the stage.

42

Blunt fell out into the cold, gasping for breath as the door shut behind him. He knew he wasn't having an actual heart attack—the readouts told him that much. Still, he clutched his chest and bent over at the waist, the butt of his holstered pistol biting into his hip.

What had just happened?

He'd been in increasingly contentious contact with Halstead throughout the day. He'd parked not far from Jules' apartment, forcing himself to listen. Two days ago, he thought the acrimony between Hillary and Wesley Montgomery had been severe enough to break them for good. Perhaps not the best thing for the mission, but they'd continue, she out of duty and fear, he out of lack of choice. Montgomery, though, still showed signs of mooning over Hillary— Blunt knew exactly what that looked like—and eventually they were back into something approaching a sarcastic banter. No one else would have thought they were a happy couple, found the behavior worth emulating. But the back and forth brought his rage to a steady boil, helped along by the alerts and readouts blinking against the back of his closed eyelids. There was only so much the IT guys could do, and now Blunt was stuck seeing red.

Waiting was a misery, nothing to do but sit and stew as they chattered. When they fell silent, it was all he could do not to imagine Halstead fucking Montgomery or, worse, passing herself back and forth between Montgomery and the artist. If she was capable of shacking up with a scumbag and gulping down bacon until she grew fat and clogged her arteries shut, who knew what else she would do. Depraved animals, the lot of them.

"Fuck." He'd hit the side of his head hoping to dislodge the thought—or at least the implant. He was half a second away from taking the Taser to his temple. Self-administered electroshock therapy or an attempt to fry the circuitry of the chip. He needed to get a grip. And fast. Then they started talking about the Gawker party.

A plan. A distraction. Work. It wouldn't make the anger go away, but it would bring it down to a manageable simmer.

Flipping through his contacts, Blunt settled on Bernie Stapleton, who'd been in Blunt's graduating class at the academy. Smart, passionate guy, a striver. The sort who should have rocketed to the top of even the Manhattan PD. For some reason he'd seemed content to settle into vice. There were only two reasons someone like Stapleton would do that—either he had a zeal for cracking skulls, personally sweeping the streets of scum, or he'd grown a little too used to associating with his sources.

Ten seconds of com chatter was all it took for Blunt to figure it out.

He said his hello, explained he was working deep undercover on a highly sensitive case and needed entry to the Gawker party.

"Blunt, you old son of a bitch," Stapleton declared, laughing the way men do when welcoming another man to a secret club. "Living the wild life now? Never would have pegged you for the kind."

Blunt forced a chuckle. "No, seriously. Working a case."

"Right, right," Stapleton said. "Whatever helps you sleep at night."

Disgusted, Blunt bit his tongue.

"But, hey," Stapleton went on. "I've got a standing invite there. I'll hook you up, get your name on the list and a table in the corner. Two things, though. Don't use your com chip in that place and don't go busting up the joint." He laughed at the last bit—as if arresting someone in such a den of ill-repute were the silliest thing in the world.

"Thanks," was all Blunt said.

"Would love to join you tonight. Catch up. See what old Blunt looks like with his hair down. But I have a private dinner with another source. Call it my own undercover mission. Because after a few bottles of wine and a couple of steaks, she'll be under my covers." He laughed again at his own joke, much harder this time.

"Ha, ha," Blunt said, his disapproval lost on Stapleton. "Thanks again, Bernie."

"Don't mention it. But seriously, do me a favor, Blunt. Try to enjoy yourself tonight. Life's too short. Sounds like you're about to give yourself a heart attack."

Blunt clicked off without further comment just in time to see three people leaving the apartment building. It took a moment for the woman in red to register as Hillary. A groan escaped his lips. He gripped the steering wheel tight. What fresh hell was this? Everything he wanted, everything he couldn't have —his desire, his torment—all wrapped up in a vision of unalloyed beauty and walking off into the evening on the arm of another man. His heart tripped.

Involuntarily, his right hand moved to his forehead, to his heart, his left shoulder. It wasn't until he'd tapped his right shoulder did he realize what he'd done. He'd made the Sign of the Cross. Aside from funerals and weddings, he hadn't set foot in a Catholic church since high school. His mother had insisted on his attendance every Sunday. Baptism, Confession, First Communion, Confirmation even. And then nothing. He'd left easily enough, therapy taking over that portion of his life. But no therapy now for over a week. Suddenly this artifact from 18 years of childhood programming came floating to the surface, and he grabbed at it like a drowning man reaching for driftwood.

"Christ," he said.

He was in a bad way, no two ways about it. It wasn't only the stress and the missed therapy sessions. He'd run out of meds earlier in the week and hadn't stopped by the infirmary to pick up refills.

Despite the chemically unbalanced cyclone sweeping through his mind, Blunt managed not to cause a scene at Hiroshima. But just barely.

With so few cars on the street, he couldn't tail the trio closely, so he'd had to rely on GPS and Halstead's com set. Still, it took a good ten minutes walking up and down the street to find the door through which they'd gone. The "Hiroshima" name plate was designed to be seen by those who already knew it was there. Not that getting inside did him any good. No reservation—no "appointment" as the shark-eyed bitch in the reception room had put it, looking at him as if he'd come in off the street with a shopping cart full of garbage. On the verge of telling her he was a cop, maybe flashing his gun, he held back. No need risking the attention—especially that of other cops. He told himself they were close to the end. Really close. No use in throwing it away in a public fit of anger. Besides, he suspected the badge wouldn't impress the receptionist unless it was backed by a substantial transfer of dollars. So he took a deep breath and left. There was no practical use to go in, he told himself. None. Still, it galled him that someone like Jules could gain such easy entry, yet a protector of the law, an officer of the fucking peace, couldn't get so much as a glass of water. The Federation should be a better place than that.

He drove downtown, parked a block away from the entrance to the Gawker party and waited until a hundred or so people had gone in. He had no trouble at the door. In fact, the bouncer had given him an "Alright, alright, alright" and slapped him heartily on the back before calling him "My Hampton Vice."

For Blunt, the cavernous space hadn't been an auditory assault. There weren't that many in the place yet and the music, though loud, wasn't cranked nearly as high as it would be later in the night. No, what caught Blunt was the smell. An unholy mix of alcohol, cigarettes, fried food. His nostrils flared, his eyes stung. The busts he'd made on the East End were small scale. The parties tended to stick to one or two genres of law-breaking. Not only was it expensive to get food, booze and tobacco lined up, but it made it that much harder to hide the resulting aroma—especially once the booze kicked in and people got careless.

Blunt had never smelled anything quite like this.

It enraged him. How could this happen? How could they be this brazen? How could Bernie Stapleton live with himself?

Blunt was led to his central table, where he was forced to choose between a $3,000 bottle of vodka and a $5,000 bottle of champagne. He chose the champagne just to stick it to Stapleton. The bottle sat there, a mockery of the law, a personal affront, until two scantily clad pudgy girls approached and asked if they could join him. His shrug was all they needed. Planting themselves on either side of him, one opened the champagne while the other ordered a basket of fried pork nuggets, again on Stapleton's tab.

"You a friend of Bernie's?" one asked, wiping grease off her plump lips with the heel of her hand.

"We love Bernie," the other said, "He's pretty cool for a cop. You a cop? Want some champagne?"

"I'll pass," he said through clenched teeth.

She wasn't really interested in his answers. As long as the booze and food kept coming, they didn't mind if he just sat there saying nothing.

As revolting as he found them, he was happy to let them run up Stapleton's tab, glad for the distraction. Sitting there, showering them with contempt, he could almost forget about Halstead and Montgomery, about the fact that this latter-day Gomorrah was sitting under King Mike's nose. Not for long, though. Not if he had anything to do with it. He was going to bring it all crumbling down. So what did it matter if these two simpering idiots stuffed their slobbering faces with fat and washed it down with alcohol? When they were both 75 years old, it would be because he had put an end to it, saved them from themselves, finished the job King Mike had started.

Soon enough, the place filled up and the sound grew oppressive. The two girls tried to draw him out onto the dance floor, but he managed a smile and told them to go enjoy themselves and charge whatever they wanted to Stapleton's tab.

"Go crazy," he said.

As they walked away, his com set beeped, alerting him to Hillary's presence. He heard a bit of conversation between her and Montgomery before Jules told them to switch off. Blunt switched his off as well. The alerts, though, continued to flash, less an annoyance now that he was surrounded by strobing club lights. Just another layer of visual pollution.

After waiting fifteen minutes, hoping in vain Hillary's team would take the last open table next to his, he gave up and entered the crowd, heading for the massive central bar. There, he found Hillary. In that red dress, she was hard to miss. Leering fat men stood to either side of her. One of them, the fatter one, was practically on top of her, a drink in one hand, a fried chicken leg in the other. Blunt walked up to them, unnoticed, just in time to hear the fat man working his charms.

"C'mon, babe, you're hot. I'm loaded. Let's go back to my place and fuck until I have a heart attack. Because I'm thinking you could kill me with that ass."

Hillary, uncharacteristically, laughed. "You sure know how to charm a lady."

"Look," he said, a piece of dark meat stuck to his bottom lip. "Why beat around the bush? I like what I see, I go for it. So what?"

"I'm flattered," she said. "But I'm with someone tonight. Thanks, though."

He placed both drink and chicken leg on the bar and wiped his hands.

"I don't see how that matters. He left you unattended. You leave him. Happens all the time." He raised a pudgy paw and stroked her bare arm.

Like a snake, Blunt's hand shot up, grabbed the guy's wrist and twisted it behind his back. "Learn to take a hint, fat-ass," he shouted into the man's ear.

"Blunt!" Hillary said.

The fat man didn't make a move to resist. "Do you have any idea who I am?" he asked.

"I don't give a shit," Blunt said. "Now get the fuck out of here." He let go of the wrist and pushed the fat man clear, but not overly hard. The guy turned on him and Blunt pulled back his jacket, flashing his badge in case the guy got any stupid ideas.

The fat guy pointed a finger at Blunt, smiled and walked away, shaking his head.

"Are you out of your mind?" Hillary asked. She turned toward the bar, waving over a bartender.

"What are you doing?" he asked.

"What's it look like I'm doing. I'm getting a drink. Want one?"

"You're on a job!" he said, grabbing her hand.

She turned back toward him. "A job? This is some hell of a job. I've broken every law on this job of yours. You're going to worry about a drink?"

His heart was speeding up again. He could feel his face flushing.

"Hell," she continued, "it looks like you need a drink. Seriously, chief. I'm not being a smart-ass. You don't look so hot."

For some reason, that pissed him off even more. "You don't have a right to worry about me."

She looked at him, shrugged, said "Whatever" and turned back to the bar. When she faced him again, she had a drink in hand. She put it to her mouth and, as if watching a video, Blunt saw his right hand dart out and slap the glass to the floor.

The action caused a ripple of silence in the space immediately around them.

She made as if to speak, but he cut her off.

"Save it. You have a job to finish. Now you fucking finish it or I finish you—the both of you. You hear me? I will—"

Before he could say anymore, he was tackled from behind and dropped to the floor. In his younger days, even this element of surprise wouldn't have been enough to best Blunt. Big as he was, he was lithe, and a scrapper. But he was older now and in bad shape after the last week. Even his rage wasn't enough to get the bouncer off his back.

"Just a misunderstanding," Blunt communicated. "She got a little lippy."

"I don't give a shit," the bouncer said. He pinned Blunt's arms behind his back, lifted him to his feet and marched him out the door.

And there he stood, gasping for air, enraged and humiliated, his heart hammering in his chest, blood rushing to his head.

Someone stumbled out of the club, lit a cigarette. "Dude," the stranger said. "You okay? You don't look well."

Blunt tried to put a hand up to wave the smoker away. Instead, he fell to the sidewalk.

"Panic attack," he managed. He hoped.

The stranger smiled. "That it? Then take a pill or something."

Blunt shook his head. "Out. Forgot at home."

The stranger pulled a packet out of a jacket pocket and flipped through what looked like a folder of patches. "Here," he said. "Do you mind?"

Blunt nodded consent. He didn't want to, but didn't see much another option. Patch on, he started calming down within a minute. Five minutes later, even the heart-rate alerts had turned off.

"Thanks," he finally managed.

"No worries," the stranger said before moving off into the night.

"How long?" Blunt shouted after him.

"That one? About four hours. You might want to get home, get to bed before it wears off."

"Yeah, of course," Blunt answered. "Sure thing."

He went back to his car, turned on the heat and waited. He figured it was the drug working through his system, but he felt a little better now, a calm resignation. He was going to finish this job tonight. The parameters had changed, but in police work, such things were bound to happen. There was only one way this was going to end.

Four hours. That would be plenty of time. It had to be.

43

With Blunt gone, Hillary pitched the second drink and ordered a water. Whatever was going to happen at the end of the night, she'd need to have her wits about her.

Bad enough Blunt had seemingly gone off his meds even as Wes was stewing his brains with alcohol and patches. She tried not to worry about Wes, but was finding it impossible. Blunt, she didn't feel responsible for. Not any more, at any rate. Wes, on the other hand, she'd had a hand in breaking. Whatever influence his old man had had on him, however Alpha male he tried to be, he was sensitive. It had taken her awhile to figure out how he was put together. He cared little for what colleagues and strangers said or thought about him. He hadn't been too crippled by insecurity or neurosis because he was a big fish in a small pond—and because he'd kept others out. Her, he'd let in, and she'd cut him to the bone.

It was what it was. There was no undoing the past, no matter how recent. But she knew that he was hurt—and currently lost, scared and swimming in a chemical cloud.

Yes, she felt guilty. There was no shame in that. She was feeling something else, something she had trouble identifying. Despite being told not to, she'd been turning on their implants for one-minute intervals. She kept quiet, observed only. Wes didn't notice. Or if he did, he didn't act like he had.

"Hey sweetness," someone said to her.

"Leave me alone," she said, without looking at the guy. Instead, she looked up to the wall of glass above the dance floor and stage to see if she could spot Wes and Jules. She triggered the implant, heard

Jules going on about blowjobs, heard Wes laughing, saw that his eyes kept drifting over to the one called Jezzie.

She switched the implant off, waited a minute, maybe two, switched it back on. Wes was now ogling Belle's muffin top, his head bobbing up, down, swiveling around. How messed up was he? What the hell was he doing? She wanted to tell him to focus. To lay off the patches and the booze. To quit staring at these media bimbos. Especially that one, with her shiny black skin and her perfect muffin top.

"Shit." She switched off again, recognizing the emotion now. Jealousy. It was almost alien to her, but there it was, as worrisome to her as Blunt's outburst. She was going to have a hard enough time wrangling cats tonight without her own emotions coming into play. She'd spent a decade—if not more—maintaining composure, keeping her chin up. She could make it a few more hours, right?

Right.

But as The Gawker and his bloggers walked out onto the stage and the crowd erupted, she felt doubt.

The adulation, the fame, the women throwing themselves at Wes. How could he say no to that? He'd be almost crazy not to. Tonight, after the show, he could sit in that back office and just wait. What was Blunt going to do? Wes had the support of the King of all Media and his army of lawyers, something that had often proven itself an equal match to crusading cops and prosecutors.

And what hold had she over him? None, ultimately. Obviously. He'd already tried to escape once. He'd made a break for it from Jules' house, but had been caught. Blunt had told her. That stung. She could admit that much. He may have fallen for her at one point, but what was she other than an undercover cop who'd ruined his life? And now he'd been to the mountaintop and had been offered the world.

Was her envy giving way to fear? Was that what was happening? Perhaps the craziness afflicting Blunt had been contagious. She couldn't have this. Envy, at least, was actionable. Fear only lead to incapacity, to trouble. To hell with that.

She turned back to the bar. "Bourbon," she barked. "Neat."

44

Wes found himself on the center platform standing right next to The Gawker. To their right stood Jezzie and Belle, who'd gone from shouting at each other backstage to fondling one another on stage. If Wes hadn't been so nervous, he may even have honored the sight with an erection. To the left were Lawson and Politicunt, Lawson dancing up a storm and Politicunt standing stock still, as if too dignified to engage in frivolity.

The Gawker began to move around Wes on center stage, stomping about to the music, gesturing to dignitaries in the crowd and then throwing his arms up and out—each time tripling the volume in the auditorium.

Wes watched in amazement. He'd seen bits of this on video—clips leaked out by insiders. But up close and personal, it was something bordering on miraculous that a man so fat could move so fast. No wonder he'd been storing up his energy all night. No wonder he'd warned Wes away from the red pills. If it could get three hundred and fifty pounds of blubber whizzing across the stage like a ballerina, it would have rattled Wes' skeleton right out of his skin.

Running to the front of the stage, The Gawker wound his arms around a few times to build the audience up and then made a safe-at-home gesture. Save for a few murmurs, the crowd fell silent.

The Gawker put a finger to his lips. "Shhhhh," he said, his voice coming through loud speakers and, Wes discovered, through the implant.

Once inside, once the show started, there was no escaping the voice of The Gawker.

"Shhhhhh," he said again. He bent forward, his hands on his knees, a crocodile grin on his face. He looked to his left, then to his right. Then, with a dramatic stage whisper, he said to the crowd, some 5,000 of the Federation's best and brightest, richest and most famous, "My bitches."

And with one voice, they answered, "Hey-hey!"

The Gawker put his hand to his chest and stumbled back as if bowled over by the response. He wasn't exaggerating much. Wes felt the wave of sound in his chest, in his head. He reached for the flask.

The Gawker ran back to the front of the stage and, a little louder this time, said again, "My bitches." He put his hand to his ear.

"Hey-hey!" The crowd roared, louder than before.

The Gawker brought a finger to his lips, silencing the crowd again.

"Ladies and gentlemen, welcome to our little secret. What happens here, stays here. So no telling the fuzz, the feds, the pigs or the coppers."

The crowd, including the fuzz and feds present, booed and laughed at the same time.

"Now, I present to you," he paused, turning to Wes for a moment to build expectation. But he pointed the other way and called out, "Jules!"

Sure enough, on a side stage in front of a giant white canvas stood Jules. A dance-club remix of the classic "Boyfriend" started playing, and Jules attacked the canvas with aggressive brush strokes while dancing and stomping around the stage like an angry retarded child, glaring at his work as if it had personally offended him. Every once in a while, he'd put a hand to his ear and the crowd would erupt. By the end of the song, he'd completed a painting of Justin Bieber— the young version, not the later tragic one—leading to further riotous applause and a bidding war, the prices flashing up on the video screens until it sold for $150,000.

What surprised Wes wasn't the clamor over populist schlock, it was that Jules had painted a recognizable portrait.

The auction finished, The Gawker stomped back to the edge of the stage.

"Ladies and gentlemen! We live here in the heart of freedom, the best city in the best country in the world. Our cross-eyed cousins to the South clamor to get in. Our friends across the oceans model themselves on our example. But a country is only as strong as its best voices, those crying out to keep them honest."

Wes wondered who "them" was.

"So we gather you here, in the presence of great artists." He pointed to Jules.

"And we offer you the best journalists on the continent," he continued, motioning to Jezzie, Belle, Lawson and Politicunt. "Who daily tell it like it is, who hold a mirror up to society, who deal in—" Here, he turned back to look at Wes. "Who deal in Truth."

The crowd erupted.

"Capital T Truth," he said to more applause.

"Dissent, as John Kennedy said, is the highest form of patriotism!"

Wes wanted to put his fingers in his ears, but knew it was pointless. Between the loudspeakers and his chip, there was no escape.

The Gawker let the commotion die down before continuing. "But tonight, we have a special treat. An old-fashioned outlaw. A scalawag. A man who may be in prison by this time tomorrow."

The crowd booed. The Gawker put his hand up to silence it. "And! And to top it all off, the man is a journalist."

If Wes had any doubts before, it was clear now that he'd pissed off the fat man.

"One of the last print journalists in fact. Ladies and gentlemen, I give you Wes Montgomery. Your bacon and egg man!"

As an explosion of applause washed over him, Wes found himself jogging to the front of the stage, one hand waving. He noticed himself on the giant vid screens, comments scrolling across too fast to read as commenters typed or muttered into their chips. He reached into the sack and started flinging food into the audience. Pandemonium ensued. Because of the stage lights, he couldn't see the action on the floor directly, but the vid screens were doing a good enough job picking out the best of it. Two scantily clad, incredibly gorgeous women fought over a chicken leg, shredding each other's clothes until they were down to their underwear, the rolls of their flesh glistening like forbidden pastries under the bright lights.

After emptying his bag, Wes took a deep bow as the crowd took up a chant. "Bacon! And! Egg! Man!" While they did so, stagehands brought out a matching pair of thrones. The Gawker led Wes to the middle of the stage and motioned for him to sit.

At that point, the others took over the show. Lawson, lacing actual sentences between his "Ha!" outbursts, went through the week's best and worst vid moments. Politicunt covered politics. As they showed their clips and posts and played audio, comments streamed in, the funniest and nastiest being frozen momentarily on the vid screens for all to appreciate the brilliance and wit and originality of that particular commenter.

Then it was Jezzie and Belle's turn. There seemed to be a bit of hesitation, and Wes heard The Gawker's voice clearly in the stream of noise channeling through his ear. "Do it," was all he said.

At that point, the image of J.A.—always the most popular of the cast, the funniest, the prettiest, the sweetest, the bitchiest—graced the screen. There she was, a modern day fertility goddess.

The crowd started to applaud. Over the years, the J.A.'s had always been the crowd favorite because, unlike the others who were hired based on education and some discernible set of skills, J.A. was always scooped up from the unwashed masses and sculpted into pure product.

But when a bright red X was stamped across her face, the audience fell into a confused muttering.

"Ladies and gentlemen," Belle started. "I think it's time we admit the truth about J.A."

"And that truth is," Jezzie chimed in.

They finished the sentence together. "That bitch is T. O. W.!"

"Tired! Old! Whore!" Jezzie yelled out in a solo refrain. "Tired! Tired! Tired!"

"T. O. W." Now it was Belle leading the throng in a chant, as photos and clips of J.A.—all unflattering, all caught behind the scenes, all likely archived just for this moment—flashed across the screen. What followed was two minutes of frenzied hate as commenters hurled at J.A.—a woman they'd been prepared to hold up and worship only minutes before—every insult ever dreamed of for woman or man.

Wes squirmed in his seat, fishing out the flask. What would his mother have thought of this? He tilted the flask back, the silver glinting in the stage lights.

The Gawker leaned over to him. "Don't get caught up in guilt, Wesley. She lived by the sword, she died by the sword."

Wes kept quiet and drank.

Eventually, the tide of hate ebbed and J.A.'s face disappeared from the screen.

The camera started casting about the auditorium and The Gawker leaned in again. "Now here's where I want you to sit very still. Here's where you really earn your passage."

The cameras found Hillary and locked on her. The crowd fell silent, waiting for direction from someone in authority.

"Now that's one hot bitch," The Gawker said, his voice bounding throughout the place before it was overtaken by applause.

On screen, Hillary looked about, unsure at first what all the commotion was about. Then she saw herself on the screen, comments starting to stream in again.

"I'd hit it."

"I'd eat that ass for breakfast."

"Custom built. For my cock."

And a few dissenters.

"I've seen better."

"Skinny bitch. Eat a pork chop."

Wes turned away from the screen and looked at The Gawker. "What the fuck?" he said, starting to stand.

The Gawker grabbed his arm. "You sit your ass down," he said, the smile never leaving his face.

Wes fell back into the seat. He wasn't so sure he would have made it far anyway. The alcohol was reasserting itself with a vengeance.

Hillary smiled into the camera, a look that Wes recognized as her eat-shit-and-die smile. She said nothing. Didn't move, except to raise a middle finger to the camera, causing the crowd to go nuts again.

So calm and composed, wasn't she? She had a mission to complete, didn't she? And if this was what it took, then this was what it took. Hadn't she slept with him, pretended to love him? Hell, this was nothing.

Wes drained the rest of the flask and waited for the show to end.

As the lights went down and the DJ cranked back into action, The Gawker stood up and helped Wes out of the chair.

"Not so bad, Wesley. Very professional. If you got over yourself, you could make a career out of this."

Wes struggled to find his balance and his words. "Yeah, well," he started, then stopped. The Gawker held the keys to the next step in the plan. No use pissing him off any further. "I don't think I'm built for the celebrity racket. If it's all the same, I'd just like to get the hell out of dodge."

"Suit yourself," The Gawker said, turning to walk away.

Wes grabbed his arm. "The dealer?"

"Oh. That. For whatever reason, he agreed to meet with you. A car will pick you up at 2 a.m. That gives you two hours."

"A car? Where's it taking me?"

"I have no idea," The Gawker said, turning and leaving Wes alone on the stage.

45

Wes looked around, his head swimming. He needed to find a set of stairs down to the main floor. He needed to sober up. He needed to find Hillary.

He needed to piss.

"Damn," he said to himself. When was the last time he had gone? He couldn't remember, but there was no denying the pressure on his bladder. He worried he might not make it to the bathroom in time.

After finding the stairs down from the stage, he forced his way through the crowd as far as he could. People were following him, clapping him on the back, shaking his hands. Women hugged him, kissed him, grabbed his crotch. He felt a little rude not returning the gestures, but such was the life of the celebrity.

After making no progress, Wes climbed back onto the stage, pushed his way through the curtains and stumbled around in the darkness until he spotted the white light of a bathroom. He stood in front of the urinal for what felt like minutes, unable to think of anything but the relief. He groaned two or three times, well aware that he sounded like he was having an orgasm. After one final shudder, he zipped up and turned to leave.

His path was blocked by Belle. Beautiful and big, she seemed furious about something.

"Hey," she said, grabbing him by the collar, pulling him close. She kissed him softly on the lips—a feminine gesture that surprised him. She hooked a finger through one of his belt loops.

Wes stepped back. "No." A silent afterthought occurred: "Why not?"

She stepped them toward a wall. "Why not, Wesley?" She kissed him again. "I heard you were leaving us, that you didn't want to stay."

"I can't," he stuttered.

"No? It's not a bad life. Pay's good. Food's good. Perks are good. And, look, that stuff in the VIP room, that's as much part of the act as anything. Tina—you know, Jezzie—she and I are really roommates, totally best friends in the world. She's got a boyfriend, stays home most nights and cooks."

His back was against the wall now. "And you?"

She smiled and smacked his chest. "Now, Wesley. Are you flirting with me?"

He didn't say anything. He didn't know what to say. If he opened his mouth, whatever came out would be wrong.

"I don't know if I'm ready for a boyfriend, Wes," she said, kissing him again. "But I'm not going anywhere. And you are cute. It'd be nice to have some fresh blood in here."

Was she a normal human being? Was she letting her guard down? Or had The Gawker sent her in here, another undercover woman sent to trap Wesley Montgomery? Suddenly, he was convinced that's what she was—bait. This was all an act.

So what if it was? He was probably trapped in the Federation regardless—his only out at this point was tonight's poorly defined mission that was as likely to get him killed as anything. So why not ride it out here? Shack up with Belle for a while, roll in piles of cash, try to put Hillary out of his mind, maybe pick the next J.A.

But that was it, wasn't it? Nothing to guarantee *he* wasn't the next J.A. He tried to recall his revulsion in the VIP room, on the stage. Lou's disdain for the whole scene. His old man's voice.

Hillary.

He saw her in bed on a Sunday morning. Across from the table during one of their meals. Her standing in Jules' apartment, looking like a goddess but unsure of herself all the same.

"No," he said, pushing Belle back. "Thanks, but no."

"What do you mean, 'No'?" she whined, tugging on his pants.

"It's not for me. I'm leaving."

She pushed him against the wall again. "C'mon," she said.

"No means no," he mumbled, pushing back, a little harder this time.

"That's how you like it?" she said, her tone changing now, her eyes becoming harder. "You want to choke me? You want to hit me? Go on." She pinned him against the wall with all her weight. She was breathing heavy now. "That shit turns me on. I'm dripping wet right now. You should feel it."

The lizard part of his brain—the part still flying his cock at full staff—wanted to feel it. Badly. He was boiling over with frustration, alcohol, booze, heartbreak. A violent hate-fuck was just what the doctor ordered.

"No," he said again. With all his strength, he twisted her around so that her back was against the wall.

She smiled. "You gonna fuck me or hit me?"

That hadn't occurred to him at all.

"Go on," she said. "Hit me. Whatever you want, Wes. That's the whole point. Whatever you want to do."

Why would he want to hit her? Still, he found himself pulling his fist back, looking at it. Looking at her. No. That wasn't going to happen either.

But before he'd had a chance to move, his fist was gone, twisted down and pinned behind his back. He was thrown against a wall and then through the door of the handicap stall where he fell against the toilet.

Hillary stood over him. "What the fuck are you doing?"

Before he could answer, Belle was behind her. "What is *he* doing? What the fuck are you doing?"

"You shut up and get out of here," Hillary said without looking at her.

"Ohh, the hostility," Belle answered. "We can share if you want. You're not so bad yourself."

"I said get out of here."

Belle dropped the playfulness from her voice. "You best check yourself before you wreck yourself."

Wes wondered why someone would quote a vintage t-shirt in the midst of a confrontation.

Belle continued. "You'll never work in this town again, see? You don't know who I am, who you're messing with."

Her reserve of patience used up, Hillary released Wes, spun around and pinned Belle to the opposite wall, forearm pressed against the bigger woman's throat.

"Your real name is Emily Allison. You're—holy shit!—42 years old. You graduated Ivy League, not on scholarship but as a legacy. You couldn't even fuck your way into school—or here for that matter. Your daddy got you into college, then he got you the gig here. And—wild guess on this one—someone else writes most of your material."

"Fuck you," Belle said.

"Some feminist you are," Hillary answered.

"Girl's gotta do what a girl's gotta do. Or, in your case, who's she gotta do." She cast her glance at Wes.

"Ha!" He couldn't help himself.

Hillary shot him a look then turned back to Belle.

"Tough girl, huh?"

"You don't know the half of it," Belle said.

Hillary shook her head as if to clear it. She removed her arm from the other woman's throat, then suddenly jerked the same arm back and brought her fist smashing into the side of Belle's head. Belle dropped like a sack onto the bathroom floor.

"I know it was you who said I needed to eat a pork chop."

Hillary turned to Wes.

"So it's okay for you to hit her?" he asked.

"You shut your hole," was her answer. She bent over Belle, turned her head this way and that and checked her pulse before cuffing her to the drainpipe of one of the sinks.

She was out of breath. Flushed. "I don't know why, but I expected better from you." Disappointment tinged her voice.

"I'm sorry," he started. "I don't know what came over me." But as the words formed, he had a flashback to their fight in the police station parking lot. Here he was apologizing again. He hit his head against the wall, looked up and the ceiling and pinched the bridge of his nose. With the adrenaline wearing off, he just felt tired, woozy and, increasingly, nauseous. "Why the fuck am I apologizing?" he said with a weary laugh.

"Because you were about to punch a woman in the face, you asshole. And then probably fuck her."

"What? No, I wasn't going to do either. Anyway, that's not what I mean. Why am I apologizing to *you*? Again? *You* got me into this mess. You! I wouldn't be here, drunk, drugged and fighting off crazy women if not for you. And *you're* disappointed in me? *You!?* Are you kidding me?"

He tried to stand up, but couldn't find his feet. He slid back to the floor.

"At the risk of sounding like an idiot, like a big fat vagina, I loved you, you know. Maybe still do. And now it's all I can do to finish this stupid mission or whatever so I can fucking escape this misery."

He was pretty sure he hadn't meant to say that out loud.

She considered him a moment. "Boy, are you something else. That's quite a story you got worked out. Poor little Wesley in love. And with the big bad police woman who ruined his life! Yeah, you're so in love, then why the hell did you try to leave me? That's your idea of love? Escape in the dead of night without saying goodbye?"

She kicked him in the thigh. Hard.

"Ow! What the hell?"

He rubbed his leg. She kicked again, this time catching one of his fingers.

"Answer me," she said.

"Goddamnit," he screamed, trying to wave the pain out of his fingers. "What the hell are you doing?"

She pulled her leg back to kick him again, but he managed to catch it and knock her to the ground.

"What are you talking about— leaving you in the dead of night? When?"

"Thursday night. At Jules'. Blunt told me you tried to escape, but he stopped you."

"Blunt? What? No." He couldn't help but chuckle at that. "I didn't try to escape. I mean, I did. But I had you with me. Fucking Christ, Hillary. I was taking you with me. You were passed out drunk."

"Bullshit," she said.

"That bruise on the side of your head? I did that getting you across the threshold. Rammed your head right into the door. But, yeah. Blunt caught me at the end of the driveway. Threatened me with kidnapping charges. I think he might have threatened to kill me, too. So I just brought you back and kept my mouth shut."

She sat motionless for a moment, processing the story. Then she punched him in the chest.

"Ow!"

She hit him again and again. "You tried to kidnap me? Kidnap me? What were you going to do? Wake me up on the submarine somewhere off the coast of South Carolina? Did it occur to you I might not want to move to the South?"

He curled into a ball and covered his face. "What the hell's wrong with you?" he shouted from behind his hands. "You're insane! One minute you're kicking me for leaving you, and now you're punching me for trying to take you with me. Are you out of your fucking mind?"

The second her punches slowed, he sat back up and grabbed her wrists. "Calm down," he said, knowing full well he couldn't control her if she wanted to start swinging again. But she seemed spent. "You make it sound like I started this. I didn't. I was minding my own business. You guys set me up. You led me into this trap. You lied to me. You and Blunt came looking for me."

She was shaking her head now. She tried to pull her wrists free, but he wouldn't let go. As if to compensate, she shook her head even harder. "No. No. No. No. No," she muttered. "No. No." Tears welled in her eyes.

"What now?" he said, worried about her suddenly, disgusted with himself because he was powerless against her tears. "Stop it. Don't you start crying. That's not fucking fair. What are you crying for?"

"I," she said but had to stop to work a few solid sobs out of her chest. "I didn't go to trap you," she said.

"What?"

"It wasn't part of some elaborate plot. C'mon. Blunt's not smart enough for that. I really was just at that party. When we met. That was real, Wes. I swear."

"I don't understand. That doesn't make any damn sense."

"I know. I know. Shit. Look. I had a month of vacation saved up, but nowhere to go. So I was just kicking around, and I met you, and we started hanging out and next thing I know I'm ten pounds overweight, stupid happy. And then Blunt caught on to me. I was the one who got trapped. Me. By Blunt."

Him again. "What's his deal?"

She blushed a little. "He may have had a thing for me."

"What?" Wes said. "I fucking knew it."

"It was nothing. Never went anywhere. Decided we'd be friends. And since then, he's always tried to be a mentor, big brother, trying to prove he was a big man and could let it go. Always making a big show about how he watched over me and helped me move up the ladder. But when I came back from vacation, he went batshit. Put an undercover on me. And when he found out about us, he really lost it. Went berserk. And forced me into this scheme. I didn't have an escape plan. No money saved up. No one else to turn to. I didn't know what to do." She started crying again. "Shit, Wes. You're right. Of course, you're right. I owe you an apology. I owe everyone an apology. I'm fucking sorry. Really. I am. I swear."

She lost control again, tears and snot now running in a torrent down her face. He pulled her head down onto his chest and stroked her hair until the sobs subsided some. He was afraid to consider everything she'd just said. It was too much to believe in at the moment. Too much hope. What if it was dashed all over again?

"So," he said. "You're not the world's most devious detective, sleeping your way through the criminal underground."

She lifted her head, leaned back and raised a clenched fist.

He flinched.

She laughed. "No, asshole. I'm not." She put her head back onto his chest.

"Now what?" he asked.

"I don't know," she said. "I really don't."

"What time is it?"

"One."

He thought. "Well, I've got a ride to the dealer. Assuming he's good on his word, maybe we can escape somehow."

She looked up at him, and he braced himself for another argument.

"Not exactly how I pictured my life turning out," she said. "But I guess we don't have any options at this point."

He laughed. "I always wanted to be someone's least worst option." He leaned his head back against the stall wall. The room slipped around him again, reminding him that he was still drunk, that this clarity was only a momentary reprieve brought on by heightened emotions. He closed his eyes. "What about Blunt?" he asked. "Shit. He's been listening this whole time, hasn't he?"

She sighed. "No. He caused a scene earlier, trying to stop me from drinking, and they kicked him out. And there's no unauthorized com traffic getting into or out of this place. But the minute we get out of here, he'll lock onto us. I don't know that he has any connections around here worth a damn. Probably used his one solid IOU to get into the party. We might get a little bit of a head start, but not much. It actually helps that we don't know where we're going."

"Shit," Wes said. "What's the worst that could happen? Life in prison?"

"Yeah, guess so," she said, pushing herself up off the floor.

She reached down to help him up and out of the stall, but standing was his umpteenth mistake of the night. It all came flooding over him— the booze, the pills, the food, the stress, the likely prison sentence.

"Oh no," he said, crashing back into the stall and spewing vomit into the toilet.

"Christ, Wes. You've got such great timing," she said.

"Jules," he managed to say before puking again. "Get Jules."

46

It took 45 minutes for her to track down Jules and bring him back. But by the time 2 a.m. rolled around, Wes was back on his feet and, thanks to a Clear patch, feeling no worse than if he had a mild hangover.

"Thank God for modern medicine, huh?" said Jules, leading them out into the night air, where the temperature had dropped to zero.

They'd half expected to find Blunt waiting for them, but he was nowhere to be seen. The only sign of life on the streets was a black BMW.

"That'll be inconspicuous," Hillary remarked.

"Look at it this way," Jules said. "You're rich enough to have a car and a weekend permit, you're too rich to pull over."

"Depends on who's looking for you," she said.

"We should get going," Wes said. He just wanted to sit and hoped the ride would be long enough for him to close his eyes for a moment. He turned to Jules. "Thanks for the help, bud. Guess this is goodbye."

"I don't think so," Jules said.

Wes managed a laugh.

"I'm not joking, chief," Jules said, opening the car door and climbing in. "Not hopping off this ride now."

Wes and Hillary looked at each other.

"C'mon, Jules," Wes said. "You've done enough. I wouldn't be able to live with myself if something happened to you."

"Something happened to me? Again, you vastly underestimate my connections. Besides, you're the one who needs a guardian angel. Argument's over. Get in."

Wes looked at the car, then back at Hillary.

She shrugged.

"Well you two come on," Jules shouted from inside the car. "Letting all the hot air out! Shit!"

Hillary shook her head. "Whatever. You get in first, Wes. That man can't keep his hands to himself."

It wasn't until they were inside, the door shut and the car moving that the driver spoke.

"Good evening," he said with a thick Iranian accent. "Please remember to buckle up. We should arrive at our destination in fifteen minutes."

"Good stuff, Sharif," Jules said. "Good stuff. Where we headed?"

"I am not at liberty to say," the driver responded, turning onto an approach ramp of the Brooklyn Bridge.

Jules looked to Wes and Hillary, then out the window. "Well ain't that some shit?"

With a sinking feeling, Wes remembered the old man's letter from all those years ago. "Whatever you do, do not go into Brooklyn." And here he was being driving by a complete stranger—an Iranian no less—into a land ruled by Sharia law and hostile to interlopers.

But that wasn't their only problem. Blunt had picked up on Hillary's signal. "Yes," she was saying. "Relax. It's under control. Just relax."

"To whom are you talking, miss?" the driver asked, looking into the rear-view mirror.

"Don't worry, Achmed," Jules said. "She's just trying to calm down her boyfriend here. He's a little racist and a lot scared." He looked at Hillary while he said it, raising his eyebrows and smiling.

"Gee, thanks," Wes said.

"Don't mention it," Jules replied. "That boss of yours sure is persistent," he said to Hillary. "Works some strange hours."

Hillary didn't respond, remaining silent as they crossed the bridge. There was no traffic heading toward Brooklyn, and they were over the river in seconds. An old exit named Cadman Plaza was sealed off, funneling them down to a checkpoint at the foot of the bridge. Wes had a moment of panic, convinced that Blunt and a horde of police would drag them out of the car. But he reminded himself that, as far as

Blunt knew, Hillary and he were still on the mission and had no plans of escaping.

Jules prattled on even as they were waved through by one of the guards.

"Haven't been out here in years," he said, waving at the guard. "Problem's not getting through going in, it's getting back. Now *that* checkpoint is a capital-b bitch. Metal detectors, bomb detectors, dogs, biometric scans. And that weekend fee for non-residents."

They drove through downtown Brooklyn, a different country altogether. Hookah bars, dance clubs, street vendors serving grilled meat in the freezing cold. And all the patrons were white. The data coming through the AR didn't match the buildings. The AR listed them as import/export shops, halal butchers—all with Persian names.

"What the hell?" Wes asked.

Where were the angry men with automatic weapons? Where were the women in burkahs? Why did this look like 20th century New Orleans instead of the Islamic Republic of Brooklyn?

"City this size needs its releases," said Jules. "And not everyone has a taste for that Gawker bullshit. A little cash and a lot of courage and you can have almost a normal night out."

"Isn't it dangerous?" Hillary asked.

"Not if you stay within the lines," Jules said.

"But," she glanced at the driver. "I mean doesn't this upset the..." She didn't know quite how to finish the sentence.

The driver spoke. "The locals? Yes. A little. But one does not kill the goose that lays the golden egg. Especially if that goose belongs to heavily armed Iranian men and the communities they pay off to look the other way. We are not all fanatics. Indeed, some of us have a very secular view of the world. But certain illusions can benefit both sides. And just as the fundamentalists can be persuaded to see the upside of sin, the secularists can see the upside of keeping the fundamentalists happy."

Wes shook his head. If the night progressed at this pace, they'd learn at some point that the laws of gravity were nothing but a sham.

It was only a minute before they'd driven beyond the few blocks of nightlife, and the driver was making a left onto what looked like a deserted street.

"Court Street," Jules said, reading one of the signs. There were lights on in some of the windows, but otherwise no signs of life at this late hour.

Then Wes saw something that defied all belief.

"Stop the car," he said.

The driver, showing no signs of surprise, pulled to a smooth halt.

"Holy shit," Wes said. "Is that thing real?"

"What?" Hillary and Jules said at the same time.

"Look!" Wes pointed out the window. There it was, a Popeyes Chicken and Biscuits. His old man used to rave about the place. In one letter alone, he'd devoted five or six paragraphs to the rapture of a three-piece dark meal. Spicy. Wes had seen the ads as well on American video. And here one was in Brooklyn.

"Is it real?" Hillary asked now.

"It can't be," Wes said. "No way."

"It most certainly is," the driver said. "We may have rules, but we do enjoy some of the finer things in life."

"But how do they supply it?"

The driver chuckled. "I think you'll find my employer is a very capable man."

47

He started driving again, but only went a couple of blocks before pulling to a stop in front of what looked like an old bank on the corner of Court and Atlantic.

They climbed out of the car and waited as the driver opened the doors to the building. Once inside, he produced a flashlight and led them to the far end of the cavernous space, their footsteps echoing off the marble floor. They followed a staircase into a cellar and only then did the driver turn on a light. He punched a four-digit code into a keypad next to the light switch, and a massive filing cabinet on the opposite wall slowly slid to the left revealing a hole hacked into the bricks, leading into a dirt tunnel.

"Well, that certainly looks familiar," Hillary said.

"No shit," Wes responded.

They walked about forty yards of dirt track before emerging in another tunnel, this one old, brick-walled and massive. A set of train tracks ran from where they stood into the darkness to their left. The driver hit a switch and a row of lights on the ceiling fifty feet above them flickered on.

"Whoaaaa," said Wes.

"Long Island Railroad tunnel," explained the driver, as if this was part of a tour he was accustomed to leading. "Built in the 1850s before your countries split the first time. Shut down not long after. Lost for years until rediscovered in the 1980s. Lost again just before the most recent split." He looked over his shoulder at Wes. "Lost things, as you may know, come in very handy." He began walking again, leading them down the tracks, chatting the whole way. "Of course this wasn't bored through bedrock. Records indicate they simply dug a trench down this length of Atlantic big enough for two locomotives. They then bricked up the sides, built a ceiling and covered it up again. The tracks, you'll see, are new. Used for transporting from the loading dock to the distribution building."

At the end of the tracks, they found a small electric locomotive attached to two flatbed trailers. Beyond that was darkness—and the faint but unmistakable sound of water lapping at a wall.

"I'm starting to get a strange sense of déjà vu," Hillary said.

"Yeah," was all Wes could think to say. It wasn't exactly a pleasant feeling. It was like he'd woken up in a parallel dimension, one in which everything was off just by a fraction of an inch. Everything was familiar, nothing was right.

"This way," the driver said, leading them to a heavy door set in a wall and pushing it open.

Inside was what appeared to be an office. Book shelves and filing cabinets lined the wall. A massive desk sat near the back of the room. Behind the desk was a chair. In the chair sat a man.

The man rose to his feet.

"Hello, son," he said.

Wes felt something click in his head, felt the world just go a little more off-kilter. He opened his mouth, but no words came.

"What?" Hillary whispered. She looked at Wes, looked at the man. Looked at Wes again, looked back at the man. "This makes no sense," she said.

Wes finally found his voice. "I don't understand," was all he could think to say.

"It's me, Wesley. Your old man."

"Holy shit," Hillary said. She ran her hands through her hair, paced back and forth a couple of times, her body seemingly channeling some of Wes's confusion. "Wow."

"Yeah," Wes said, looking around, lost, as if someone in the room might offer him some sort of explanation. "Yeah." What was he saying "yeah" to? There just wasn't any room left in his brain to process this sort of thing. "I mean, I understand, but."

And then he closed his mouth again. Words failed him.

"Obviously, this wasn't the way I'd planned things," the old man said.

"Planned?"

"Well, yeah," he said. "You know, you hop on a sub in Montauk, escape to the South. Retire in wealth."

That sounded like Wes's plan, but what the hell was the old man doing here? "What the hell are you doing here?" Wes asked, looking around again. Hillary's eyes were wide, taking it all in. The driver stood to the side, his face passive. And Jules—Wes couldn't make out the expression he was wearing.

"I'm working, Wes."

"Working? Here? I thought you were down South. I thought you. I thought. I."

"Look, it's complicated," the old man said. "Well, not really. But I can explain it all once we get you on the sub."

"The sub? You've been on the sub all these years?" And he'd never thought to climb out, say hi?

The old man sighed. "No. Not *your* sub. And I'm not the driver. Look, we got the call on Thursday and headed up."

"You got the call?"

Hillary, a little calmer now, tugged on his sleeve. "Wes, would you like me to assemble this puzzle for you? I don't think it's that hard."

He looked to her and a couple of pieces seemed to slide into place, but when he looked back at the old man, his brain short-circuited again. He'd always been such an abstraction, yet there he was. It was like coming face to face with Santa Claus or Jesus.

Or Darth Vader.

"So you supply the city?"

"Yes."

Okay, that was easy enough to understand.

"But why would you answer my call?"

The old man opened his mouth to answer, but Hillary cut in. "Because he's your supplier, too, dumb-ass."

Wes looked back at her. "No, he's not. We quit talking years ago. My supplier is—"

"Clark Butler." The old man finished the sentence for him. "He works for me."

"But. All these years. Why didn't you tell me?"

"I didn't think it would be prudent," the old man said.

"No, I guess it wouldn't have been," Wes said, trying to force his mind to absorb the information. He, Wes, was the dealer on the East End. That first guy who approached him all those years ago was actually an employee of his father. He'd been working for his father this whole time.

And? And there was something else, wasn't there? What was it? One last detail that Wes knew he should be focusing on but couldn't because it was all so much. He tried to shake his head clear of this massive information dump. What was that little practical matter tickling the back of his brain?

The door behind him flew open, banging against the wall, and Blunt stepped in.

Oh. *That's* what he was trying to remember.

48

Blunt had a gun—a real gun—in his hands. He swept the room with it.

"I hate to break up this little reunion," he said. "But the first one of you assholes who moves, I shoot in the face." He herded them all to the same side of the room. All except Hillary, who he took as a human shield.

"Crap in a bucket," Hillary said.

"Shit, indeed, you little fucking back-stabber," he said.

"What the hell is this all about?" the old man asked.

Now it was Wes's turn. "It's a little complicated," he stuttered.

"This is about your son leading the cops directly to the biggest dealer in the Federation," Blunt said, pointing the gun at the old man. "With the added bonus of me getting to see this little emotional play. Reunion! Betrayal!"

"The cops?" the old man said.

"That's right," Blunt said. "The police."

"Do you have any idea who you're dealing with?" the old man asked.

Blunt paused for a second, thrown off by the question. "Yeah. I do. You. The man who's poisoning the entire Northeast, apparently. The man who's got the NYPD so corrupted, he's slinging this shit right under the nose of the President."

"Ha!"

Wes half expected to see Lawson jump out from behind a filing cabinet, but it was the old man.

"The President?" he said. "You mean King Mike? Teddy?"

Oh boy, Wes thought. He was going to get to experience a rant in the flesh.

The old man continued. "Who do you think I work for?"

Wes and Blunt spoke at the same time. "What?"

The old man directed his answer at Blunt, laughing while he did so. "So you think I've evaded all the non-corrupt cops in this city? And the Feds? And the special services? And you, some third-rate East End detective, were able to crack this huge mystery all by yourself?"

"Well, here I am. And there you are," Blunt said, his voice wavering a little now.

"No denying that," the old man said. "No denying that. But ask yourself this: How the hell am I getting a submarine in and out of New York Harbor? Think that's happening without someone's tacit permission?"

"That's bullshit," said Blunt. "Bullshit."

"That's one way of looking at it," the old man answered. "Another way is to consider me just part of a delicately balanced faith system, one that needs its releases, its vice, its devils. I provide those things— and more. I also happen to keep the top one percent of the population happy enough that they don't abandon the Federation in one mad rush, crippling the tax base."

"But why?" It was Wes now.

"Why? Why what? In order to function, the Federation needs these people."

"Why keep them happy? Why not let them leave? Let the whole thing collapse and be reabsorbed into the rest of the country? All those letters? All those rants?"

The old man shrugged. "Old age mellows a man. As does unimaginable sums of money and exclusive vendor contracts. Besides, the South wants nothing to do with the Federation. The South needs its bad guys, too. Everybody's happy."

"Lies," said Blunt. "All of it. The Federation wouldn't allow it to happen. You're poisoning people, taking lives."

"You don't honestly believe that, do you?" the old man said.

"Truth is truth," Blunt said. "The science is settled."

"Believe what you need to believe," the old man answered. "But you think about it for more than two minutes, my story is the only thing that adds up."

Blunt fell silent as he considered the old man's words. Suddenly, a smile crept across his face.

"Let's say you're right," Blunt said. "Let's say the government is complicit. That doesn't make it right, now does it?"

"Of course not," the old man said. "It just makes it reality."

"So," Blunt continued. "What happens if I shoot you right now? You and your son? And everyone else here? Set fire to this place? Sink the sub? Blow the whole thing wide open?"

Now it was the old man's turn to look puzzled. "Huh," he said. "I hadn't thought of that."

"I bet you hadn't," Blunt said, pulling the hammer back on the revolver and putting it to Hillary's temple. "This is going to hurt me almost as much as it hurts you."

"Drop the gun," Jules shouted, producing one of his own, pointing it in the general vicinity of Blunt and Hillary.

Wes turned to Jules. "What the hell, dude?"

Jules shrugged. "Told you I was connected," he said. "Drop it, Blunt."

"No," Blunt answered.

"Listen up, chief. Best you can hope for at this point is to get one of us. Could be the girl, could be Wes, could be the old man. It ain't going to be me. You got one shot, so you might as well make it count."

Blunt swung the gun toward Jules. Then the old man, then Wes, then back to Hillary.

"I don't think you have the balls to let me kill her," Blunt said.

"You have no idea who I work for," Jules said. "Let's just say I've got more notches on my bedpost than you do."

"Wait!" Wes shouted, his mind racing for a stalling tactic.

All eyes turned to him expectantly. There had to be something he could offer Blunt. Anything. A deal. But what? Not Hillary. Wes couldn't stand that. And at this point she wouldn't have satisfied Blunt's need for justice.

"The Gawker," Wes said.

"What?" Blunt asked. "Why would I want that when I've got you?"

Wes needed to make something up and quick. "You don't have us. Like Jules said, one shot and you're done. C'mon. The Gawker is the biggest customer, the biggest conduit for this stuff. And he's teaching an entire generation to snub their noses at the law."

"That doesn't stop the flow, though," said Blunt.

The old man spoke. "You'll never do that. As long as there is a border and supply on one side and demand on the other." He looked at Wes. "But, yes, taking down The Gawker would seriously disrupt business on both ends. And take down half the Manhattan police force, perhaps a few politicians."

Blunt looked around the room, considering his options. "How? Like you said, he's been untouchable."

Wes knew Blunt had a point. Even if he and Jules and Hillary had recorded the entirety of the party, it wouldn't have mattered. Cops and politicians were typically in the VIP room. The only people with the kind of evidence necessary to bring down that ring were already in on the business.

He turned to the old man, made a conscious effort to form the word: "Dad?"

The old man looked at him. "Wes?"

"You can do it." He was getting excited. He just wanted that gun away from Hillary's head. "You can give Blunt the evidence. Enough at least to bring The Gawker down."

"Wesley, do you have any idea what you're asking?"

Wes looked to Hillary—her eyes considering him, not betraying the fear that had to have been coursing through her—then back to the old man. "Yes."

"This is going to throw a major wrench in my operations, in my cash flow. This thing I've built up over all these years. The East End. Manhattan. This isn't a fly-by-night operation." His voice was lifting now, getting ready to launch into a full rant. "This is a major corporation. Jobs are at stake. Producers. Supply chains. Distributors, Customers. Millions—no billions—of dollars. Lives will be affected.

My life. This is my life, Wes."

"Yeah," Wes said, "I know it's your life. What about hers?" He paused. "What about mine?"

With that, the fight went out of the old man. "Shit. Fine. Okay, Wes. For you." He turned to Blunt. "Let the woman go and I'll hand over the files. All of them."

"You have files?" Blunt asked.

"This is a business. Might take a little detective work to put names to numbers, but The Gawker will be obvious."

Blunt considered them all. "How do I know I can trust you?"

"There are enough files in this office to nail whoever you'd like to nail."

Blunt removed the gun from Hillary's head and pushed her across the room toward the rest of them. As he did so, a shot rang out and Blunt's right arm went limp, his revolver clattering to the ground. Before he could move, Jules had rushed in and picked up the piece.

"You fuckers!" Blunt roared. "We had a deal."

"No," Jules said. "You had a deal with them. I just felt like shooting you."

"Jules," the old man said.

"We can just off him and be done with it," Jules replied.

"No," the old man said. "Wes made a deal. We'll honor it. Besides, the jungle needs a new king. The Gawker's been on top for too long."

Blunt was on his knees, holding his shoulder. "Son of a bitch."

"Quit your bitching," Jules said. "You'll live."

The driver grabbed a first-aid kit and went to work on Blunt. The old man called Jules over, and they started pulling relevant files from the filing cabinets.

Wes stood still, unable to move, unable to process.

Hillary tugged on his sleeve. "You okay?"

"I don't know. You?"

"Yes. I think so."

Wes grabbed hold of the old man's desk chair. "I need to sit," he said.

EPILOGUE

Wes and Hillary sat under an umbrella at a Popeyes, sweating even in the shade, the summer sun beating down on New Orleans. They looked out on the still waters of the oxbow lake formed when the Army Corps of Engineers finally lost control of the Mississippi and it found a new route to the Gulf via the Atchafalaya River.

Five months after the old man had dropped them off on a dock in South Carolina, they were still adjusting to the environment. They'd fallen back into their own relationship, as if the multiple betrayals they'd inflicted on one another in New York had canceled one another out. Now they were strangers in a strange land, a team trying to get accustomed to the culture—the vast American one, and the weirdness specific to New Orleans.

Wes was also slowly getting to know the old man. He wasn't exactly loving everything about him, but neither could have lived up to the other's imagination after all those years. What helped was that the old man seemed content in his marriage to his job and wasn't around every day of the week.

Jules made visits sporadically, and was much less obnoxious now that he didn't need to play the part of famous artist in front of them. Of course, Jules technically was a famous artist in some parts of the world, even if the role had been created in part to cover for his multiple other roles as spy, saboteur, and lord knew what else.

The biggest problem Hillary and Wes faced—aside from how to spend the piles of money from his years of dealing now unlocked from those secret accounts—was weight gain. No longer forced to abide by strict rules, they'd packed on the pounds quickly. Wes liked to think they wore the weight well—Hillary did at any rate—and they certainly enjoyed eating their way around their new country.

But they'd quit working out, too. And just that morning, after a brief bout of sex, they found themselves panting for air and slightly nauseous. Neither talked about it, but Wes had been more than a little embarrassed and suspected Hillary was as well.

The woman at the table next to them—morbidly obese, flushed in the face, sweat soaking her blouse—ordered fried calamari as an appetizer and half a fried chicken. Her husband, who matched her in size, ordered fried chicken fingers and the fried seafood platter.

"And two Diet Cokes," he said.

The waitress turned to Hillary and Wes. "What can I get for yall?"

"I'm going to have a garden salad and a glass of water," Hillary said, handing over her menu.

"I'll have the same," Wes said.

They looked at each other and laughed, their bellies jiggling along to the joke.

CPSIA information can be obtained at www.ICGtesting.com
Printed in the USA
BVOW041354240213

313996BV00001B/3/P